David Shepherd was born in Bolton-le-Sands, near Lancaster, in 1942. He was educated at Abbotsholme School in Derbyshire and at St John's College in Durham. He has written two postgraduate theses: "Yugoslav-Bulgarian Diplomatic Relations, 1918-1941" (M.A. 1968) and "The Royal Dictatorship in Yugoslavia, 1929-1934" (M.Litt. 1976). After University, he was a probation officer in Linlithgow, West Lothian, and a student at the Episcopal Theological College in Edinburgh. From 1968-1979, he was Chaplain of St Paul's Cathedral, Dundee, and Anglican Chaplain in the University of Dundee from 1973-1979. Since 1979, he has been Rector of St Mary Magdalene's Church, Dundee. He has served on many boards and committees of the Scottish Episcopal Church, most notably as Convener of St Serf's Home, 1976-1992 and as Convener of the Diocese of Brechin Administration Board since 1984. In 1985, he opened the Meadowside Bookshop which has now sold over 100,000 books.

In November 1986, he married his wife, Patricia, whose love of foreign travel and sunbathing provided him with the welcome opportunity of writing a number of detective stories. To celebrate his 50th birthday, he decided to publish his first novel under the imprint of MEADOWSIDE CRIME.

MEADOWSIDE PUBLICATIONS

WHO KILLED SOPHIE JACK?

DAVID SHEPHERD

WHO KILLED SOPHIE JACK?

A DETECTIVE NOVEL

BY

DAVID SHEPHERD

MEADOWSIDE PUBLICATIONS

DUNDEE
1992

Meadowside Publications
75 Meadowside, Dundee

© *Meadowside Publications, 1992*

Printed by
Burns & Harris (Print) Ltd.
Dundee, Scotland

*The characters portrayed in this
novel are all imaginary and bear
no intended resemblance to any
person alive or dead.*

ISBN 0 952 06320 4

Meadowside Crime
is a © imprint of
Meadowside Publications,
Dundee.

CONTENTS

The story is set in a small university town in England in July 1988.

1 *The New Man*

Detective-Inspector Raynes settled himself behind his large office desk for the first time. It was an old desk which had accommodated many generations of detectives before him. It had a faded, torn, green leather surface; the locks on the drawers didn't work and it had a blue plastic ashtray sitting in a corner waiting to be filled. Raynes picked up the ashtray, looked at it critically and threw it into the cheap raffia waste-paper basket. He wouldn't be needing it. He was a non-smoker.

He looked at the walls. To his left, a calendar kindly left by his predecessor. Nothing erotic. Just boringly practical. To his right, a map of Grasshallows – much used – showing the four sub-stations into which the city was divided and for which he was now responsible. In front of him a glass partition wall with windows and door looking out into the main office. Secretaries and more desks. Photocopiers and files. The peaceful hum of routine activity at the heart of what was acknowledged to be one of England's safest and quietest cities.

He pressed a small button on his desk which said: "Call". It was 8.30 am – a little early perhaps for a call – but Raynes had only arrived in Grasshallows the night before and it seemed desirable to create a good impression. A young detective, Carlisle by name, had also figured that his new superior might favour an early start. He answered the call very promptly.

"Good morning, sir. Detective-Constable Carlisle."

"Good morning, Carlisle. I'm the new man here."

There was a note of challenge in the soft voice. A pair of deep brown eyes watched to see if that challenge was taken up. But the younger detective had done his homework carefully. He knew that Raynes had been "moved" to Grasshallows. There had been a scandal in his last job and he had been obliged to leave. Raynes had had the reputation of being one of the most brilliant young detectives in Britain and yet that brilliance was accompanied by a streak of wilful irresponsibility that irritated and offended those about him – especially those in authority.

9

As a professional sleuth, people always spoke highly of Raynes but their praise was qualified by the rider that he was not an easy man to work with. He was a loner. He was rude. He was unscrupulous. After the latest episode, which allegedly involved a Chief Constable's wife, Raynes had been railroaded out of the mainstream of police life. Placed in a siding. Grasshallows had been selected as that siding – a suitable place of punishment for an unorthodox and unsuitable man. Carlisle knew that the detective sitting behind his desk must be feeling very raw, very bitter and very angry – and that he must tread most gently to avoid explosions.

"We're very glad to have you here," he said.

And meant it.

He looked at the bare, miserable office with its tatty desk, the old map and the pathetic waste-paper basket ... and felt ashamed. It was almost an insult.

He said: "You'll be needing a few things in here, sir. A filing cabinet. An in-and-out tray. A dictaphone ..."

"I don't use them," said Raynes. "I don't expect to be in the office much. If there are reports to be written, someone else can write them. My job is to be on the spot where a crime has been committed. To question the people involved. To form opinions. To think through solutions and to get results. Other people can do the donkey-work. Do we have a car?"

"There's an old Jaguar and a new Granada."

"Well, that's something! We'll take the Granada!"

Carlisle smiled.

"Sit down," said Raynes.

"There's no chair!"

"Well, sit on the desk."

Carlisle perched delicately.

"Tell me," said Raynes. "Tell me, what goes on round here? What sort of crimes do people commit?"

Carlisle reflected.

"Grasshallows is basically a very quiet, law-abiding place," he said. "We have the usual runs of petty theft. Mostly by teenagers. We have no football hooliganism because Grasshallows Athletic has never made it even to the fourth division.

We have sudden outbursts of fraud. The University students get drunk, peddle drugs and smash shop windows – mostly towards the end of term. There's an occasional rape. An occasional murder. But most of the time is taken up with traffic offences, lost property and keeping our expense accounts up to date. Extremely boring!"

"Extremely."

Raynes stared with unseeing eyes through the glass partition into the main office.

"Is there anything special happening at this moment?"

"Nothing in particular. I think there was some report about sheep-stealing last night but it hasn't come through yet."

"Cattle rustling!" said Raynes to himself. "What next?"

Carlisle did not smile. He could appreciate the frustration the new man must feel. The prospect of an unrelieved diet of petty crime. A mind tuned up like a racing car reducing to delivering milk. In fact, to be honest, he felt pretty bored himself.

Raynes seized at one final straw.

"Are there any unsolved crimes on our books? Anything that defeated my worthy predecessor, Detective-Inspector Parkinson?"

Carlisle's face lit up.

"Well, there was a murder last year. Quite a sensational murder. But the scent will have gone pretty cold by now. Even when it happened, there wasn't much to go on."

"Who was murdered?" asked Raynes quietly.

"A local lady – emphasis upon the 'lady' – Sophie Jack."

"Were you involved in the case yourself?"

Carlisle nodded.

"Tell me about it."

2 *Sophie Jack*

Carlisle began.

"Sophie Jack was born in February 1946. I can't give you the exact date without looking up the records. Sometime at the end of February anyway …"

"A V.E. baby?"

"Precisely. Her mother was unmarried. A Scots woman called Macmillan, who was working down here – on parachutes, I think it was. Anyway, she celebrated the victory over the Germans a little too enthusiastically and was – to coin a phrase – left up the spout."

"Sophie was brought up by her mother – now a barmaid-cum-cleaner who later married a chap who worked on the railways. George Jack. Quite a nice fellow by all accounts. Treated Sophie well. Brought her up as his own daughter – and all that."

"Sophie was educated at the C of E primary in Riverside Road; then at the secondary modern out at Henslea and left school in 1961. I think she got a couple of 'O'-levels. Records would tell us. Anyway, like her mother before her, she soon fell pregnant. She was working in a coffee bar near the University and one of the students knocked her off. She had a baby – a boy it was – who was brought up by his grandmother and the long-suffering Mr Jack, who themselves had three other children of their own. That was before the days of abortion. A family either did its stuff or the kid was adopted."

Raynes nodded.

"Sophie then embarked on a passionate love affair with one of the Italian blokes who ran the coffee bar. He married her but I don't think the marriage could have been all that much of a success because she ran off to London with one of her husband's in-laws and I believe there was a rather unpleasant incident – a knifing – in Hammersmith. Or Bayswater. Somewhere in London anyway. One of these Italians put her on the game and she was on it for about twenty years. On and off. No shrinking violet, our Sophie!"

"She was in London till she was about thirty. I think she got married again – but I can't be certain. Needless to say, it didn't work out and she came back home about 1975 or 1976 to nurse her mother who was dying of cancer. Breast cancer, I think it was. Rest of the family had grown up, gone away, got married and had families of their own. George himself was killed the year before. He was killed in a shunting accident down at the railway yard. It was a pity that. If he'd lasted another year, he'd have been in line for a pretty handsome redundancy payment."

"When was Grasshallows station closed?"

"About 1975. I think they might have left it open. Would have made quite a nice little tourist attraction. It had lots of hanging flowers in baskets, you know." Carlisle was waxing poetic. Raynes brought him back to the point.

"So Sophie came home to look after her mum?"

"Yes but she died fairly quickly."

"Did she leave any money?"

"Not that I know of. She'd been a working woman all her life. Had five children to bring up. They had a Council house. Sophie kept it on till her son joined the Army as a cadet. Then she bought a flat of her own. Over a betting shop – Pleydells – in Riverside Road …"

"She hasn't moved far in life!"

"No. She's always been around the same area. Very well known. Very well known indeed. She had no enemies as far as we know. The local women bore her no ill will, even though some of their husbands must have had her at one time or another."

"So Sophie lived above the betting shop in Riverside Road from about 1976 onwards?"

"From March 1977."

"Did she entertain her customers there?"

"Some of them, certainly. It wasn't far from the betting shop. Just up the stairs. But in the evenings, she often used her car. She had an old red Marina. A bit rusty! She used to drive out along the road to the Meadows and meet her customers there. Normally she would go off in their car – to their flat – or whatever. You would normally see Sophie's car there most evenings. When things were quiet, she'd sit there chain-smoking, waiting for trade to arrive. It was done very discreetly but everybody knew about Sophie – and where to find her. In fact, she was a bit of an institution in Grasshallows!"

"Did you ever pull her in?"

"I don't think so. She was quite useful actually. She used to pass on bits of information to us when they came her way. People often told her things – and if it was important, she used to buttonhole one of our officers and give them the guff …"

"Did they buttonhole her?" asked Raynes with a mischievous smile.

"I don't know," said Carlisle. "It probably wouldn't have done them any harm. Her health record was good. She took all the necessary precautions. I think that she probably did a lot of her trade with the kinks, people who like to be beaten or tied up with chains …"

"Are there a lot of people like that in Grasshallows?"

"Oh, I'm sure that among the University people, there are a good number of perverts. We've had one or two lecturers up for receiving obscene publications. Mostly in the Theological Faculty! It was really quite funny …"

Carlisle digressed.

"… We've had quite a few reports of orgies – well, wife-swapping parties – which got a bit out of hand. The local news-papers had quite a field day with the stories. Then there were several very juicy divorce cases. Sophie was in on quite a few of the parties. That all came out in the investigations after her death."

"Where did she die?

"Down at the Meadows. Her old stomping ground. It's a stretch of parkland over the river – a place much frequented by loving couples."

"And what happened?"

"Well, as usual, she must have been out with one of her customers. She was blindfolded. Tied to a tree. Naked. She had been strangled with a rope – round the tree. And then stabbed several times in the stomach. It was pretty horrible. Some children found her next day – which made it even worse."

"Did she die a rich woman – or poor?"

Carlisle paused.

"That was the problem. She died a very rich woman. She left at least £60,000 plus the sale of her flat."

Raynes whistled through his teeth.

This was real meat!

"And who got the money? Her son?"

Carlisle shook his head. "You won't believe it. I didn't. With the exception of a few small bequests – £500 here, £500 there – she left the lot to St Benedict's Parish Church! Virtually every penny went to them."

"£60,000?"

"Nearer £100,000 by the time they were finished."

"Were they needing the money?"

"Not really. As a Church, they're pretty well endowed. Lots of shares, gilt-edged securities and so on. They're quite a rich church. But they lashed out after they got her money."

"Did they?"

"Yes. They're in the middle of re-building their organ. These things are pretty expensive. I think it's going to cost them something approaching £100,000."

"And all on the strength of Sophie's immoral earnings?"

"I think their Treasurer's prepared to overlook that point. Money is money wherever it comes from. I mean, they've probably got shares in South Africa and other places – equally immoral if you think about it."

"Who is the Treasurer of St Benedict's?"

"He's a banker."

"And the Rector – or Vicar?"

"Canon Murray. He's been at St Benedict's for about twenty-five years."

"So he probably knew Sophie quite well?"

"Everyone did."

"And she left him nearly £100,000!"

Raynes ran his mind over the picture Carlisle had painted. Here was a case to tempt his palate. A really juicy murder. The scent all but lost. The murderer – or murderers – quietly confident they had pulled off their hideous deed with total impunity. Re-opening the case would be very interesting. Very interesting indeed. Raynes looked at his watch. It was still only 9.15 am. He looked up at Carlisle.

"The day is young," he said. "If we have nothing better to do than sheep-stealing, I think we should go out and look at the scene of the murder."

"I'll go and get the car," said Carlisle.

"Make sure it's the Granada," said Raynes.

3 *In the Meadows*

It did not take long to drive out of Grasshallows. There were no traffic jams to speak of, but the University students riding their bicycles were a nuisance. They drove three or four abreast down the High Street, turned left or right without the slightest warning and were inclined to stop with dramatic suddenness when they espied some friend on the pavement. Within three minutes of leaving police headquarters, Raynes was bowling down Riverside Road and two minutes later they had entered the lush acres of parkland which many generations of Grasshallows had called quite simply "The Meadows".

The entry was through a mock gothic stone gateway, called the Royal Arch, erected on the occasion of Queen Victoria's Diamond Jubilee. Then there was a long, curling avenue of plane trees, creating the effect of a large green cathedral. This lasted for about half a mile. The car then debouched into a very broad stretch of grassland, dotted with occasional trees and bushes. This was much favoured as a picnic area in summer. A row of willows and a small stream marked the boundary of the picnic area. An old stone bridge crossed the stream and on the farther shore there was the imposing Meadowside House – formerly a stately home – now a cafe-restaurant and Resource Centre for Grasshallows Education Committee. To the left was a large car park and an eighteen hole golf course. To the right, a wilder stretch of woodland interspersed with many lanes and paths which were used by the Pony Club (or the Equestrian Centre, as it was called) who had their stables behind Meadowside House. This wild woodland occupied about three square miles. It was here on summers' afternoons that children got lost. It was here that courting couples walked arm-in-arm and dreamt dreams of love and marriage. It was here, on dark evenings, that cars crept into dark corners and illicit passions were voluptuously enjoyed. It was here, of an evening, that Sophie plied her trade.

16

Detective-Constable Carlisle drove down the main avenue quite briskly. There was nobody about at this time of day and he felt good. He was glad that Raynes had decided to take up Sophie's case. Everyone at Grasshallows' police station had felt very angry when the body was discovered. It seemed most unfair that someone who had given her body so readily to others and who had become something of a local legend – should have been dispatched in such a cruel and heartless manner. Strangled in bed would perhaps have been understood – and accepted. An occupational hazard! But to be tied up, naked, to a tree, stabbed and then left there as a public spectacle, was disgraceful and degrading.

Carlisle knew several of Sophie's long-standing clients who would have done the same and worse to her murderer if they could have got their hands on him – or her. Even now, the case was not forgotten. Once people had had a couple of drinks, the question often turned to "who dun it?". The number of suspects could not, it was felt, be more than two or three hundred at the outside. The investigating team had been able to reduce that number to nine or ten – but nothing had been proved against any of them.

Carlisle drove the Granada through the uncharted tracks with an experience and confidence which Raynes remarked upon.

"You obviously know this part of the woods quite well?"

"I used to bring quite a few of my young ladies out here, sir, in time past." He paused. "In fact, my wife and I did most of our courting here before we got married."

"How long have you been married?" asked Raynes.

"Two years, next month," replied Carlisle. "We're expecting our first baby just before Christmas."

"That's good," said Raynes. "Something exciting to look forward to. I shall expect to be chosen as the godfather!"

Carlisle smiled. He was surprised that Raynes was proving so friendly. He had expected him to be cold, hard and sarcastic.

"Are we there yet?"

"Just round this corner, sir."

Carlisle pulled the white Granada off the track. Both men got out of the car. It was a rather dark and sinister part of the woods. Several large old trees blocked out the light of day. Underfoot, the ground was sandy with many seasons of pine needles providing a dark carpet.

"It was over there."

Carlisle pointed to a chestnut tree which stood in the background, hidden by several pines and a yew. "This one."

Raynes paused and looked at the tree.

"Was she facing this way?"

"Yes."

Raynes turned and looked behind him.

The track along which they had come could no longer be seen.

"A good place," he said.

They walked towards the tree.

Raynes stopped again about seven feet away from the trunk and tried to picture the actual scene. "What time did she die?"

"About 7.00 pm. That's what the police surgeon said."

"Quite early then? It would still be light?"

"Yes, it was June."

"What was the actual date?"

"Saturday June 27th."

"Just about a year ago?"

"A year ago last Saturday."

Raynes walked round the tree looking for signs of a rope cutting into the wood. There was none.

"How was she tied up?"

"Hands. Feet. And one rope round her neck."

"Any signs of a struggle?"

"No."

"Do you think she was strangled before she was tied up to the tree?"

"I believe Inspector Parkinson did mention the possibility. But I think the police surgeon said the marks on the neck corresponded directly with the point of strangulation. The rope round her neck had been pulled tight then knotted."

"Unusual knots?"

"No. Conventional."

"Fingerprints?"

"Gloves."

"And she was blindfolded?"

"Yes. A black silk scarf."

"Hers?"

"I don't know. I heard it was quite new."

"A woman's scarf?"

"Yes."

"Anything to say where it was bought?"

"No."

"That's odd. Why do you think she was blindfolded?"

"So she couldn't see what the murderer was doing."

"Could be." Raynes looked thoughtful. "It could be because she might see who the murderer was."

"You think she didn't know?"

Raynes shrugged his shoulders. "Who can tell? People in this line of business do some strange things. The tricks that people pay for would seem bizarre to you and me, but it gives them kicks. Imagine that Sophie got a telephone call … no, that'd give the game away … imagine Sophie got a note from her client saying: 'I want you to meet me on Saturday night beside your car in the darkest part of the woods. I want you to wear nothing but a black cloak and a black blindfold. I shall lead you over to this tree, tie you up and make passionate love. See if you can guess who it is. I enclose £100 for the trick.' Do you think Sophie would have done it?"

"For £100. Yes, I think she would."

"The other alternative – perhaps the more likely one – is that she did know the murderer, as you suggest. If she was dealing with a total stranger, she would be taking a great risk letting him tie her to the tree. She could have been robbed – or murdered. Sophie must have had plenty of close shaves in her time. She wouldn't allow herself to be trussed up by someone she didn't know."

"That's what I thought."

"What about her clothes and handbag?"

Carlisle shook his head. "That's the strange bit. Her clothes were returned to her flat. Her handbag and keys were returned to her car."

"Where was her car?"

"In the car park beside Meadowside House."

"Was her flat burgled?"

"Not to our knowledge. There was quite a lot of money in her flat but it hadn't been touched."

"So, the suggestion is that the motive for the murder was not money? It was lust, hatred or revenge?"

"It points that way."

Raynes returned from his speculation to the events at the tree a year before. "And then she was stabbed. Stabbed before death or after?"

"The police surgeon said it was after."

"How many stabs?"

"Three."

"Was there a lot of blood?"

"A small pool of blood at the foot of the tree. But by the time she was found, most of it had dried into the soil."

Raynes looked at the ground.

"It was all taken away to forensic," said Carlisle.

"Her blood?"

"Yes."

"No weapon?"

"No, but the police surgeon said it was a hunting knife that did it."

"A hunting knife? But why stab her when she was dead? Was it a ritual killing? Was any blood smeared on her face or arms?"

"It didn't look like it. Just three random slashes to the abdomen. Must have been a very sharp knife. Some of her innards came out …"

If Carlisle had hoped to upset Raynes' delicate stomach, he failed. Raynes was quite used to inspecting gory scenes. He viewed them with complete professional detachment. He looked beyond the act of murder to the psychology of the person who had done it. "He must have hated her very much," he said. "Not just to kill her; but to disfigure her body as well. Either it was an act of revenge – or the act of a complete pervert. Or – a third possibility – we are being asked to think of it as the act of a pervert when it was nothing of the kind."

Carlisle said nothing.

Raynes continued: "The murderer slashed at the body. He wiped the knife on ... on what? On her underwear, presumably? Was that found?"

"I don't think so."

"He leaves the body, goes back to her flat ... in his car or hers? He returns her clothes. Steals nothing from the flat ... Are we sure about that?"

Carlisle shook his head. "We don't know; but we've got a complete inventory back at the station."

"Was there any blood on any of the stuff back at the flat?"

"No."

"No damp clothing recently washed?"

"I don't think so."

"And what about the rope. Was it bought locally?"

Carlisle shook his head again. "No, it was old stuff. Clean but old. Someone's old clothes line. Cut with a sharp knife."

"Of course," said Raynes.

He looked round the scene once more. Even at 10.00 am on a summer's morning, it looked vaguely spooky. He sighed. "I don't think there's much more we can do round here. We must go back to the office and have a look at your list of suspects. Perhaps on the way, you could point out her flat and the bookies? Perhaps you would like to take a bet on this case? A tenner either way that we solve the mystery by the end of next week?"

"Not me!" said Carlisle. "I'm a born loser."

Raynes shook his head sadly. "No faith," he said. "No faith!"

4 *Consider the Facts*

After a leisurely cup of coffee and an introduction to the other staff at Grasshallows police station, Raynes got down to the question of suspects. Whilst they were having their elevenses, all the relevant files on the Sophie Jack case were brought up to Raynes' office and there was a visible outburst of excitement that the "new man" was about to have a fresh look at Sophie's murder.

"I hope he gets the bastard!" said one officer.

"A year's a long time," said another.

Raynes settled down to read up the case notes. First of all, he looked long and hard at the face of the victim. It was a very ordinary face – neither fat nor thin; neither square nor pointed. It was the sort of face one might easily pass in the street without a second's glance. The eyes were tired and dull; the lips not particularly passionate. The style of her hair made her look younger than her 41 years. It had been dyed blonde but the darker roots were plainly visible.

"When was this photograph taken?" asked Raynes.

"About two years ago," said Carlisle. "It was taken at a charity dinner dance in the University. For Ethiopia, it was. I believe they raised about £500."

"Who took the photograph?"

"The local paper."

Raynes looked at the other photos in the file. They were more gruesome, being the pictures taken by the police photographer after her death. Raynes looked carefully at the way she had been tied to the tree, at the knots, at the blindfold, at the three savage cuts in her abdomen. He looked at her figure critically. She had long legs, thickening hips and small breasts. She seemed to have no distinguishing marks of any kind.

Her record was pretty much as Carlisle had described. He noted the names of her two husbands, her step-brothers and sister, her son and his wife – the next of kin. He read through the inventory of all the items found in her flat and car, together with photocopies of all her personal documents – passport, birth certificate, insurances, bank accounts and bills. Looking at these more carefully, Raynes could see that Sophie was both consistent and methodical in her finances. She went to the bank twice a week – on Mondays and Thursdays. Each time, the amount she banked was £200. Every two months a sum of £1500 was transferred to a high-yield investment account. She had bank books for four different building societies. No shares. No national savings. No complicated deals requiring an accountant. Now and again, there was a larger sum paid in which suggested a lucrative weekend. Other times, a week or two would pass with no deposits, suggesting a holiday away. Her current account which seemed to be used mainly for bills, was kept topped up to £500. It seemed that Sophie had earned something in excess of £400 per week and kept anything over that sum in the shape of ready cash. When she died, a sum of £343 had been found in her flat. From the evidence of her bank books, it was easy to see how she had accumulated a nest egg of £60,000 over the years. It was also plain to see that she had no pimp or protector. Sophie was very much her own boss.

Raynes next looked at her birth certificate – 18th February 1946. Her baptismal certificate – 27th March 1946. Her name then was Sophie Macmillan. She had been baptized in St Benedict's by the incumbent, Archdeacon Walton, who had also prepared her for confirmation in May 1959.

Both her marriages had been in the registry office – once at Grasshallows, the other in London. She had become Mrs Luccione in October 1963 – occupation "waitress" – and been divorced in May 1971. She had taken the plunge again in July 1974, becoming Mrs Harrison – occupation "sales assistant". The second divorce had come a little quicker – in April 1978 – just after her mother's death when she had set up home in her flat above the bookies.

Raynes looked at specimens of her handwriting – large round letters with generous loops top and bottom. Neat lines across her "t"s. A fairly open character. Limited education. High spiritual endeavour. But a somewhat reserved sense of humour – the dots over her "i"s being very precise. It told him nothing new about Sophie, but it was interesting to see the evidence in full.

Whilst Raynes was reading through the case, Carlisle was busy sorting out the different files which had at first been dumped on the floor – there being nowhere else to put them. However, Carlisle had insisted on two extra tables and a chair being brought in to the office and these had now arrived. Carlisle steadily assembled the previous investigations into some sort of order so that he would be ready to face the deluge of questions that he was sure would soon be coming his way.

For almost two hours Raynes ploughed through the case, absorbing copious facts and registering many small points of detail which he thought might prove important. At last, feeling hungry, he looked up:

"It's lunchtime!"

"1.15 pm," said Carlisle, for whom it had been a very long and energetic morning.

"Where do you normally eat?" asked Raynes.

"In the canteen upstairs."

Raynes looked out of the window like a bird peering out of its cage. "I think," he said slowly. "I think I should prefer to go out to a good restaurant to eat a hearty meal and consider all the likely suspects over a sparkling glass of wine. Would you like to join me?"

It was an offer the younger officer could scarcely refuse.

"Which is the best restaurant in town?"

"The *Grosvenor* has the best English food. *L'Escargot* is more exotic ... more French."

"Where would we be least likely to be overheard?"

"Oh, the *Grosvenor*. The other one's very small. Little tables and candles and things. Ideal for an evening out. The *Escargot*'s very good. It's got several awards for cuisine ..."

"But it's a bit of a security risk?"

"I should think so. Especially at lunchtime."

Raynes led the way out of the office, feeling much more confident about the new job. How long it would take to track down Sophie's killer, he did not know, but at least he had something to bite on – something to occupy his mind. It didn't really matter whether he was in London or Grasshallows. As long as something was cooking, he was a happy man. He decided he would have fillet steak and roast potatoes, two glasses of Beaujolais and something deliciously creamy and fattening to follow. He wondered if he could charge it to expenses? Better not.

5 *Dramatis Personae*

Whilst they waited for the food to arrive, Raynes launched into the inevitable question of suspects. Carlisle had been in on many of the original interviews so he was able to give Raynes not only the facts but also his personal impressions.

"The No. 1 suspects were two brothers, Eddie and Jim Reid. They run a garage on the outskirts of Grasshallows. They sell second-hand cars. They do them up first then they sell them at inflated prices. Most of their workmanship is pretty lousy and a number of people have had nasty accidents driving their cars. About eighteen months ago, Eddie Reid was taken in for questioning about a Fiat whose steering had failed – almost at the first roundabout! And that despite a brand-new MOT. Nothing could be proved, but one of the mechanics who worked for Eddie told Sophie a thing or two – and she passed it back to us. I think that they had diddled her too once before – so she wasn't all that pleased. Anyway, what the mechanic said put Eddie squarely in the dock. He was fined £1500 and his garage lost its MOT licence. Quite a good source of income, I should think. Well, it didn't take Eddie long to find out who spilt the beans. The mechanic was sacked and there was quite a scene in a pub one night when Eddie threatened Sophie in public. He said he'd make sure the dirty bitch was strung up. Since he said that about two weeks before Sophie's death, he and his brother were obviously prime suspects …"

"But they had a perfect alibi?"

"Well, they both said they were at home with their wives and children. Their wives swore blind that they were at home all evening. We went back several times but nothing would shake them. I still think they knew who did it. They had a guilty look. Their answers didn't ring true. They're the sort of people who would get someone else to do their dirty work for them. If it was a contract killing, it was they who put out the contract – but, as I say, they maintained their innocence most vigorously. It'd be difficult to shift them."

"Motive – revenge," said Raynes.

"Our second pair of suspects were Sophie's son – and his wife."

"John and …?"

"Linda. He's been in the Army for nearly seven years. He's on a twelve year commission. He's married – with two children.

He didn't like his mother. Didn't want to be associated with her. But when he was in a tight corner, he wasn't too proud to ask her for money. A born gambler, John is. Compulsive to the point of folly. When he has the money, he goes wild. Linda's left him several times. Taken the children away. But John's been lucky; his mother helped him out many a time. But John was now twenty-three. Sophie didn't like forking out her money and for the last six months before she died, Sophie had been saying: 'No'. John came to see her twice in the month before she was murdered. He admitted he had been through her bank books … he knew what she was worth. And he had every reason to suppose that, in the event of her death, some at least would come his way."

"But it didn't."

"No. He says that she told him she was leaving most of it to the Church. That's his alibi. He claims that he had no motive for murder. He told Detective-Inspector Parkinson that he stood to get more out of his mother alive – than dead. But he was alone in Aldershot on the night she died. His wife, Linda, and the children were away at the time, so he had the opportunity to come up to Grasshallows and do her in. But whether he would kill his own mother in that way – I just don't know …"

"It does seem unikely," said Raynes.

"But he had been pretty desperate for money. There were letters in Sophie's flat – pretty menacing. He doesn't deny writing them …"

"And he didn't remove them after the murder?"

"No."

"But he had the motive and the opportunity. I suppose even loose cash would have been acceptable?"

"He'd already stolen £200 from her on his last visit. She was very upset about that. She went to see Canon Murray to ask what she should do."

"And what did he suggest?"

"Well, I think he wrote to the Army padre responsible for John's unit. I think they patched things up. John promised to keep away from his mother. Linda returned to him – plus children. And since his mother's death, John has been a reformed character. All debts paid. Never looks at a crap table. It's apparently little short of miraculous."

Raynes and Carlisle tucked into their fillet steak, their knives clattering on the black cast-iron plates. Raynes cut deeply into his medium-rare and was very pleased to see the meat cooked precisely to his instructions. He sipped thoughtfully at his Beaujolais.

"Anything on Linda?"

"Well, she didn't like Sophie either. She put John against her. She comes from a very puritan background. Family disapproves utterly of fornication and prostitution. Her father is a part-time Methodist preacher. Sophie wasn't even invited to the wedding or the christenings. There were several nasty letters from Linda – Sophie kept them – accusing her of corrupting the young and warning her of the wrath to come. Divine punishment with all the trimmings."

"A nice lady!"

"At first sight."

"Had she an alibi?"

"No. She was supposed to be staying with an aunt. Her parents were looking after the children."

"Where was she?"

"She was at a disco and went home with this bloke who was the DJ."

"Oh dear," said Raynes.

"Precisely! She begged us not to let on to John. Wouldn't even give us the name of the bloke. In fact, I'm not even sure if she knew his name …"

"People in glass houses …" said Raynes, finishing off his first glass of Beaujolais.

"Yes," said Carlisle, "she certainly blotted her copybook, if that's really where she was. But I often wondered if she was using one sin to cover another."

"Whoever murdered Sophie, hated her. That's what we are supposed to believe."

"Well, Linda's a fanatic. There's no doubt about that. But since the murder, she and John have been O.K. At least they were last November. That's when the case went dead. I don't

27

know where they are now. Could be in Germany or Northern Ireland …"

Raynes saved up the last of his roast potatoes for a final mouthful and envied Carlisle who had been talking so much that his steak was still half-eaten. Raynes poured himself a second glass of wine and thought about the picture so far.

Carlisle eventually put down his knife and fork.

"Next?" said Raynes.

"The next one was a Commander Kenworth. A nice old guy. About sixty-three. Grey hair. Blue eyes. Thirty-five years in the Navy. He lives alone in Grasshallows. His wife died some years ago – in Malta, I think it was … or Gibraltar … somewhere in the Mediterranean. Commander Kenworth is one of our kinks. He enjoys tying up young ladies with ropes and chains. He pays generously for the pleasure. He was one of Sophie's regular customers. She used to visit his house quite often for bondage sessions. She catered to all his whims."

"So Kenworth was a prime suspect?"

"Yes – except that he did all or most of his philandering at home. I don't think he'd go out all the way to the Meadows to tie someone up to a tree. Not when he had all his equipment at home."

"It seems unlikely."

Raynes' train of thought was upset by the arrival of the waiter who cleared away the dishes and asked if they would like to see the sweet trolley.

"Strawberry pavlova for me," said Raynes.

When the waiter had gone, he resumed: "And where was the Commander on the night in question?"

Carlisle smiled. "He told us that he was having dinner in London with a friend. He told us his dinner guest was a certain Joanne Ritchie. Now we discovered that he did have a girl-friend called Joanne Ritchie but she was in the south of France at the time. I don't think he knew that. He had hoped she would vouch for him, but she wasn't around for him to contact. He didn't know where she was. We found out quicker than he did. She was in Nice or St Tropez or some such place on a package tour. No likelihood of her being in London at the same time."

"So – no alibi?"

"No. Most embarrassing! Fortunately, he did give us the name of the restaurant. He goes there quite often. They recognized his picture. But they couldn't remember whether he was there Friday or Saturday. He often goes down to London for the weekend. But he was certainly with some woman ..."

"Did you identify her?"

"We did – and it was most interesting! She was a woman called Rosalind Hayman who comes from Grasshallows. She's one of the University crowd. Her husband was a lecturer in English. He and she got involved in one of these wife-swapping parties and he eventually left Rosalind and moved in with someone else. It was a pretty bitter separation. She went for the other woman at some University function. Attacked her like an animal. Then she went and poured paint stripper over his car. After that, she poured petrol through his letter-box and threw several lighted matches after it. Fortunately, they all fizzled out but it gave him a nasty shock. He was a friend of Sophie's. At least, she used to go and see him. She was with him the night the petrol came through the letter-box. There is evidence to suggest that Rosalind knew Sophie was there that night. She had it in for any woman associated with her husband. Another time, she slashed the tyres on Sophie's Marina when it was parked down at the Meadows – so we can be quite sure there was no love lost between them. Mrs Hayman was unrelenting in her venom. Not even a couple of prosecutions could calm her down. She made her husband's life in the University quite impossible. He left last year – just after Sophie's death. I believe he got a post in America."

"So Commander Kenworth, one of Sophie's regular customers, was dining with Rosalind Hayman, one of Sophie's proven enemies?"

"Yes. But Mrs Hayman's on the downhill path. She's taken to drinking a lot during the past year. We've had to take her in for being drunk and disorderly. She hasn't been charged but she's been warned. She's a tough cookie. Square face, big eyes, long nails – very long nails with red paint on them."

"And she and the Commander have become friends?"

"I think he's been supporting her. Since her husband left, her financial position has much improved. She's bought a new car. And there's talk in the University that they might be thinking of getting married."

"Did she admit to being the Commander's alibi?"

"She did. But, of course, he got to her first, whilst we were still looking for the invisible Joanne. He put us off the scent for several days but once we found it was a load of rubbish, he eventually came clean and said he was simply trying to protect a lady's reputation. That made us laugh, I can tell you! But all the time we felt he was laughing at us. He didn't seem to be all that upset by Sophie's death. In fact, I think he got rather a kick out of it. Sort of thing he would have liked to have done himself. And, as for that woman – she was capable of anything!"

Coffee was poured. Raynes liked his thick and creamy and ordered a Benedictine to go with it. Carlisle refused a liqueur saying that he would prefer to keep a clear head.

"You've done very well so far," said Raynes. "Who comes next?"

"Oh, rather a curious one – Paul Brown, a student at the University. He was trying to convert her."

"Convert her?"

"Yes. He believed that she should turn from her evil ways and be saved." Carlisle smiled sadly. "Bit of a forlorn hope, I would say. But she liked him. He used to drop round to her flat about teatime and have a chat. An earnest young man with a tweed jacket and brown suede shoes."

"Not a very likely combination?"

"No. But it's amazing the cross-section of society which Sophie attracted. He's a fanatical member of GUCU."

"GUCU?"

"Grasshallows University Christian Union. He was secretary, I believe."

"How on earth did he come to meet Sophie?"

"I think he was taking a walk through the Meadows one evening and they got talking about the flora and fauna. Probably thought she was a member of the RSPB! It was some time before he realized why she was there. I think he represented the sort of son she would have liked to have had and she was a sort of mother-figure to him."

"Some mother!" murmured Raynes. "How did he come to be a suspect?"

"He was the last person to see her alive. He dropped in for a cuppa at about 5.00 pm. They chatted for about forty-five minutes and he left to return to his college for dinner. That was at 6.30 pm. She told him she had an appointment at 7.15 pm. He says that he tried to persuade her not to go. She told him that she had to earn her living and that this was 'a good one'."

"What did she mean by that?"

"I think she meant it was a rendezvous which didn't involve sex."

"I see."

"So he said 'Goodbye' and returned home for tea. She went out to the Meadows and got murdered."

"Nothing to suggest he might have been responsible?"

"Very little. He's very naive. I don't think he realized the half of what Sophie got up to. He used to persuade her that she could get an equally good job in a shop or as a waitress."

"Did she leave him anything in her will?"

"No."

"So – no motive?"

"None except disappointment that she wouldn't listen to his advice. People have been known to kill their mother-figures before now. And we have only his word to go on that their relationship was entirely innocent. Incidentally, he had a very sharp hunting knife in his room at the University. But it wasn't the one used on Sophie."

"Why did he have it?"

"Apparently, he used to be a boy scout."

"Did you examine his background? Before he joined GUCU?"

"I don't think we did. I think Detective-Inspector Parkinson took him at face value."

Raynes scowled. "A great mistake," he said.

There was a brooding silence for a couple of minutes.

"No. 8?" said Raynes. "And yet this is only the tip of the iceberg."

31

"That's the annoying thing," said Carlisle. "After all our investigations, it could end up being a complete stranger. Someone who murdered her on the spur of the moment."

"But you don't think so?"

"I don't know."

"No. 8?" repeated Raynes.

"No. 8 is a lawyer. A respectable lawyer who lives about six miles outside the city. Derek Coates-Smythe is the name. He's a smoothie. Very soft voice; very gracious manner. All angles covered. Thinks before he speaks. Tends to ask you questions rather than the other way round. 'Why should you think that, officer?' Quite maddening!"

"Where does he fit in?"

"Mr Coates-Smythe runs a legal practice here in Grasshallows. It's an old family firm and he's the senior partner. He has a reputation as a womanizer so his connection with Sophie came as no surprise. He used to phone her up about once a month or when he felt the urge. They used to meet at her flat or down at the Meadows in the back of his car."

"Is he married?"

"Indeed he is. A charming wife. Very long-suffering, I would say. She loves him – that's obvious. They have three children and he's devoted to them. But he just likes to pick up what's going. An attractive client ... A young secretary ... A stable girl ... If he feels in the mood, he can't resist making a pass."

"And Sophie had known him for some time?"

"For at least the last ten years. He was her lawyer. He did all her legal business for her."

"Drew up her will?"

"Probably."

"So he would also know where her money was going?"

"I suppose so. But he wouldn't know how much."

"Wasn't Sophie a bit old for him?"

"That's what Inspector Parkinson asked him. He's about the same age. 42. He described himself as very catholic in his tastes. When Inspector Parkinson asked him if he would describe his tastes as weird rather than catholic, Mr Coates-

Smythe said: 'One man's mate was another man's perversion!' I think he liked to shop around. Sophie was about the bottom end of his womanizing. I fancy he liked to do some pretty bizarre things with her."

"Why d'you think that?"

"Well, one of Derek Coates-Smythe's hobbies is photography. He has quite a collection of photographs …"

"How did you discover that?"

"Well, Detective-Inspector Parkinson regarded him as the most likely suspect apart from the Reids. So he did a full-scale search of Mr Coates-Smythe's home and office, looking for the murder weapon. Needless to say, we didn't find it. But we did discover this large collection of erotic photographs in his safe. He liked taking weird pictures. It would've been quite in character for him to have rigged up the scene in the woods and then have tightened the noose."

"There were shots like that?"

"Quite a few. That's what made him so … possible. We had him in for questioning several times. We turned his house and office upside down. As you will see, back at the office, his is the largest file. We even thought of holding him on suspicion and taking his passport away, but he hired the best London lawyers to act for him and they said we had no definite proof – which was true. I'm sure that if he had murdered Sophie, he'd have hidden away those pictures. They're so suggestive … suggestive of the things they got up to. It was just asking for trouble. But Derek Coates-Smythe's too clever to get caught like that."

"What was his excuse?"

"Golf. He claimed that he had played a couple of rounds at Skipper's Hill – that's about six miles west of Grasshallows. He says he was finished by 5.00 pm. He then drove to his office and checked some details for a man he met on the golf course. He says he then went for a drink with one of his partner's wives …"

"Is that confirmed?"

"Well it wasn't at first. The partner's wife was adamant she hadn't seen Mr Coates-Smythe that night. But when it became obvious that only her alibi could save him from a murder rap, she admitted that he'd been with her till 7.00 pm. He drove home from her house to his own home where there was a dinner party for some University folk at 8.00 pm."

"Was there any possible motive?"

"None that we could see. Money isn't a problem for Mr Coates-Smythe. He wasn't being blackmailed. Quite a few people had seen him with Sophie so it was no secret about him and her. Like her son, John, he seemed to have more to gain from Sophie being alive rather than dead. But there's one thing I haven't told you … one of his visiting cards was found on the ground about fifty yards away from the tree …"

"Really?" Raynes' eyes brightened considerably.

"That rattled him. He couldn't explain it. All he could say was that many people must have had one of his cards. Over 3000 had been printed. And if anyone was going to pin the blame on him, that was the easiest way to do it."

"What did you think?"

"It wouldn't have surprised me if Mr Derek Coates-Smythe had put it there himself. So that, because the finger of suspicion pointed so obviously at him, it almost certainly proved his innocence. Legal minds are warped minds."

"Indeed they are," said Raynes; "but what did his wife say about all this?"

"She has stood solidly beside him all the way through. She completely believes in his story. She knows what he gets up to but she doesn't think he's a murderer."

"So he's really Mr Clean?"

"Not really. There's one final twist to the story. His first wife, Constance, claims that he once tried to strangle her. She claims that she left him because of physical and mental cruelty. But his present wife declares that he is a very gentle, sweet-tempered man and that his only vice is young women. Given the dangers of venereal disease, you'd hardly think she viewed his peccadilloes so lightly."

"Do they sleep in the same bed?" asked Raynes.

"No."

Raynes and Carlisle were now the only two people left in

the restaurant and the waiters were busy clearing the tables and tidying up. Raynes asked for the bill and for a second cup of coffee – black this time.

"The final pair?" he said.

"Emilio Zaposito. He's been in and out of jail most of his life. He was one of the Italians Sophie was associated with when she ran away to London as a teenager. He's an absolute brute! He was running a number of call girls in Notting Hill and selling drugs in Carnaby Street in the 'swinging sixties'. He was responsible for killing Carlo Luccione, one of Sophie's brothers-in-law by her first marriage. He was knifed to death in a midnight brawl in West London. Emilio was found guilty of a particularly nasty murder – with a knife you will notice – and his release was delayed because of his violent behaviour in the prison itself. But he was eventually released and there were strong suspicions that he had tracked Sophie down and finished her off."

"Revenge again?"

"Well, she was a leading witness in the trial that sent him down. She wouldn't have been his favourite lady. I'm sure his anger had plenty of time to fester – all those years in jail. I was only present at one interview with Emilio so I can't remember what his movements were – or who was his alibi – but there was certainly nothing all that obvious or we'd have pulled him in. But I always thought he had the best motive and the worst criminal record. I thought that a combination of the Reid brothers and Emilio would have been pretty lethal. The Italians seem to find killing so much easier than the English. The spirit of the vendetta lives on. I think Emilio would repay a closer inspection. For all I know, he may be back in jail again – or even have gone abroad. But I expect someone's keeping an eye on him."

Raynes nodded.

"Bound to be."

"And finally, there's the park-keeper. The man who looks after the Meadows, Ernie McCulloch. He's a queer character. Used to be a pilot in the Fleet Air Arm but was invalided out on health grounds. He was unemployed for a very long time –

couldn't keep a job for more than a week. Just gave it up – without any excuse. He's not married. No family that we know of. The City Council eventually took pity on him and offered him a job as groundsman at Meadowside House. Since then, he's never looked back. Done the job excellently for the past twelve years. Enjoys the outdoor life. The only complaint against him is that he occasionally upsets courting couples by spying on them in the woods. I caught him once watching my wife and me. That was before we were married! Still, he's never done anyone any harm. He's more of a nuisance – a practical joker. Hiding behind trees and scaring the life out of people by suddenly appearing out of nowhere. But everyone knows Ernie. Sophie did. Even if he couldn't account for his movements – and he couldn't or wouldn't – I think it unlikely that he would actually kill Sophie. Tease her, yes. Annoy her perhaps. But not strangle her. The only thing that did surprise me was that he didn't discover her body the following morning. He's always up and about at 6.00 am – even on a Sunday morning – and he's normally the first to report anything suspicious. In fact, it was he who found Mr Derek Coates-Smythe's visiting card. Picked it up and handed it in. But he didn't notice her body. I find that strange."

"Is that the lot?" asked Raynes.

"Well, Detective-Inspector Parkinson reckoned they were the most likely bunch – but we couldn't make anything stick."

"What about the Vicar?"

"Canon Murray?" Carlisle shook his head. "You can't imagine him doing it. As I told you, he's a very gentle soul. Wouldn't hurt a fly."

"That makes him doubly suspect!" said Raynes. "Think how much he stood to gain by all this! One hundred thousand quid! That's quite something. Did you pull him in for questioning?"

"I think he was seen by someone; but I'm quite certain he didn't know anything about the legacy until after the funeral. It took everyone by surprise."

"Not everyone," said Raynes. "Her son knew."

"That's true."

"Well, I think we should start with Canon Murray," said Raynes, "if only to clear the decks."

6 *The Canon*

With the clergy, Raynes' approach was one of maximum offence. Quite frankly, he despised them. So, having been ushered into the genteel sitting room at St Benedict's Rectory, Raynes launched immediately into the attack:

"How long have you been in Grasshallows, Canon?"

"Twenty-five years this October."

"And St Benedict's is quite a wealthy church?"

"Well it was till we started rebuilding our organ ..." Canon Murray smiled a sad smile. "I'm afraid it's going to cost us a pretty penny!"

"How much?"

"Well, it was going to be in the region of £60,000 – plus VAT of course. But now they're talking in terms of something over £90,000. After we've paid all that, I think we shall be a rather poor church!"

"But you received a very generous legacy?"

"We did."

"Was it expected?"

"Not at all. It came completely out of the blue."

"Did you have any scruples about taking the legacy – knowing where the money had come from?"

"I did. But I don't think my Treasurer did. To him, money is just ... money. And this organ business was hanging over our heads. It was really quite a godsend, coming when it did."

"Immoral earnings!" said Raynes aggressively.

"I know."

"Earned every night in the Meadows!"

Canon Murray was silent.

"Did you know Sophie well?"

"I would say so ... Yes. I first met her when she was about sixteen. She'd just had a baby and I baptized him. Must have been one of the first children I ever baptized here. Christmas 1962. He's a soldier now. A gunner, I believe. He was brought up by Mr and Mrs Jack but I rather think he took after his natural father. He's a wild fellow. Very impulsive … Then of course, I buried her father and mother. He had a dreadful accident down at the station and she had cancer. Sophie came home to nurse her mother and she's been here ever since. I think she was always very grateful for the way I looked after her mother …"

"Grateful enough to leave you one hundred thousand?"

"It was a very large amount of money."

"Did you know she had written her family out of her will?"

"Yes. I was very sorry to hear about that."

"Her son got nothing?"

"None of her family got a penny. Mark you, they didn't treat her very well. Her son was always pestering her for money. He beat her up once or twice … and his wife wasn't much better. She was always trying to sponge off Sophie."

"Did she tell you about all that?"

"She did. She used to come to one of our midweek services and occasionally we had a chat about things. She was prepared to help him out. In fact, she did help him out – a lot. Mainly because of the children, I think. But she didn't consider giving him money was the best way. She wanted him to be independent. But his wife was no help. No help at all."

"Do you think he killed her?"

"Well, I thought so at the time. So many murders are committed within the family. About 80%, I believe. I assumed that he was after her money."

"But he didn't get it!"

"No."

"You've got it!"

"Yes."

"Have you ever considered, Canon Murray, that you yourself might be a prime suspect? After all, you stood most to gain from Sophie's death?"

The Vicar shook his head in gentle disbelief, amazed that anyone could connect him with such a crime. Raynes pursued his point with quiet malice: "Did anyone suggest to you – this time last year – that you might be involved?"

"No one suggested anything of the kind! I'm not in the habit of murdering members of my congregation!"

"Not even rich ones?"

"Certainly not!"

"Someone who told you, confidentially, that she was going to leave St Benedict's one hundred thousand pounds, which you needed so much for your organ!"

Canon Murray's face went bright red.

"Mr Raynes, you are being extremely offensive! I am a man of the cloth. I spend my life caring for my people. Praying for them. Rich or poor. If we had needed the money, we should have organized a public appeal, an organ fund, like anyone else. But we had enough invested to pay for the job. If we'd needed more, we'd have had to mount a special campaign. We wouldn't have wanted to use up all our reserves. The fact that we were left such a generous … sum meant that we didn't have to appeal. But if it had been necessary, that is what we should have done."

Raynes decided to move the conversation on to safer ground.

"Your treasurer's a banker, I'm told?"

"That's right. Peter Bridges. He's a manager at the Midland. High Street branch. A very good man."

"How long's he been treasurer?"

Canon Murray paused to think. "Fifteen or sixteen years, I should think. He knows St Benedict's backwards. He's a bit old-fashioned. A bit stubborn. Very tight-fisted. But that's what you want a treasurer to be."

"You get on well together?"

Canon Murray pursed his lips.

"If I'm to be honest, he's not really my cup of tea. He's a typical banker. Thinks only about money, balance sheets, budgets and bottom lines. Mark you, he's very devout. Always there every Sunday at 8.00 am. But even whilst he's waiting for the sacrament, you feel he's counting the cost of the six candles burning at the high altar. I told him that once!"

"Did he laugh?"

"Oh yes. He's got a good sense of humour. A bit dry per-haps. 'Got to keep an eye on you clergymen burning away our

39

profits!' That's what he said. But I can't deny he's been a very good friend to St Benedict's. A very good friend."

"You mean in terms of money?"

"Yes. He's always been most generous."

There was a slight pause whilst Raynes considered the answers he had received. They seemed a little too smooth for his liking.

"I wonder, Canon Murray," he said, "whether you would mind giving me some personal details about yourself?"

"Most willingly."

"When were you born?"

"May 13th 1924. In Edinburgh."

"Full name?"

"George Erskine Murray."

"Are you married or single?"

"My wife died six years ago … cancer. She was only fifty. I miss her very much." Tears welled in his eyes.

"You were at school?"

"Fettes. In Edinburgh."

"University?"

"After the war."

"You were in the Army?"

"Artillery. But the war ended before we were sent abroad."

"Demobbed?"

"September 1946. I was at Jesus. Then at Westcott House."

"Ordained?"

"Deacon in '51. All Saints', Peckham. Priested the following year."

"Any family?"

"A son and a daughter. Both grown up and away. They live in London."

"And where were you before you came to Grasshallows?"

"Five years in London – at Peckham; then six and a half years at a church in Edinburgh, I've always been a high churchman. Bells and smells, you know?"

Raynes nodded thoughtfully.

He was an atheist himself.

"Last year," he said, "you were interviewed by the police?"

"I was asked about Sophie. What I knew about her and her family. Whether she had any enemies and so on. I told them what I could. I tried to explain to them what Sophie was like. She was a very kind person. A very good person, really."

Raynes decided to heave a massive boulder into the tranquil pool.

"Canon Murray," he asked, "did you ever have any dealings with Mrs Jack in a professional capacity? Her professional capacity, I mean?"

For a second or two, Canon Murray looked at Raynes with complete disbelief. Then he exploded with anger: "You are a very rude and offensive man!"

"I'm after the truth, Murray, nothing more and nothing less. A lady has been strangled and mutilated. Tied up to a tree and her stomach slashed open …"

"I thought the case had been closed?"

"A murder case is never closed. This is one of the most brutal murders ever committed in Grasshallows. The murderer still walks free. A year has now passed." He turned to Carlisle. "A year ago last Saturday, was it not?"

His assistant nodded.

"… And I am here to get to the bottom of this."

"Well, I can assure you, Inspector, that I didn't murder her. I didn't know anything about it till I had a visit from a young policeman who told me she had been killed. He didn't say how it had happened but I read about it in the paper. It was a dreadful business."

More tears welled in the Canon's eyes.

"It was terrible. That anyone could do such a thing to her. She wasn't vindictive. She was a very kind person even though she was a … loose woman. She had a warm and generous heart. And because she was a member of my congregation – a black sheep, perhaps – but nonetheless a regular worshipper, I felt it particularly strongly. We've never had anyone murdered before. You can understand what I felt."

Canon Murray took out a handkerchief and wiped his eyes.

"You haven't answered my question," said Raynes.

"Which was that?"

"Whether you knew Sophie in *her* professional capacity?"

"What sort of clergyman do you think I am?"

"Canon Murray," said Raynes patiently, "I would be very grateful if you could answer my question. Did you or did you not encounter Sophie Jack in her professional capacity as a whore?"

"I most certainly did not!" said Canon Murray indignantly.

He's lying, thought Raynes.

"Do you have a police record, Canon Murray?"

The vicar stared at the policeman.

"You mean traffic offences?"

"Criminal offences."

The Canon looked down at the carpet.

"Think carefully," said Raynes. "Don't perjure yourself."

The silence was long and deep.

"Even if you don't tell me, I shall soon find out from Records."

The Rector shrugged his shoulders.

"Are you thinking of retiring soon?" Raynes asked pointedly.

"In a couple of years."

"And where would you live when you retired?"

The Canon relaxed perceptibly as the tone of the questions became less menacing. "On the south coast," he said. "That's where everyone goes."

"Do you have property there?"

"Yes. How did you know?"

"I didn't."

"My wife and I bought a small flat down there a number of years ago. For holidays, you know, and retirement. We didn't get away often but it's nice to know it's there."

"Where is it?" asked Raynes.

"In Rye."

"Beautiful place, old streets, the Mermaid ..."

"Yes. And a lovely old church ..."

Raynes decided that the interview had gone on long enough. He was quite sure the elderly Canon was being less than honest with him. But now he must give him time to sweat out his conscience. Raynes got up out of his armchair.

"And where does your treasurer live?"

"46, London Road. A large white house. You can't miss it."

"Is he married?"

"Yes. He has a charming wife. Does a great deal for the Church."

"We must drop in."

"Well, you won't catch him till Wednesday. He's away at a Bank Managers' conference. In Bournemouth, I believe. He goes there every year at this time. But he should be back by Wednesday night."

Raynes nodded.

"Thank you for telling me what you have, Canon Murray. I wish you could have told us more. I shall read what you told the young policeman last year and I shall make a point of consulting police records. And then, if necessary, I shall return. If you want to see me, all you have to do is phone. In the meantime, I shall leave you to write your sermon!"

Raynes turned on his heel and walked out of the door. Canon Murray turned to Carlisle.

"What an unpleasant creature! Who is he?"

"He's the new chief. He took over from Detective-Inspector Parkinson this morning."

"Well, I don't think he'll go down very well in Grasshallows if he treats people like that!"

"It was a pretty horrible murder."

"But surely, he didn't think I'd do a thing like that. I can assure you that I've never thought of murdering anyone. Not even the President of the Womens' Guild – though she's a real pain." He chuckled to himself. "Certainly not Sophie. She was a very kind person … very kind."

7 *The Mechanics*

Eddie Reid was standing beneath the hydraulic jack examining the underside of a particularly run-down Toyota. He poked a screwdriver gently against a rusty piece of metal which crumbled instantly. He said to his brother: "That sill's completely gone. No chance of patching it up. No chance at all …" He realized that his brother was not listening to him. Jim was looking over his shoulder into the garage yard where a large white Granada had just pulled up.

"Pigs!" said Jim.

"Not again!" said Eddie.

"'Fraid so."

"Would it be the Rover?"

"Hope not."

"There's two of them. Who's the new guy?"

"Dunno."

Eddie continued to examine the entrails of the Toyota whilst Jim watched the advancing policemen with studied contempt.

"Afternoon! Mr Reid?"

"Yep."

"And your brother?"

Jim nodded.

"Can we go somewhere and have a chat?"

Jim indicated the office which was a pre-fabricated box set in a dark corner of the garage. They walked past several heaps of chain, a recovery lorry and two much-mangled cars before they reached the small dingy room which passed as an office. The air was thick with tobacco smoke. The walls had many streaks of dirt and grease. Two pin-up calendars enlivened the room and a half-open filing cabinet showed a remarkable lack of records. As Carlisle had said to Raynes: "They don't keep much on paper."

Raynes introduced himself in a pleasant fashion.

"I think you knew Detective-Inspector Parkinson?"

Jim Reid nodded.

He knew his predecessor all too well.

"Well, he left recently and I've come to take his place. My name's Raynes."

Eddie quietly added the name to his Encyclopedia of Demonology.

Raynes continued: "I'm not here about any cars – or any accidents, but I want your help to clear up a mystery which has been bugging the police for over a year."

Raynes felt that he could not have been more agreeable. The fact that no car was involved immediately improved the

44

atmosphere but with the mention of "a year", a cloud returned.

"Sophie Jack," said Raynes.

"Her!"

"Yes. Her."

"We thought we'd heard the last of her!"

"Well, I'm afraid you haven't. The police never close their files – and this one was a pretty gruesome murder. I can see from records that you two were high on the list of suspects this time last year, and I'd like your help. We can discuss it here – or we can pull you in for questioning. The choice is up to you."

The brothers sat sullenly in the cheap plastic chairs. Neither one looked at the other. Both looked at the floor. Eddie ground out his cigarette. Jim wiped his hands over his brown overalls. He decided to be the spokesman.

"Well, we didn't do it. Everyone thinks we did. A lot of nasty things have been said. Rumours and such like. Eddie got his eye bust in a fight last November. Chap accused him outright of carving her up. Eddie lashed out; five chaps bounced him and he ended up in hospital. Lucky to still have his eye!"

Carlisle nodded. He remembered the incident.

He said: "You made it pretty obvious you had it in for her. You said that you'd like to string her up – the dirty bitch!"

"So I did. She lost us a lot of trade. Her and Mitchell …"

"Mitchell was the mechanic," explained Carlisle.

"… and he's dead too," said Eddie. "Can't blame us for that. Got knocked down by a lorry outside that supermarket …"

"Serve him right too. He did the dirty on us …"

"… Bit the 'and that fed 'im!"

Raynes felt that the introductions were now complete.

"How long had you known Sophie?"

Jim looked at Eddie.

"Since we were at school."

"So that's about thirty-five years?"

"On and off, yes. Of course, she spent a lot of time down in London. On the game with those Italian blokes …"

"You knew her when she was working in the coffee bar?"

"Not us. We didn't go into no coffee bar. It wasn't for the

45

likes of us. We preferred the pubs and the flicks. The coffee bar was for all them 'versity types. Gasbags and tarts."

Clearly, Mr Reid did not think highly of the University community.

"When did you renew contact with her?"

"Eh?"

"When did you meet up with her again?"

"Oh? When she bought a car here."

"That would be about ten years ago?"

"Couldn't say."

"What kind of car did she buy?"

"God! You don't expect me to remember that! Not after all these years. Blimey, if I could remember all that ..."

"It was a Renault 4," said Carlisle.

"Was she satisfied with it?" asked Raynes.

Neither Eddie nor Jim said a word.

"I imagine she brought it back several times?"

Silence.

"It was a complete banger?"

"I don't think she paid much for it. You get what you pay for."

"Indeed you do," said Raynes. "But you sold her a dud car and she was pretty annoyed. She didn't buy any more cars from you?"

"No."

"Avoided you like the plague?"

"Expect so."

"So she was hardly likely to have happy memories of Reid's Garage?"

There was no reply.

"I take it therefore that neither of you two gentlemen ever visited her in a professional capacity?"

"You mean – screwed her?"

"Not bloody likely!"

Eddie and Jim both looked up with righteous indignation.

"Never had to pay for it yet!"

"Wouldn't want to get the clap!"

"But you met her in pubs and things?"

"Came across her occasionally."

"Did you ever say anything to her?"

Eddie laughed. "Jim used to say she was the most vintage fanny in town! Both her front wings were sagging! Rusty innards and a faulty exhaust! Doubt if she'd ever pass an M.O.T. even from us! She was a complete cow!"

Jim continued the attack:

"How any chap went with her, I just don't know! She was well past it …"

"Yet they were all shagging her. They say people used to queue up in the Meadows for a quickie!"

"Perverts!" said Jim. "Bloody perverts!"

"You two are both happily married, I believe?" said Raynes.

"Yep."

"Wives and children?"

"I've got three. Jim's got two."

"So you don't need to go and sow your wild oats? Never a whiff of scandal? Pure as driven snow?"

Eddie was about to say: "That's right!" but Jim looked at Carlisle – a suspicious look. Even if Raynes didn't know the brothers, the young constable did. He'd been brought up in Grasshallows. He knew all the gossip.

"Not entirely," said Carlisle. "There were a couple of barmaids, weren't there? One of them got pregnant. An abortion, wasn't there? And someone got caught out with that long-distance lorry-driver's wife? Caught running home with no pants!"

Eddie shrugged his shoulders at the memory.

"The joys of sex!" said Raynes. "But this is a serious business. Sophie Jack was murdered. Brutally. You had it in for her. You said publicly that you would string her up. Strung up, she was. And strangled. Both of you have lousy police records. Eleven assault cases between you, I'm told. You're suspected of selling any number of dud cars. And you're responsible for quite a large number of innocent people being injured …"

"And three others killed!"

"It's a lie!"

47

"Lie or not, the two of you have a violent reputation in this city. You both have a track record of crime with violence – especially after a drink. You've taken your revenge on many people who have crossed you in the past. Sophie Jack may have done the dirty on you …"

"Didn't half!"

"But you publicly threatened revenge only two weeks before she was found dead at that tree. Why shouldn't the police regard you as the No. 1 suspects?"

Eddie shook his head.

"We didn't do it."

"We thought of doing something to her car …"

"You did several things to her car," said Carlisle with anger. "You cut her brake pipes and it was probably you who re-adjusted her exhaust so that the fumes fed into her car! …"

Both brothers were silent.

"… so don't say you did nothing! You know you had a good try. Lucky for you nothing serious happened!"

Raynes waited till the atmosphere was less charged.

"I imagine Detective-Inspector Parkinson has dealt with most of this," he said. "What I want to know is what you were doing on the night she died?"

"We've already told the pigs!"

"I'm not sure they believed you."

"Too bad!"

"From what you've said, quite a few other people in Grass-hallows didn't believe you either. They know you were out to get her."

The brothers said nothing.

"Where were you on the night she died?"

"At home," said Jim.

"Whose home?"

"Both our homes."

"Unusual to be in on a Saturday night?"

"Very unusual," said Carlisle. "Normally they're in one of the pubs – playing darts."

"But you weren't that night?"

"We were at home …"

"… and that's all we're saying!"

"You expect us to believe you?"

"You can believe what you like, mate! …"

"… That's our story and we're sticking to it!"

Detective-Inspector Raynes looked at the brothers coldly.

"Don't you think that's a very stupid attitude to take? You're just adding to your troubles. We know you weren't at home. You know you weren't at home. We're going to keep on at you till we get the truth. Detective-Inspector Parkinson may have given you the benefit of the doubt. I certainly won't. I shall take you into custody and after a couple of hours with one or two of our young constables, you'll be ready to squeal. You're not very popular in Grasshallows so no one's going to shed any tears if you get hurt. Quite a few people are itching to get their hands on you and by the time they've finished, your balls will be pretty sore!"

"Another bent copper!"

"It's the best way to treat thugs like you. You go round throwing your weight about but underneath, you're yellow cowards. I shall give you one last chance. Come clean with what you know about Sophie. Tell us where you were that Saturday night – and no trouble. Hold out on me and I promise that you'll be doubled up in pain and crying for mercy. After that, you'll sign anything!"

Pure hatred shone in the eyes of both brothers.

"You better watch your step, copper!"

Raynes kept his voice calm and reasonable.

"I want the truth. If you bumped her off, I want to know. If you took out a contract, I want to know whom you paid. I shall give you one week – till next Monday – then we'll pull you in."

"All for that shagbag!" said Eddie.

"She didn't deserve to die like that."

"That's what you think!"

Raynes shook his head – more in sorrow than in anger. "Goodbye," he said. "I shall look forward to hearing from you between now and next Monday."

He left the garage at a fairly quick pace and was glad when he reached the Granada unharmed.

"Not very nice," said Carlisle as he started the engine.

"Poisonous," said Raynes, looking back.

But of Eddie and Jim Reid there was no sign. They were still in the office.

"Are you going to tell 'em?" asked Eddie.

"Well, I'm certainly not going to get my balls kicked in by his mob."

"He's a bastard!"

"Yep, he's a right bastard – and he means it!"

8 The Park-keeper

Raynes and Carlisle found themselves caught up in a traffic jam. It was 4.45 pm and Grasshallows' version of rush-hour was about to begin. Raynes ground his teeth with impatience. He turned to Carlisle:

"Have we time for one more?"

"A quick one perhaps?"

"The gamekeeper – Ernie something?"

"The groundsman."

"That's right."

Detective-Constable Carlisle looked at his watch.

"Would you mind if I phoned my wife. She was expecting me back at 5.15 pm. But it's been a much more hectic day … much busier than I expected."

"That's all right," said Raynes. "I promise we'll finish by 6.00 pm. I'll even drive you home. Do you think we'll catch this Ernie fellow?"

"No problem. He's there all day."

The traffic suddenly cleared and Carlisle took a sharp right-handed turn which led them through a maze of back streets and brought them back on to the road which led to the Meadows for their second visit that day.

Ernie McCulloch was cleaning out the toilets – a job which he always felt was beneath his dignity as a retired naval officer. Why, he asked himself, did people have to relieve themselves all over the floor? Presumably they didn't do it at home – so why do it elsewhere? Ernie had cleaned out the gents and was halfway through the ladies when he was suddenly conscious of two dark shadows falling across the wet tiled floor. He looked up with surprise. Policemen.

Carlisle said: "Ernie, this is Detective-Inspector Raynes, our new C.O. He wants to ask you a few questions. Can you spare us a couple of minutes?"

Ernie put down his mop.

"Anything's better than cleaning toilets!"

He wiped his hand on a towel and rolled down his sleeves.

They sat down on a low stone wall beside the river. The late afternoon sun shone down warmly upon them.

"Mr McCulloch," said Raynes, "I'm told that you know everything that goes on round here?"

"Pretty well," said Ernie.

"Well, I want you to tell me everything you know about Sophie Jack."

"Sophie? Heavens! I could write a book about her! Poor Sophie! Place hasn't been the same without her. She was almost a fixture round here. Come rain – come shine, you'd see her car parked over there." He pointed to a small car park on the other side of the bridge. "She always parked in that corner beside the rhododendrons – the purple ones. Her car was there most evenings from 7.00 pm. When things were quiet, I used to go over and have a fag with her – just to pass the time. But that wasn't often!" He smiled. "She was in constant demand, our Sophie! By 7.15, the first car would be rolling up. Off she would go. Back into town – or into the forest." He looked at Raynes. "That's what we call that wild bit. Jungle might be a better word!" He laughed.

Raynes noticed that he had very white teeth.

"Some nights she'd be back and forrard like a yo-yo. Other times, she'd be away two or three hours and people would be hanging around waiting. I recognized quite a few of them. Councillors … lecturers. On Sundays, you'd see them here with their wives and children; then, on Wednesdays, you'd see them coasting around in their 2CVs. Most uncomfortable, I should think!" He laughed. "Sophie did her best. First come, first served. Into the wood – she always went to the same place.

51

And they always dropped her outside the ladies. A quick wash and brush up and she was ready for the next one. Like clockwork, she was."

"Been here almost as long as you, hasn't she, Ernie?"

"Just about. She started off before her mother died. That must be – what? – ten years ago. She was a bit more uppity in those days. Cut you dead when she felt like it, but she got more ... more mellow as the years went by. Became more of a friend. Yes, we miss her very much round here since she died." He wiped away a tear. "Sentimental old bastard," he said apologetically.

"You were the last person to see her alive, Mr McCulloch. Can you remember that evening?"

"Well, after the grilling I got from you people last year, I'm hardly likely to forget. I don't know how many times I was questioned. Again and again – same story. She arrived here about seven o'clock as usual. Parked her car in the usual place. Walked over the bridge. She was wearing a red dress, gold belt and gold shoes – and a black handbag – I remember that ..."

"She crossed the bridge alone?"

"Yes."

"On foot?"

"Yes. That surprised me. Normally, she drove into the forest – either in her car or someone else's. You often saw her walking out, but not normally walking in."

"What did you think?"

"I thought she was going to the ladies to freshen up. I wished her a good evening. Last thing I saw was her walking up the path beside that pine tree."

"Did you think she was meeting someone?"

"Well, obviously! He must have got there first, I thought. Not many people around at that time. Bright summer's evening and all that. She's probably late, I thought. Or else he didn't want to be seen. There's quite a few like that – but Ernie, he sees them all!" He winked in a particularly lecherous fashion.

Raynes smiled.

"Did she seem frightened or worried?"

"No. I've thought about that again and again. I can't say she was. Looked quite cheerful really. Had her best dress on …"

"How do you know that?"

"Well, I knew her wardrobe pretty well. Had seen it all, many a time. Black winter coat with a gold brooch, pink track suit, blue trouser suit, brown cloak, you name it. I'd seen her in most of her outfits. And her wigs …"

"Wigs?"

"Yes. She chopped and changed. Now and again, I'd see this brunette and I'd say: 'Hold on. Who's this?' and it was her. She had a black one with curls – even a red one – well, orangey. She had a green velvet dress that went rather well with that – and her gold belt. Sometimes you might think it was a completely different woman – but then you realized it was Sophie. Made her look younger, I thought."

"She wasn't wearing a wig that night?"

"No. She was just herself. Just herself."

"And the last thing you saw was her going into the wood? At about 7.00 pm?"

"That's all."

"You didn't follow her?"

"Heavens, no. I've seen it all before."

"I'm sure you have," said Raynes.

He thought for a minute.

"You say it was unusual for her to set off into the woods on her own – on foot?"

"It was. I'd seen her do it before – but not all that often. Normally, on a Saturday, she'd have to wait. Specially on a summer's evening. People didn't turn up till nearer 8.00 pm, when it was getting darker … when they'd had a drink or two. Dutch courage – or dutch something." He laughed in a rather crude fashion.

"And her car stayed there for the rest of the evening?"

"Never moved. Sat there till you people broke into it on the Sunday afternoon."

"What did you think had happened?"

"Well, it's not unusual to see the car there overnight. Quite often it was still there in the morning. Specially if she had an all-nighter. The car'd often be here till 7.30 or 8.00 next morning. They'd drop her off on the way to work. Or she'd get a taxi. Sometimes the car wouldn't start. On a frosty morning in winter, I used to clean her points and give it a drop of wet start – and off she'd go. Always gave me a fiver."

"Very generous?"

"Very. Though sometimes we had to call out the garage."

"Not Reid's?"

"Not bloody likely! Load of crooks, if you ask me. Wouldn't touch 'em with a bargepole … and neither would she! Not after what they did to her."

Raynes nodded.

"They came up here and cut her brake pipes. Tried to gas her."

"So I've heard."

"Nasty lot. It's a wonder you don't pull 'em in."

"You didn't see them round here that night?"

"Oh no, you don't see them round here. Not in the Meadows. They've other fish to fry. From what I've heard."

"Did you see anyone you knew that night? Any of Sophie's regulars?"

"Well, there were a few of them hanging round later. Parked their cars. Stomped around. Had a fag. Visited the toilets. Went up for a walk in the forest. Some of the other girls looked after them. But, eventually, they all drifted away."

"So you saw nothing unusual that night? No big car streaking away?"

"No. Nothing."

"Could someone have come in some other way? Across the fields?"

"Could have. Not all that easy. Lot of hedges and so on. It's about a mile to the nearest road."

"From where the body was found?"

"Yes."

"And that was at the back of the forest?"

"Yes. Right at the back."

"Not her usual place in the woods?"

"No."

"Why d'you think she was there?"

"Wanted a bit of privacy, I should think. I heard it said that maybe the murderer wanted to take some saucy pictures. That'd be quite a good place. Quite bright of an evening. Quite quiet. Very few people go that far. No peepin' Toms! I should know!" He laughed again.

"So all you saw was an empty car?"

"Well, almost. I did think at one point she came back to her car. About 9.00 pm it was. Perhaps a bit later. It was getting dark by then. I could have sworn I heard her car door bang. The passenger door. You had to bang it hard to get it shut. I heard it go. I thought: 'She's back' but the car never moved. When I happened to look down the avenue, there was a car parked – I saw its red lights – and I saw someone getting in. I said to myself: 'She's off again'. But I couldn't be sure. It might have been one of the other girls …"

"But her handbag and keys were found in the car?"

"I know. So it must have been her – or the murderer."

"That's right," said Raynes.

It was getting near 6.00 pm. Raynes moved to his two final questions.

"How was it," he asked, "that you didn't find the body? I thought you kept a close eye on all this property? How come you missed her?"

"Well, that was because she was a bit off the beaten track. I did my rounds as usual – looked in all the normal places – but I wasn't expecting to see her. I assumed she was off on an all-nighter. And then those kids found her. That made it worse. I saw her. It was a pretty ghastly sight." He shuddered at the memory.

"Well, you may not have found Sophie, but you found that visiting card."

"You couldn't miss it. Stood out a mile. I was on the back ride … only about a hundred yards from the body (only I didn't know it then) when I saw it lying there at the side of the path. 'Hello', I said to myself, 'who's been a naughty boy then?' I looked at the card. Mr Derek Coates-Smythe! Respectable lawyer, I said to myself. Well, perhaps not so respectable …"

"Had you seen him in the woods?"

"Not that night. But he used to come quite often in the old days. Afternoons and evenings. Quite a lad, our Derek! Mark you, he's been much better since he got married again. And since last year, we haven't seen him hardly at all. Reformed character, if you ask me!"

"So the card didn't surprise you?"

"Well, in a way it did. Most people don't leave their names and addresses behind 'em. Old condoms, bras, pants and other things – but not usually their visiting cards!"

"Do you think it was deliberately left?"

"Could have been."

"But you didn't see this lawyer here that Saturday night?"

"No. I'm quite certain about that."

"How long d'you think the card had been there?"

"Well, it wasn't there on Saturday afternoon. I'm sure about that. So it must have fallen out on Saturday night or early Sunday morning."

Raynes looked at his watch. It was nearly 6.00 pm – and Carlisle's wife would be on the warpath. He looked at Ernie's brown, wizen face. "Thank you," he said, "you've been most helpful."

"Always glad to oblige!"

Raynes stood up and stretched his legs.

"Were you ever yourself one of Sophie's customers?" he asked.

The question was designed to take Ernie by surprise just as he thought the questions were over. Raynes watched his reaction closely.

Ernie laughed. A rather sad laugh.

"Never had the offer, sir."

"Surely it's not a question of 'offer'?" said Raynes. "It's a question of inclination – or cash?"

"Never had much of either," said Ernie. "I'm not really one for the ladies, sir, being an old navy man. You know what the Navy traditions are, sir! Rum, sodomy and the lash!"

Raynes smiled.

"You just stick to the rum," he said.

9 *The Green Man*

It had been a long day.

Detective-Inspector Raynes returned to his hotel well-pleased with the way his new job had begun. At 8.30 am that morning, he had been in the pits of despair, contemplating a future of unremitting boredom. By 7.00 pm, he was deep into a savage murder hunt which provided him with a fascinating professional challenge. In the process, he had plunged vigorously into the life of a small University town and won immediate approval and support from the staff at Grasshallows police station. Yes. It had been a good day.

He went upstairs, had a shower and tried to decide what sort of outfit would be appropriate for dinner in Grasshallows' premier hotel. He selected a dark green cord jacket, dark green trousers, a white shirt with thin, pale green, diagonal lines – and a plain green bow-tie. After all, he reflected, it was called *The Green Man*.

Despite the substantial lunch which he and Carlisle had enjoyed, he was by now feeling extremely hungry. He entered the dining room and was shown to a single table near the window. He ordered stilton and cauliflower soup, medallions of pork and lemon meringue pie. Whilst he was waiting and in between courses, he looked through the *Evening Echo* to see what properties Grasshallows had to offer. There was no hurry – but he could not afford to remain in *The Green Man* indefinitely.

The food was good and the service too was satisfactory. The waiter proved attentive and obliging. Raynes asked him where the best local talent could be found. "Female talent" Raynes added, lest the sight of his green bow-tie should perhaps create the wrong impression. The waiter assured him that he need look no further than the cocktail lounge where the *jeunesse doré* of Grasshallows sipped their gin-and-tonics in genteel splendour. To be sure, Monday was not the best of nights but it was certainly more congenial than Friday or

Saturday when the place was filled to capacity with students. Fortunately, most of that crowd had now departed on vacation but, in a fortnight, they would be back again with their parents for the Graduation and the place would once more be in turmoil. Raynes thanked him for his information and left a generous tip.

He strolled into the deep orange glow of the cocktail bar and immediately noticed two very shapely young women sitting at the bar deep in conversation. Although there were perhaps fifty or sixty people in the room, his professional eye immediately identified them as Sophie's *cordon bleu* sisters. The one on the left had dark hair and wore a black velvet dress. The one on the right was a blonde with bare shoulders, wearing a tight, shiny, electric blue dress. What caught Raynes' eye was her bottom, sitting perched on the bar stool. It was deliciously round and shapely. He decided to make its acquaintance.

He realized of course that this was not exactly in the best detective tradition. Sleuths did not go round picking up young women. You could not imagine Hercule Poirot finding himself in this position: "Oh Madame, I fear I must resist your obvious charms." Or Lord Peter Wimsey: "I say, Bunter, what would the Duchess of Denver say about this?" "I don't know, my lord, but I'm sure she would disapprove." Too right she would! Sherlock Holmes, certainly, had always tried to immerse himself in his part – to attain local colour, but cocaine and cabmen had been his portion. Miss Silver and Miss Marple would certainly have disapproved: "Oh, my dear, I was most shocked! They would never do such things in St Mary Mead!" But they were all fictional characters. He, Raynes, was a real, flesh-and-blood, live detective. He had his passions and failings – but often, he found, he could turn his vices into virtues. This he proceeded to do.

He walked up casually to the bar and laid his evening paper on the counter. He ordered a malt whisky with plenty of ice. Even though he had not as yet looked in their direction, he sensed that he had been noticed. He hoped that he did not look or sound too much like a policeman. That could be awkward.

Having collected his glass, he turned in their direction and smiled shyly as he caught their eye.

"You must be the local talent!" he said teasingly.

"We are!" said the girl in black.

"The best!" said the girl in blue.

She was older than he had thought. About 30 to 32, but she had a cheeky, interesting face. The darker girl was plain and wore too much make-up.

"I was wondering what this little place had to offer."

"Are you a visitor then?"

"I'm here for a few days. I was wondering what the property prices are like round here. Are things expensive?"

"We are!" said the girl in black.

"I can see that," said Raynes, "but what about houses and flats? Which is the best area to go for?"

"The Meadows!" said the girl in blue, with a laugh.

He noticed she had nice teeth.

Being a visitor, Raynes could not be expected to know anything about the Meadows. He let the joke pass over him. The girl in blue explained: "That's where all the courting couples go in Grasshallows. It's very dark, very wild …"

"… and very romantic!" added the girl in black.

Raynes raised his eyebrows.

"That sounds just the place. And you say it's very expensive?"

The girl in blue changed the subject.

"What brings you to Grasshallows? Are you in the University?"

"I sell wine," said Raynes without the flicker of an eyelid. It was a little white lie which he had often found useful. Everyone had an opinion about wine and his revelation was greeted with enthusiasm. A lively discussion followed about French wines and German wines, Spanish wines and Italian wines. Which were good and which were to be avoided. All the wines they had ever drunk were given an airing. Could he supply them with a box or two of their favourite tipple?

"At a price," he said – with a twinkle in his eye.

Touché.

As a friendly gesture, he treated them to a fresh round of

gin-and-tonic. The girl in black wondered whether she should have a cocktail but then decided it would be wiser not to mix her drinks. Raynes steadily directed most of his conversation towards the girl in blue and her partner was not slow to get the message. After a final gulp of her gin, she espied an old friend at the other end of the bar and left them.

"Fiona and I have been friends for twenty years," said the girl in blue. "We were at school together."

"In Grasshallows?"

"Yes. I've always lived here. Where do you come from?"

"Bristol. The West Country." It was better to be vague.

"And you're thinking of settling down here?"

"Got to have a good base. This seems as good a place as any. We sell quality wines and there seems to be quite a good class of people living round here. The University and so on."

The girl in blue did not like the University people. They were snobs, she said. They were very clannish. Now and again, there were terrible scandals.

Professors ran off with lecturers' wives. There were wife-swapping parties. Yes, she had been to one or two. She didn't think much of lecturers as lovers. Too much talk. Not enough action. Always trying to analyze your feelings. Not happy unless you had at least one orgasm.

"Was he married?"

No, said Raynes. He'd been divorced. About five years ago. She had been divorced. Twice.

Raynes agreed that no one in their right mind would endure matrimony willingly. He had found that people treated each other more kindly – and more honestly – when they were free to come and go. The girl in blue agreed.

Raynes asked her name.

"Debbie May," she replied.

"On the other hand, Debbie might not!" he joked.

She assured him that although she was picky-and-choosy, when she liked someone – and when the price was right – Debbie was not the girl to say no.

Raynes said he was glad to hear it. It was a bit lonely being a stranger in an unfamiliar city. Would she like another G & T?

He had settled himself on the bar stool where Fiona had been sitting. He looked at the brown breasts sloping under the electric blue dress and told Debbie how much he admired her bottom. It was the first thing he had noticed when he came into the room. Debbie giggled happily. She told him – *in vino veritas* – that underneath her dress, she was wearing no pants and only a small bra. The information aroused Raynes – as it was meant to do.

Debbie narrowed her eyes and moved closer.

"Would you like a little run down to the Meadows?"

"How much would it cost me?" he asked cautiously.

She looked at him speculatively.

"Fifty quid for a couple of hours."

"How much for the whole night?"

Debbie brightened up at the prospect.

"For you," she said. "A round hundred!"

"God!" said Raynes. "That's more than my quarterly telephone bill!"

"And so it should be," declared Debbie. "Think of what you're getting!"

"A long-distance trunk call," joked Raynes.

Debbie giggled again.

"Well, you did say you wanted to see my bottom!"

"For a hundred pounds," said Raynes, "I shall expect the entire works! Gym slip and black suspenders. Bondage and leather gear. Whips and manacles."

He paused to watch her reaction.

None.

She was obviously into most things.

He wondered if she had known Sophie. He would soon find out.

Debbie sipped the last of her gin.

She asked if he could smell her perfume? Chanel No. 19?

Raynes leaned forward and put his nose close to her soft, warm cleavage. He breathed in the deep, warm, satisfying smell of womanhood. She stroked his face with her hand. "Let's go," she said; "your place or mine?"

"I'd prefer yours," said Raynes, anxious not to blot his copybook too publicly. "Then I shall know where to send the wine."

Debbie put her arm round his shoulder and climbed down from her perch. "Am I getting the wine too?"

"Of course," said Raynes. "You do your best for me and I shall do my best for you. A great night – and a case of bubbly shall be yours!"

He escorted her through the back door of the hotel into the car-park where his Rover was parked. He ran his hands round her waist and cradled her left breast. It felt soft and bouncy. He stroked her bottom as she bent down to get into the car. No, she was wearing no pants.

Raynes drove his happy hooker home.

10 *The Happy Hooker*

"A cigarette?"

"I'd prefer a drink of something."

"Whisky, gin, martini …?"

"Orange juice, if you've got it?"

"Sure."

Debbie rolled out of bed and went off to the kitchen.

Raynes lay back peacefully and looked at the ceiling of the basement flat. It was white. Everything was white. Furniture, carpet, chairs – even the pictures seemed to be in various shades of white.

"You like white?" he asked when she came back.

"Brightens the place up," she said. "Makes me look browner," she added.

"It certainly does," said Raynes, admiring her all-over tan.

"Ambre solaire?" he asked.

"Porto de Pollensa."

"Where's that?"

"Majorca. Went there for a break at the beginning of June. It was ever so hot." She settled back with her cigarette and shut her eyes. Raynes sipped his orange juice slowly.

"Don't you ever worry about being on your own with strange men?" he asked. "Aren't you frightened that they might suddenly bash you over the head – or strangle you – without warning?"

"Every single bloody man I have ever known has asked me that question!"

"Oh," said Raynes, slightly deflated. "It's just that I remember reading about some murder round here last year when a girl got strangled. It was in one of the Sunday papers ..."

"Sophie Jack."

"I couldn't tell you what her name was, but she got bumped off. Did they ever catch the chap that did it?"

"No."

Debbie opened her eyes. They were deep hazel brown.

"Wasn't you, was it?

"Certainly not!" said Raynes. "I never set foot in Grasshallows till last night. It just stuck in my mind as a nasty piece of work."

"Stuck in my mind too," said Debbie, "and Fiona's. We've been much more careful who we go with. We always start off together and if she thinks someone is a bit odd, we warn each other. We have a password. See?"

"Very wise," said Raynes.

"Mark you," said Debbie, "it's sometimes the odd ones that pay the most."

"More than wine salesmen?"

Debbie smiled.

"I haven't had a wine salesman before. But some of those kinky types are so glad to have someone who'll do for them, they'll pay well over the odds. I had a bloke here yesterday afternoon – just for twenty minutes. All he wanted was to be tied down and spanked with my sandal. Nothing more than that. I did it good and hard. When he left, what d'you think? He gave me a £50 tip – over and above my normal! I mean, it was amazing for twenty minutes." She paused to calculate. "At that rate" she said, "I'm worth £240 an hour!"

"More than that!" said Raynes putting his arm around her.

"You think so?"

"I do."

"Are you an expert then?"

"I know a good body when I feel one!"

"Gee! Thanks!"

"Did you know this girl that got murdered? Sophie …"

"Everyone knew Sophie. Everyone in Grasshallows. She'd been around for so long. She was quite old you know. In her forties, I think. Didn't look it though. Made herself up well. But we didn't fish in quite the same pool … if you know what I mean?"

"Snob!"

"No, I'm not. But it's true. She was dirt cheap. I go with perhaps one or two blokes a day – but she used to have seven or eight. We used to call her a well-buttered bun! That's probably why she got bumped off. She took anyone. She used to specialize in all the queer customers – people who weren't particular. The whips, the rubber men, the real perverts. They pay well – but you have to handle them very carefully. I don't mind a bit of good honest sex – well, you know that – but some of these men are real shits. They want to … to humiliate you. Pee on you. Take dirty pictures of you in really horrible poses. Most girls avoid them like the plague but you never know what people are like till you get them on their own. Then they come out in their true colours. Then you see what they're really like."

"So you think it was one of them that killed her?"

Debbie paused.

"No one really knows. The word around town is that it was a couple of blokes who run a garage who did her in. She shopped them to the police and they threatened to string her up. Fiona was there when they said it – so there's no denying they said it. Other people say it was her son. He was in my brother's class at school; he said he was pretty rough with his hands. And then there's one of those blokes she worked for down in London. A gangland killing, they said. But we don't have any gangs up here."

"But you have your own idea?"

"I'm not sure. Something tells me it was one of these kinky types who just went too far. I know who it might have been. He's a real weirdo. And yet he seems such a nice, gentle old soul. White hair, blue eyes, retired. Lovely house. I went there once. Never again! He tied me up – upside down! Almost strangled me! I scratched his arm – so as the police would get

64

his blood group off my nails. He was one of Sophie's. It could have been him." She shuddered. "Who knows?" she said.

She looked at her watch – on a little white strap. The roman numerals suggested that it was 2.30 am. "Come on!" she said. "Let's do it again and I'll make you breakfast!"

* * *

Raynes awoke to the clink of knives and forks and a strong smell of bacon and eggs. His watch said that it was nearly 8.00 am. He rubbed his eyes – amazed at such VIP treatment. Breakfast as well!

"You've been very kind," he said to Debbie as he came into the kitchen – all white, with red pans.

"I don't do it for everyone," she said.

"In that case, I consider myself very lucky."

She smiled and shovelled two sausages on to his plate.

"You won't forget the bubbly?"

Bubbly? Oh, yes. The bubbly!

"No," said Raynes. "I shan't forget. I'll put in an order right away. First thing I shall do!" He tucked into the two fried eggs and munched a piece of toast.

"You see," Debbie said, "I was afraid you might forget."

Her bright hazel brown eyes mocked him across the table.

"I have an excellent memory," said Raynes.

"People do promise you the earth. Then, after they've laid you, they tend to forget awfully quickly! Tea or coffee?"

* * *

As he left the basement flat ten minutes later, he looked at the number on the door.

"No. 18."

"l8B. May. Mrs D. May."

"I'll not forget."

"I hope not, Inspector. Have a nice day!"

Raynes almost stumbled up the steps.

"That was clever," he said. "How did you know?"

Debbie smiled broadly.

"We girls have our methods!" she said.

But that was all she would say.

As Raynes walked back to his car, he examined his wallet

and his pockets to see if there was anything which could have given her a clue. There was nothing at all. As he drove across the river, he kept saying to himself: "How did she do it?" It was a question that puzzled him all day.

11 *The Diary*

Tuesday morning started – by mutual agreement – at 9.00 am. Raynes arrived five minutes early and made himself known to some of the other officers who were stationed at Grasshallows. As he expected, they were a good crowd – a little bored perhaps in their work – but with a strong sense of duty and a pleasing turn of humour. Working with them would be no problem. From even a brief conversation, he realized how eager they were to solve the mystery of Sophie's death and to find the killer. Raynes promised no miracles but said he would do his best. He entered his miserable office to discover that his popularity had visibly increased – even in 24 hours. A vase of flowers had appeared on his windowsill. "How very nice!" he said – and meant it.

When Carlisle arrived, it was agreed that Derek Coates-Smythe would be the target for the morning. A telephone call would be made to arrange a suitable time for a visit. Police records would be consulted to discover any reference to George Erskine Murray. The University accommodation office would be asked to find the whereabouts of Paul Brown. The Army would be approached to pinpoint Linda and John Jack and the London police would be asked whether Emilio Zaposito was still at large or back in jail. In the meantime, Raynes wanted to look at the inventory of Sophie's flat. He wanted to examine her address-book and diary. And, while he was doing this, Carlisle could do all the routine stuff, dictating a brief report on their Monday visits so that an official record might be kept. Not that Raynes had much time for written stuff …

However, he had to concede that Detective-Inspector Parkinson and his team had done a power of work investigating Sophie's death. Her flat had been full of bits and pieces, mementos and treasures of all sorts, letters, papers, books –

all boxed away – and now stored in the basement of Grass-hallows police station. Every item had been catalogued and numbered. Raynes said that he wished to examine her address book and diary for 1987 and before he had even settled to his first cup of coffee, both had appeared.

The address book was a rather battered red book, falling apart at the spine. It was about fifteen years old and was so full of names and telephone numbers that many appeared on the wrong pages because the correct pages were already full. Inside the front cover, Sophie had written her car number, her insurance number, her national health number, her car engine number and her car insurance number. Then she had a list of vital people like dentist, doctor, hairdresser, chemist and vet. Raynes noted that there were very few changes over the years.

He counted the pages and looked to see if any had been torn out. No. The book was remarkably intact. He looked up each of the main suspects to see how they figured.

Canon George Murray appeared under "B" – St Benedict's. So did the Treasurer. Both men were accompanied by their telephone numbers. Raynes reached for the local telephone directory to see if the Treasurer's number was for his home or his office. He discovered that it was the number of his Bank. He noted that beside Canon Murray's name, there was a small tick. Beside the Reid's entry – under "G" for Garage – there were no ticks! Their names had been in for some time but they had been scored out with a thick black pen and she had written "crooks" in the margin. Paul Brown had his University address and his home address plus phone numbers. No tick there either.

Emilio Zaposito did not figure anywhere in the book. Nor did Ernie McCulloch. Rosalind Hayman appeared as "Mr & Mrs G. Hayman" but the "Mr" had later been struck out. Gordon Hayman re-appeared under a separate heading with several different telephone numbers and several different addresses. His wife also re-appeared in her own right but under page "I". A tick or two for him. None for her.

Derek Coates-Smythe had two addresses – home and office with several extra telephone numbers, including the golf club.

Along with his name were several other Christian names, Ralph, Beaver, Cecil and Wynn … plus a plethora of numbers and little ticks. They had all sailed in the good ship Sophie!

Commander Kenworth was an old entry. He could tell that by the ink. His telephone number and address remained unchanged over the years. Her son and daughter-in-law also figured. They had occupied most of the letter "J". There were addresses in Britain and abroad, complicated phone numbers and BFPOs. The names of their children and their birthdays were recorded as were other anniversaries. For all the way that they had treated her, it was clear that Sophie cared about them. Even the unpleasant in-laws, Linda's parents were included – but no ticks there!

It was a remarkable document. Raynes counted through the names with ticks beside them – some just Christian names or initials. As Carlisle had said, the number was about 300 – mostly local people. A remarkable web of contacts. Raynes went through the book once more. From the evidence before him, Canon Murray, Commander Kenworth, Derek Coates-Smythe and Gordon Hayman could be accounted as her customers. Paul Brown, Peter Bridges, the Reid brothers and Ernie McCulloch could not. Raynes put the book to one side and turned to the diary.

He thought it was surprising that the murderer had not taken the trouble to destroy both these valuable books. He – or she – had had access to her keys and her flat. Why had he or she not removed them?

Raynes looked at the diary for 1987 which came to such a sudden end on June 27th. He looked at the entry for January 1st. "Ny Pty with NL, RG & MC. Home 7 am. Slept till lunch. C'tails with CK at 3 pm. VN + TP at 5. M for 1 hr. No T. Home. GS phoned – 1 am." Raynes looked up her bank books to see how the New Year had paid. Only £200 for the whole week. Not a very profitable start to the year.

He thumbed through the pages and suddenly discovered that five pages were missing. Each day had its own small page but the entries for the last Saturday of each month were missing. January 31st, February 28th, March 28th, April 25th and

May 30th. Raynes called Carlisle through. "Did you notice these dates were missing in her diary?"

"Yes, we did."

"You realize that these were obviously the dates when the murderer visited her – or had contact with her?"

"Yes."

"But do you see what it means? The murder wasn't a casual spur-of-the-moment event. It was planned. Premeditated."

"It could still have been done on the spur-of-the-moment."

"I don't think so. There's no sign of any attempt to tamper with the address book."

"That might have given the game away."

"But suppose the murderer's name doesn't appear in the address book at all?"

"It is possible. But why tear out a few pages and leave the rest of the book?"

"So that the other suspects would still be detailed. There's plenty of them." Raynes thought for a moment. "Were there diaries for any previous years?"

"All the way back to 1974. To her second marriage."

"Any other pages missing?"

"I don't think so."

"What did Detective-Inspector Parkinson make of this?"

"He made a lot of enquiries about what people did on a Friday and Saturday nights. It took a lot of work but it didn't lead anywhere …"

Raynes felt deflated. "Oh well! If Parkinson's already been through it …"

Carlisle departed.

Raynes reached out for the file with the photocopies of her bank books. He looked up the entries for each building society. He examined the inflow of funds after each weekend from January to May 1987. He noted with interest that after each of the "torn-out" weekends, Sophie had banked a larger than average sum in her account. He checked each book – because she switched from week to week – but the picture was clear. On the missing weekends, Sophie made more. Whoever her client was, he paid well. Very well.

12 *The Lawyer*

Whilst Raynes was still brooding over this fact, Carlisle returned to remind him that they were due at the lawyer's at 11.15 am. Raynes looked at his watch with surprise. He was amazed that the time had passed so quickly. He headed out of the station with Carlisle and walked the hundred yards or so to Derek Coates-Smythe's office in the High Street. It was a fine Georgian building, well-maintained, with a large brass plaque on the wall: Logan, Smythe & Smythe. Raynes stopped to look at it.

"The Smythes were his grandfather and grand-uncle," said Carlisle, "and Logan was the man who originally owned it. A Scotsman. The Smythes bought their way in."

The two policemen entered the building and were greeted by a smart and attractive receptionist who had obviously been well-briefed. She led them upstairs to an office at the back of the building with a splendid view over the river.

"Mr Coates-Smythe? Detective-Inspector Raynes."

"Good morning, gentlemen."

The lawyer was a tall man with sharp features and glossy black hair. He had a prominent, straight nose, dark eyes and black bushy eyebrows. His mouth was broad and sensual and Raynes' first impression was that Derek Coates-Smythe looked very like the Restoration King, Charles II.

He was wearing a somewhat loud brown-grey checked suit with a grey shirt and a dark brown tie. Raynes noted that he had large rough hands, very hairy, and it looked as if he had the unfortunate tendency of biting his nails. His voice, however, was soft and unctuous with a slightly soporific character.

Raynes outlined the reason for his visit:

"Mr Coates-Smythe, I'm sorry to intrude upon your privacy and raise matters which I am sure would be best forgotten – but I have recently taken up my post in succession to Detective-Inspector Parkinson and I have decided to review the case of Sophie Jack who was murdered just over a year ago. I'm very sorry if my visit should arouse unhappy memories but I would like to get to the bottom of this case – and, as her lawyer, I believe you can help me."

"In what way?"

"Well, for a starter, I believe you were responsible for drawing up her will?"

"Yes?"

"Well, perhaps you could tell us a little about that will?"

"Such as what?"

"Well, such as how much she left to people other than St Benedict's."

"Surely the police already have all this information?"

Derek Coates-Smythe spoke so gently and so reasonably that Raynes wanted to hit him. As Detective-Constable Carlisle had said, he had the most infuriating habit of answering one question with another. Raynes decided to be patient:

"I would like to see a copy – the original copy – of her will."

"Now?"

"Now."

The lawyer rang a bell and a very good-looking secretary in a short black dress came into the room.

"Miss Stansfield, the file on Jack, please!"

Raynes continued: "Did you draw up the will for Sophie or was it done by one of your staff?"

"Why should you think I would do it?"

"Well, because I'm led to believe you were a good friend of hers."

"An acquaintance perhaps?"

Raynes smiled. This was going to be a very slippery customer. He would have to be squashed in the opening round.

The file arrived.

It was a fairly slim file – nothing compared with those at the police station. The lawyer turned over a number of sheets – mostly involving accounts and passed the will over to Raynes without a word. Raynes read through the document quite quickly.

"Who were these other people to whom she left money?"

Derek Coates-Smythe said: "I believe that one was her hairdresser; another was her cleaning lady; the third was a female

71

friend in London; the other three are charities for which Mrs Jack felt some affection."

"Donkeys, Save the Children and Cancer Research?"

"Precisely."

"And they accounted for £10,000 of her estate?"

The lawyer nodded.

"And the residue went to St Benedict's? Were you surprised about that?"

"Nothing surprises a lawyer. Many people make the most bizarre requests in their wills. Ours not to reason why …"

"The will was signed in September 1983. She never made any subsequent wills?"

"Not to my knowledge."

"How did her family feel about the contents of her will?"

The lawyer looked thoughtful.

"Annoyed – but not surprised."

"They were already aware of its contents?"

"I believe her son had already seen a copy of her will at her home."

"Was this the cause of his beating her up?"

"It may have been. He is a very coarse, rude, unpleasant brute. He deserved nothing. He received nothing. I think Mrs Jack was very wise to make her bequests the way she did – and not to change her mind, even under threats and blows."

Raynes looked across the desk at the impassive face before him.

"Did you advise her to draw up her will?"

"I believe it had been in her mind for some time."

Raynes said to himself: "… at this rate, we shall get absolutely nowhere …" To Mr Coates-Smythe he said: "I think we would get on a little better if you could switch off your tape-recorder and we could speak man to man. If you are innocent, you have nothing to hide; if you are guilty, it will do you absolutely no good."

Carlisle watched the battle of wits between the two men with fascination. He had never guessed that the lawyer might record the conversation. But Raynes had immediately realized that there was an inhibiting factor about the conversation. A secret recording was the only solution. The two men stared at each other … possibly for as much as a minute. The silence was unbroken. Then Mr Coates-Smythe bent down and opened a drawer. There was a click and the drawer was shut.

"Thank you," said Raynes.

Mr Derek Coates-Smythe looked a little less assured.

Raynes continued:

"I am fully aware from records at the police station that you were closely involved with the victim and, indeed, that you were a prime suspect this time last year. Can you tell me frankly – and without prevarication – how long you had known her?"

Mr Coates-Smythe did not reply hastily. In fact, before all his answers, there was a distinct pause. And as each question was answered, there was an air of finality – as if that were the end of the story. For an hour and more, Raynes prised out the details.

The first fact to emerge was that the lawyer had known Sophie for almost twenty-five years. He had met her at the coffee bar when she was a young tear-away – before she had got pregnant. He had been at boarding school but he had been "around" during the holidays and, in the sixties, the coffee bar had been very much the hub around which the *jeunesse doré* of Grasshallows had revolved.

"She worked in the coffee bar?"

"She did."

"Did you speak to her?"

"Only to order expresso coffee."

"Was she physically attractive at that time?"

"Sexy – but not beautiful. Provocative – but by no means a lady."

Had he been attracted to her? Not particularly. He had had a number of different girlfriends at that time. Mostly from the riding club.

Raynes asked him to spell out the story of his life.

Derek Coates-Smythe was born in 1945. He was now just about to reach his 43rd birthday – at the end of August. He had been educated at a private school in Grasshallows, a boarding school in Derbyshire and at Balliol. He had studied Jurisprudence and had gone on to do several extra diplomas. His speciality was conveyancing. Two years after coming down from Oxford, he had married for the first time. Constance had been a girl he had met at University. She had been "a mistake". He said that he had realized this even before they walked up the aisle. But his father and mother had liked her – she was "the right sort" – and because he was working for his father and his father withheld his full wage until he got married and settled down – he had decided to go through with it.

She had been very selfish. Very greedy. Not very exciting in bed. And in a short while he had decided that she was physically repulsive. Even to a man with his catholic tastes, Constance was a complete "turn-off". He was surrounded by many other attractive young ladies who met the bill more effectively. Constance was simply "to be endured". This situation had lasted until his father died in 1976. Then Constance had come out in her true colours. She had attacked him endlessly in private – and then in public – about his infidelity and adultery. Derek Coates-Smythe had admitted nothing; denied nothing. "It was just so utterly tiresome," he said.

He admitted that eventually her nagging had driven him to violence. He had grabbed her by the neck several times. He had once tried to push her down the stairs. He did not deny it. Two years in jail for manslaughter would have been a small price to pay – just to get rid of her.

Fortunately, she had at last decided to seek a divorce. Cruelty was the ground of her petition. He did not contest it. To be honest, he welcomed it. Naturally enough, he had taken precautions to make sure that she would not break him or his firm. He had rather cleverly arranged for her to contact a lawyer who was an old friend of his. He had taken up her case with great enthusiasm but, after a long song and dance, had managed to ruin her petition with the utmost decorum. Constance had been furious at the way she had been outmanoeuvred and had never forgiven him. When he had become a suspect in Sophie's murder case, she had done everything she could to sink him.

"Do you think that she could have been responsible for leaving your visiting card at the scene of the murder?" Raynes asked.

"Had she been in the country at the time, yes," said Mr Derek Coates-Smythe. "But as she was in the States, no."

Raynes asked the lawyer when he had renewed his acquaintance with Sophie.

"Shortly after she returned to Grasshallows to look after her mother."

"Where did you meet her?"

"In the chemist's." He smiled. "Where else? I didn't recognize her, but she recognized me."

"Had she changed a lot since you last saw her?"

For once, Derek Coates-Smythe did not hesitate before speaking. "Yes. A great deal. For a start, she had dyed her hair blonde ... that was a big change. Then she'd filled out – her figure, you know. When she was in the coffee bar, she was a skinny creature. Now she had more assurance. Less strident. She had a certain tired sadness about her. You felt her life was a bit of a burden. Which, at that time, of course, it was. She picked up a lot after her mother's death."

"Had she gone back to her 'trade' at that time?"

"I think she had to – to make ends meet."

"What did her mother think about that?"

"Hated it! Just hated it! She felt it reflected on her as a mother. Whilst Sophie was in London, it didn't seem to matter all that much. But in Grasshallows, everyone talks and it didn't take Mrs Jack long to find out what was going on. She was very upset. Caused a lasting rift between them."

"But she nursed her?"

"She nursed her but there was no warmth in it. No warmth on either side. It was a case of gritted teeth on Sophie's part and endless reproaches from her mother. Sophie never liked anyone to dominate her life. She would take it for so long ... then – snap!"

"She liked being her own boss?"

"Very much so. Her first husband – and his family – they exploited her to the full down in London. It took quite a lot of courage to break away. But after that, she managed her own affairs. If she was going to earn money the hard way – then it might as well go into her own pocket."

"Which it did?"

"Which it did."

Raynes paused before moving to more delicate ground.

"Did you ever have any grudge against her?"

"No. She was always perfectly fair with me."

"You must have contributed quite a bit to her prosperity?"

Derek Coates-Smythe permitted himself a further smile.

"A little," he said. "A little."

"Did you realize she had accumulated such a large bank balance over the past ten years?"

"I had no knowledge of what she was worth."

"Even though you must have had ample personal knowledge of what she charged?"

"I had no knowledge of what she received – or spent. Quite frankly, the subject never crossed my mind."

"You were mainly interested in photography, I believe?"

The lawyer looked at him coolly.

"I suppose the police have all the details?"

"They do."

"So you won't expect me to expatiate."

Raynes assured him that no expatiation was necessary.

"How did your second wife react to your relations with Sophie? You were married again for the second time – in 1982, I believe?"

"My wife had no knowledge about any of my dealings with Sophie – at least, not until the police investigations began."

"It must have come as something of a surprise to her?"

Mr Derek Coates-Smythe nodded.

"She has stuck by you – and your story?"

"She has been an excellent wife. The ordeal has brought us much closer together. I think she understands my behaviour and my feelings much more deeply – I think I also understand myself more clearly," he added.

Raynes had no time for the lawyer's deeper feelings.

"When was the last time you saw Sophie alive?" he asked.

The lawyer hesitated and looked out over the river.

"About a week before her death, I would say. The Tuesday before. I dropped by at her place after lunch ..."

"And she said nothing to you about being frightened by anyone?"

"Well, she was always frightened about John. She always felt he might suddenly arrive and cause a scene. It was a constant anxiety. He thought nothing of hammering on the door – even when she was with a ... 'client' ... it was quite embarrassing to all concerned ..."

"Did that happen to you?"

"No. But she told me it happened on about four occasions. He would suddenly arrive, wanting money. Usually, he'd been drinking – so it was quite unpleasant."

"On the night in question," said Raynes, "the Saturday night; what were you doing?"

"Playing golf. Drinking. Fornicating – and driving home."

"That was all between the hours of 5.00 and 7.30 pm?"

"Not entirely. I finished the round at about 5.00 pm. Left the clubhouse about ten minutes later. I came in here to check on a couple of documents which should have gone off to a client. They were still sitting in the 'out' tray – never posted. I posted them first-class." He paused. "Then I went to have a drink with Hilary – the wife of one of my colleagues. He's left us now – so I don't mind talking about it. Hilary and I had a quick tumble. Another G&T and then back to Delia and a dinner party at 8.00 pm."

Raynes turned to Carlisle.

"And Hilary provided the necessary alibi?"

"Not at first she didn't! That caused quite a lot of trouble!"

"Not half!" said the lawyer. "She denied it point-blank. You could understand why. She and her husband had only been married ten months. He was away on a course. Had no idea of what was going on. I didn't want to involve her. And she obviously didn't want to say anything about me. Knew it would damn-near break up their marriage. Which it did! She went back to her mother. He left the firm. A most unpleasant business altogether. But when you're faced with a murder rap and she's your only alibi, you've got to spill the proverbial beans. Even when the police had got it out of her, it still caused me a great deal of trouble. I was obliged to call in a top London firm to defend my interests. The police were determined to break me down. I'm afraid Hilary's morals were of little concern to me. She was bloody furious ..."

"I bet she was," said Raynes.

The lawyer shook his head.

"Hell hath no fury like a woman exposed ..."

"But her alibi cleared you?"

"Well, I couldn't be having it off with two women at the same time, could I?"

Raynes was blunt.

"Where were you 'having it off' with Hilary?"

"Picton Dale. It's a charming little village about three miles north of here. They lived in a small house on a private scheme. Pretty little house. Pity they had to leave ..."

Raynes did not pay much attention to the lawyer's crocodile tears. He reckoned that Derek Coates-Smythe was a cold, unscrupulous man who thought only of himself and his own selfish pleasures. He was rich, handsome, persuasive and cruel.

"So you left Hilary at what time?"

"At about 7.00 to 7.15 pm. I got home at about 7.30 pm."

"Where do you live yourself?"

"I live about six miles east of Grasshallows. A village called Newton St Mary's." He suddenly perceived the point of Raynes' question. "I was nowhere near the Meadows, if that's what you're thinking. The A193 bypasses the town – and the Meadows. About two miles across the fields to the murder scene – and I didn't have my wellington boots with me that night!"

He smiled broadly at Raynes.

Raynes did not respond.

"Whom do you suspect of murdering Sophie? After all this time, you must have some theories of your own?"

Derek Coates-Smythe again looked out of the window for inspiration. His reply was a long time in coming.

"Someone who was particularly spiteful. I can understand her getting murdered. It's an occupational hazard for people like Sophie. But there was a humiliation about it. The knife wounds. They suggest a certain calculated bitterness. Only a few people have that sort of bitterness. *Cherchez la femme,* I would say. A bitter, twisted woman – with a male accomplice …"

"You must have someone in mind?"

"I have. But you wouldn't expect me to mention names – would you?"

"No," said Raynes. "But I could guess."

"Difficult to prove, though?"

Raynes agreed.

He looked at his watch and saw that it was nearly 1.00 pm. He had got as much out of Mr Coates-Smythe as he had expected. The interview had added a little to his picture of Sophie but it had brought him no nearer to a solution of the problem. If Mr Coates-Smythe's alibi was cast-iron, he was in the clear; but Raynes still felt there was certain information he could add which might give him the key. He returned to the question of the will:

"Just two more questions before I go. Why did Sophie decide to leave the bulk of her estate to St Benedict's? Was it her idea – or did you suggest it to her?"

"I did not suggest it to her. It was her idea."

The answer was clipped. Raynes decided to prod a little further.

"But you have some connection with St Benedict's, don't you?"

"I'm on their P.C.C."

"So you would have had a vested interest in seeing her money coming to your church?"

"I can assure you, Inspector, that I had no part in helping her make any decision about what she should do with her money. She was very fond of the Church. She had a soft spot for Canon Murray. And, in view of the way her family treated her, I think her choice was most sensible – and charitable."

"Yes," said Raynes, "that's a fair point."

79

"It's the truth," said the lawyer.

Raynes looked at him.

"And my second question is this. Did you at any time before Sophie's death, tell anyone the contents of her will? Did you give the slightest indication to anyone that her money might be going to the Church – or any individual in her will?"

The lawyer gave him a cold withering look.

"Mr Raynes, you know as well as I do that a lawyer never, repeat never, discloses his client's business to anyone. Her son knew the contents of his mother's will. He may have shot his mouth off ... but lawyers ... never."

His face clouded over – as if some memory had come to him. Something which he could not quite place. Raynes watched him.

"Are you sure," he asked, "that you never said anything to Ralph or Beaver, Cecil or Wynn? To any of your golfing chums – or your hunting cronies?" He paused. "Just because you didn't plunge in the knife doesn't mean you're innocent. A word spoken out of place may well have put the key into another man's hand. Or another woman's hand. Who knows? If you remember, tell me."

Mr Derek Coates-Smythe looked at Raynes with undisguised contempt. He had not enjoyed the interview. He was appalled to think the case had been reopened. He had the unpleasant feeling that he was going to see Detective-Inspector Raynes again.

The policemen rose.

"We must be going," said Raynes. "It's Tuesday – and I know you're busy on Tuesdays!"

13 *The Commander*

Tuesday lunch was in the canteen.

Cream of mushroom soup, shepherd's pie, apple tart and cream. A far cry from the *Grosvenor* and *The Green Man*. But Raynes knew it was important to see and be seen. His meal was constantly interrupted with introductions and messages. He seemed to be forever standing up and sitting down.

Somehow, he caught his cuff in the synthetic cream and a sympathetic waitress helped him wipe it off. He said to Carlisle: "It's all very well trying to appear like an ordinary mortal but it doesn't help when you behave like a bumbling idiot!"

"I shouldn't worry," said Carlisle. "At least it'll show you're human!"

Raynes looked at his watch.

"Quarter of an hour for coffee then we'll hit the road again. Whom should we attack next? The pervert or the hyena?"

Carlisle thought for a moment.

"If we visit Mrs Hayman, she'll phone up the Commander and warn him we're on the warpath. I think it might be better to catch him first – unawares."

Raynes stirred his coffee.

"Where does the pervert live?"

"60 Ranelagh Gardens."

"Classy?"

"Very."

* * *

The Commander's house was all that a Commander's house should be. It was a white-painted Georgian house in a terrace of fine Georgian houses. There were geraniums in tubs at the top of a short flight of steps, two fine white fluted pillars holding up a small stone porch, a broad, glossy, black front door with a large well-polished brass knocker. No bell.

Carlisle gave the knocker three stout blows.

There was silence.

"Knock again!" said Raynes.

After a long wait, the door slowly opened and an aged housekeeper peered anxiously round the door.

"Police!" said Raynes bluntly. "We're here to see the Commander."

"He's having his afternoon nap."

"Too bad!" said Raynes. "Tell him to get up!"

The housekeeper looked even more anxious.

"He doesn't like to be disturbed!"

"Well, I'm afraid, this afternoon, he'll have to be!"

He put his hand to the door and slowly pushed it open.

The housekeeper was clearly uncertain where her loyalty lay.

"You just let him know we're here," said Raynes. "There's no hurry. We're quite prepared to wait."

The aged housekeeper shuffled her way across a tiled hall and showed them into a large sitting room at the back of the house. It was a cheerful, sunny room with several seascapes decorating the walls. There were three comfortable settees surrounding the fireplace which had a beautiful teak mantelpiece. A bust of Admiral Nelson graced a mahogany sideboard and the room was littered with books and trophies collected by the Commander over many years. Carlisle stared thoughtfully at the crossed swords above the sideboard, whilst Raynes looked out of the window into a small walled garden. He always believed that gardens told you a lot about people. The Commander was no exception. His lawn was immaculately cut and all the flowers stood in regimented rows as if awaiting an inspection upon the quarterdeck.

Raynes moved back to the door to see how the housekeeper was faring. She had climbed the staircase and was clearly facing a very angry employer.

"You know perfectly well that I am not to be disturbed ..."

Mutter. Mutter.

"I don't care who it is! You should have told them to come back later."

More muttering.

"Well, tell them to wait. I shall be down in about five minutes."

Raynes turned to Carlisle and smiled.

"Knocked him off his perch!" he said.

"I don't think we shall get a very warm reception!"

"Who cares?"

The housekeeper staggered down the stairs and delivered her master's message. She shuffled off across the hall and went downstairs to the basement.

It was about ten minutes before the Commander appeared. He was wearing a dark blue blazer, a white shirt with a dark red neckerchief and grey flannels. The badge on his blazer was of some naval design incorporating two anchors. As Carlisle

82

had said, he had fine grey hair, piercing blue eyes and a ruddy, healthy complexion. He looked far from pleased as he strode through the door.

"Now look here, you chaps! This is pretty rough – breaking in on a fellow's siesta! I know you're the police and all that, but my housekeeper tells me that you just about forced your way in. It won't do!" He shook his head. "I must say I take a jolly dim view of your behaviour." His voice reminded Raynes of the film actor, Terry Thomas – an upper class rogue with an apologetic whine. However, having said his piece, the Commander appeared to mellow. "Now, what'll you have?" he asked. "A glass of port, perhaps?"

Raynes refused all hospitality and went straight to the point. "We're following up the death of Sophie Jack who died about this time last year. I believe that you were one of the chief suspects ..."

"Not me, dear boy! Not me! I was in London at the time. Got the alibi to prove it!" He laughed.

"Which one?" asked Raynes.

The Commander frowned. "I don't think I've met you before. Have we been introduced?"

"We haven't been introduced," said Raynes, "and whether you know me or not is scarcely relevant. I am the new head of CID at Grasshallows and I'm following up the investigation of my predecessor, Detective-Inspector Parkinson."

"Oh, I see?" said the Commander. "What a pity! Detective-Inspector Parkinson was such a nice man. Most refined. We used to play golf together at Skipper's Hill."

Raynes noted the insult.

"Which of the two ladies are you claiming as your alibi? Miss Ritchie or Mrs Hayman?"

Kenworth laughed. "Miss Ritchie was just a little joke. Mrs Hayman and I were having a meal together in London ..."

"... on the Friday night?"

"No, dear boy, not Friday – Saturday night! That was the night of the murder. You must get your facts right – even if you are a new boy round here!"

Raynes said: "I am perfectly aware that Saturday was the

night of the murder. What I am saying is that it was Friday night when you dined with Mrs Hayman in London. What I want to find out is what you were doing on Saturday."

"Can't be in two places at once, dear boy! Either I was in London – or I wasn't."

"That is precisely my point!" said Raynes.

"But I've already told you I was in London."

"That's what you say – but others say differently. And unless you can prove to my satisfaction that you were in London on the night in question, I fear – dear boy – that we may have to pull you in for questioning. Which would not be nice." Raynes laid on the sarcasm heavily.

Commander Kenworth looked ill-at-ease and silence fell over the room as each side considered its next move. It was unfortunate that this silence came when it did for Raynes and Carlisle both heard the distant sound of a door shutting upstairs. The Commander heard it too for he immediately started speaking in a loud voice in a most vigorous manner.

Raynes ignored him.

"See who it is," he said to Carlisle.

Carlisle opened the sitting room door to see a dark-haired girl coming down the stairs in her stockinged feet clutching her handbag and a pair of high-heeled shoes. Carlisle recognized her immediately.

"Oh, it's you!" he said. "Scoot! Off you go!"

He returned to the sitting room.

"Fiona Brown," he declared. "Local talent. The afternoon shift!"

"So much for the siesta!" said Raynes coldly.

"A rose by any other name ..." said the Commander.

He grinned feebly.

Raynes looked at him. "We're not playing games, Kenworth. This is a murder inquiry and you are up to your neck in it. Sophie Jack was one of your harem. She was here quite regularly. I know for a fact that you almost strangled at least one woman here in Grasshallows. You have a track record for violence against women. You have no alibi for the night of the murder. You tried to deceive the police last year – but it didn't work. And, as the last few minutes have shown, you are a liar …"

The Commander opened his mouth to protest.

Raynes continued: "… When people like you go to prison, they have a pretty nasty time. People don't like perverts. They beat them up. Put glass in their mashed potatoes. You've probably noticed how many remand prisoners end up getting hanged – or hanging themselves. If I have even the slightest suspicion that you are holding out on me, I shall pull you in." Raynes looked at his victim with the utmost contempt. "So – no mucking about. No more of this 'dear boy' stuff. I want the truth, Kenworth! What was your part in this disgusting business?"

Carlisle looked at his boss with admiration. He had never seen anyone squash an opponent quite so ruthlessly. Within five minutes, Raynes had secured an absolute ascendancy. He had watched him pulverize Canon Murray, the Reid brothers, the lawyer – and now the Commander. It was a mixture of blackmail and subtle threats which took the suspects by surprise and utterly unnerved them. Having blasted their complacency, the opposition crumbled. It would certainly not sound good in a court of law – or on a police complaints form – but as a means of getting to the point, it had distinct advantages. Detective-Inspector Parkinson had been too much of a gentleman to bully. Raynes was totally different.

The Commander looked tearful.

He took out a cigarette from a silver case.

"You don't mind if I smoke?" He lit his cigarette, sat back in his settee – and looked at Raynes, hoping to see some glimmer of kindness and compassion. He saw none. His face looked pale and drawn.

"Where do you want me to start?"

"At the beginning," said Raynes.

"It all began when my wife died," said the Commander. "We'd been married for twenty-five years. In fact, we'd just celebrated our Silver Wedding. We were in Malta at the time and she took a massive overdose. She'd just been to the doctor and he told her she had breast cancer. Being a nurse, she knew what that meant. Couldn't face it. Took the easy way out. I came home to find her in a deep coma. We rushed her to hospital but it was too late. She died next morning at 6.00 am."

This was not quite the beginning that Raynes had been looking for. He took the Commander back to his earliest years. He discovered that Kenworth was the same age as Canon Murray. Both men were sixty-four. The Commander had joined the Navy in 1942 on his eighteenth birthday and had spent most of the war on convoy duty in the Atlantic. The sea had appealed to him so, after the war, he applied for a commission. He was sent to the Far East and was based in Singapore until 1948. Then he had served on destroyers in the Mediterranean. Radar had been his speciality and over the years he had earned steady promotion.

He met his wife in Gibraltar. She had been a staff nurse in the hospital there. They had married in 1950 when he was twenty-six. She was five years older than him and had been married before. Her first husband had been a submarine officer who had died during the war. They had had no children. The Commander fancied that there was some genetic problem in his wife's family. Neither of her two sisters had had any children and she herself had had two miscarriages. After that, she had lost heart.

Raynes wondered if it was then that the Commander's morals had begun to go to pieces. Kenworth said not. Theirs had been a very happy marriage, completely normal apart from all the separations and adversities of naval life. They had been very close and her death had been hard to bear. He blamed himself for not coming home earlier that night – and getting her to the hospital in time. But would he have wanted her to suffer? If she had decided to take the "easy way out", would he have been right to stop her? He thought not. But, at the time, he felt confused. Confused, lonely and guilty. Naturally, in the vacuum which followed, he turned to others for distraction and pleasure.

Through his wife's connection with the hospital, he had met several eligible young ladies. They had fed him, comforted him and satisfied him in every possible way. The Commander was discreet, but Raynes was not to be fobbed off:

"When did you start beating women?" he asked bluntly.

Kenworth looked pained at the thought of going into greater detail and lit another cigarette.

It was a young nurse, he said. A rather plump, bouncy girl who had been married to a sailor but who had then been divorced. She was the sort of girl who was bored with normal sex and had provoked him into doing all sorts of outrageous things. They had tied each other up, whipped each other, done every possible perversion in the book – and, after that, it had been rather difficult to go back to normal things again. He had thought about marrying her – but she was twenty years younger and it wouldn't have worked.

"You paid her?" asked Raynes coldly.

The Commander looked hurt and silent.

Eventually, he nodded. "Yes. I paid her."

"Where did you get all this money from? You couldn't have afforded this house on a naval officer's pension?"

The Commander agreed that such a thing would have been quite impossible. In fact it would have been quite beyond his means but for a couple of legacies which had come his way.

"When did they come?" asked Raynes.

"Just after my wife died ..." said Kenworth.

Raynes instantly registered that he had been told a lie.

"... and the other one shortly after I retired."

"Which was when?"

"1977."

"You were 53?"

"I took early retirement. I'd been in the Navy over thirty years – so I'd had a pretty good innings."

"You could afford to retire in style?"

"Exactly!"

The Commander was beginning to look happier now that they were talking about money rather than sex.

Raynes said: "I'd like you to reconsider an answer you made a couple of minutes ago. You said that you received your first legacy shortly after your wife died. Was that correct? If so, I'd like to see the actual documents from the lawyers. Perhaps you could give me their name?"

The Commander went slightly red – and thoughtful.

"I believe you're right," he said. "It was about six months before my wife passed away. How did you know?"

"When people lie to me," said Raynes. "I notice immediately."

"That must be a very useful gift, Inspector?"

"Very," said Raynes.

He decided that this was the moment to make life even more difficult for the Commander. "You said that you met this 'plump young nurse' after your wife's death." He paused. "Was that correct?"

The Commander said nothing.

"Could it be that you met her before your wife died?"

The Commander sighed.

"I find it difficult to remember."

Raynes watched his victim squirm, wondering whether he would crack – and confess. "That's the first thing you've found difficult to remember this afternoon. I could have sworn that you had a very vivid memory of all that you did with that young lady. Could it be that you had wanted to marry this young Amazon for some time?"

Silence.

"Could it be that your wife found out about this affair and was very distressed about it?"

Silence.

"So distressed that she took an overdose. Not a suicide attempt? Not 'the easy way out'? Just a protest at your infidelity? A cry for help? Hoping to bring you to your senses? But, of course, it didn't. You just left her! Left her to die! Left her till it was too late!"

The Commander said nothing. He did not crumple or collapse. He just remained frozen, staring out of the window with unseeing eyes, his cigarette untouched, its ash falling in thick blobs into the deep pile of the Wilton carpet.

"Perhaps," continued Raynes, "perhaps the 'plump young nurse' – realizing what you had done to your wife – had second thoughts? Decided that after all you were not such a marriageable prospect ... even with your recent legacy?"

Carlisle, listening, realized why Raynes had come to Grasshallows with such a formidable reputation. You could see immediately why people hated him. He seized upon the weak point in his enemy's armoury, exploited it, theorized upon it and then used it to crush his victim. There was no mercy in him. He tightened the thumbscrews so slowly and deliberately.

"... And then you retired. To get away from all the bad memories. Away from all the questions which might be asked. Away from all the rumours which might be spread. Away from the 'plump young nurse' who knew so much ... I wonder what happened to her?"

"She died."

"Did she now?"

"She was knifed. But I was in Grasshallows at the time."

"Another perfect alibi?"

"I don't kill people, Inspector. You may not believe me. I came to this place to retire. To relax and enjoy myself. I don't want to hurt anyone. What you people call perversions ... I call them fantasies. It's more in the mind than anything else. Now and again, we go over the top – but it's nothing serious. Just ... acting out my fantasies. I'd run a mile from real violence ..."

Raynes was glad to have got Kenworth talking again. He decided to adopt a gentler tone of voice. "And when did Sophie come into the picture?" he asked.

"Soon after I arrived. I was at some function – I forget which – and her name was mentioned. I asked around. Made contact. And that was that. I must have known her for about ten years."

"You must have been one of her best customers?"

"More than likely, dear boy! More than likely!" He took one look at Raynes' face. "Sorry, Inspector!"

"She was living with her mother at the time?"

"She was. Didn't get her own flat till later. I never went to her flat. She always came round here. Just gave her a buzz on the phone and round she came. Most convenient."

"You never went down to the Meadows with her?"

"Never."

Raynes was listening very carefully. Had he been told another lie – or was there a slight half-truth which he had picked up?

"But you have been down to the Meadows with other women?"

"Yes. Not often though. Just now and then." The Commander chuckled. "Getting too old for it!"

Raynes said: "You must have known Sophie better than anyone. What sort of person was she?"

Commander Kenworth did not hesitate: "She was a very nice person. Very easy going. Slim figure, small breasts, a nice bottom. A very nice bottom. A little fat over the hips – not surprising perhaps at her age. Used to dye her hair, of course. Made her look younger ..."

"Personality?"

"Oh, how can I put it?" He bit his lip once or twice. "She had a colourless personality. Perhaps that's a bit unfair? She had a strong character but it didn't really show. She had a good sense of humour but she smiled rather than laughed. She smiled a lot. She was nice when she smiled. I miss her."

"Naturally," said Raynes.

"She was the sort of person who moulded herself into what you wanted her to be – and do. You know what I mean? She was like one of those lizards who take on the colour of the stones they're sitting on."

"Chameleons?" said Raynes.

"Yes. That's them. She was like that. She adapted herself to the landscape. You could do anything with her. She was passive – very passive. That's what I liked about her. She didn't object or question what you said. She just fitted in. I think she lacked drive and initiative. She was too passive – too submissive for her own good." He paused for thought. "And she was cheap. Didn't sting you for money. I always thought she was very reasonable. I used to send her an extra cheque for her birthday and at Christmas. Just to show my appreciation, you know." He laughed. "When I think back, I must have spent a small fortune on her over the years. As you say, I was probably her best customer. In fact, I'm sure I was."

Raynes nodded.

"When did you last see Sophie?"

"On the Wednesday before she died."

Raynes raised his eyebrows.

"I thought you had given up Sophie for someone else?"

"You asked me to tell you the truth, Inspector. And that's what I'm doing. Mrs Hayman and I have been seeing a lot of each other for the past three years – but there are some things that …" he hesitated.

"… that Mrs Hayman can't or won't provide?"

"Exactly. You took the words out of my mouth."

"Which is why you still need people like Fiona Brown?"

"Yes."

"But Mrs Hayman didn't like Sophie?"

"No."

"She was jealous of her?"

"Not so much jealous. She felt that Sophie had broken up her marriage … She was very bitter about that."

"So much so that she wanted to get her revenge?"

"It's not for me to say."

"Are you intending to marry Mrs Hayman?"

"She's still waiting for her divorce."

"That doesn't answer my question, Commander."

"No."

"You're not intending to marry her?"

"No."

"Does she know this?"

The Commander lit another cigarette.

"No, she doesn't."

"But she might have thought that if she got rid of Sophie, she might be in with a chance?"

"She might."

Raynes decided to fire a question at random.

"Did you ever discuss with Mrs Hayman how you might get rid of Sophie?"

The Commander looked embarrassed.

"Did you?"

"If you want the truth, Inspector, the answer is yes." He looked at Raynes. "But it wasn't serious. It was just talk. Fantasizing. How you would bump off the Prime Minister. How you would deal with the IRA. It was just general conversation. Nothing serious!"

91

"Not to you," said Raynes. "But it possibly meant more to Mrs Hayman. You may have given her ideas. What sort of death did you concoct?"

"Well, there were several ideas. Poison, I think, was mentioned. Weedkiller. Suffocation. Gassing her in her car. I think Mrs Hayman wanted to catch her at a vulnerable moment – with her pants down – and then do her in. If I remember rightly, the body was to be burned somewhere out of town – to destroy the evidence."

"You discussed all this?"

"Several times. But it wasn't serious."

"Not to you!"

"Not to her either. She just had to get the anger and bitterness out of her system."

"But Mrs Hayman was capable of doing some pretty ghastly things? Petrol through the letter-box. Slashing tyres …"

"Yes. But I don't think she would commit murder."

"Whom do you think killed Sophie?"

The Commander was silent for several minutes.

"I don't think anyone round here would have done anything like that."

"Canon Murray?"

"Good heavens, no!"

"Derek Coates-Smythe?"

"Not really."

"Mrs Hayman?"

"I think she'd have told me."

"But if you'd done the deed together, there'd be no need for her to tell you anything. You could have set up the scene – and then left her to finish it off. Just like the plan."

The Commander looked worried.

"I see your point, Inspector, but we were in London that evening …"

"I don't believe you."

There was a deep silence which lasted a very long time.

Raynes broke the silence.

"You contacted Sophie. Made a booking for that Saturday night …"

The Commander shook his head.

"… You arranged to meet her in the Meadows for a little harmless romp. You couldn't do it in your own home in case someone saw her coming in. You offered her a little more cash than usual – so that she wouldn't suspect anything. She trusted you – as an old friend. Someone who sent her cheques at Christmas. She turned up on time. In her best dress. You tied her up. You blindfolded her with one of Mrs Hayman's silk scarves. You left her there. You wanted to humiliate her – as you had often humiliated her. But she was paid for it – of course. This time, you wanted to please Mrs Hayman. Possibly, you had no thought that the incident would end in murder. But the moment you had turned your back, Mrs Hayman came in and tightened the rope. Slashed her stomach as she had previously slashed her tyres. Got her revenge. You don't know whether she did it – because you didn't see. You deliberately walked away!"

"It wasn't like that at all!"

The Commander looked very upset.

"Inspector, you've got to believe me. It wasn't like that at all. We were nowhere near the Meadows that night. We were in London. I give you my word."

"Once a liar – always a liar!" said Raynes.

The Commander went very white.

"There is a pattern in all this," said Raynes. "You may not see it, but I do. Already, once in your life, you have been responsible for a woman's death. You may not have killed her, but you let her die. And you did that because it suited your book. You were very attracted to that young nurse. She was attracted to you. Hoped to marry you, perhaps? Unfortunately, your wife was in the way. Whether she died of an overdose – or whether you … helped her – I don't know. It would be interesting to find out. But the fact remains that she was in the way … and she was removed. Even though you'd had a happy relationship for over twenty-five years. Now we have the same scenario all over again. Sophie pandered to all your perversions and kinks for ten years. She has not treated you badly. She has not overcharged you. But, in the wings, there's another woman anxious to get her hands on you. A very determined woman. A very violent woman. And Sophie is in the way. Just as your wife was. Mrs Hayman has a legacy of hatred for Sophie … an irrational hatred. Together, you discussed how Sophie could be murdered. You have admitted that. You put ideas into that woman's mind. You probably enjoyed planning it all out. You have a clever mind. A scientist's clinical mind. And Sophie died a violent death – perhaps not unlike the one you concocted together. If I put two and two together, why should it not make four?"

The Commander was silent.

"I was in London," he said. "I was in London – and so was she!"

"Yes," said Raynes, "but which night?"

"The Saturday, damn you!"

He was really angry now.

"That's not true," said Raynes. "I know you're lying!"

"I didn't do it," said the Commander. "You have no proof. And I'm sticking to my story. Do your worst! You can't force me into a confession of something I didn't do!"

Raynes smiled – a cruel smile.

"Can't I?" he said. "You wait and see!"

14 *The Writer*

"You can't say I didn't try!" said Raynes.

"He's a tough nut," said Carlisle. "Fancy him even admitting they'd thought of bumping her off!"

"People play straight into your hands," said Raynes. "They can't control their subconscious. If they've got something to tell you, they just throw up. They can't help it. I presume he didn't tell Detective-Inspector Parkinson about that?"

"He most certainly didn't!"

Raynes looked at his watch.

It was after 4.00 pm.

"I really don't feel like doing any more visits today, but if we don't deal with Mrs Hayman quickly, the scent will grow cold. They'll be able to concoct a few more tall stories – and waste our time. Where does this wretched woman live?"

Carlisle drove the car about half-a-mile and pulled up outside another terraced house – smaller and brick-built – with a dark red front door.

Through the door, they could hear a woman's voice.

"You what?" it screamed. "You stupid ..."

Raynes pressed the bell.

The voice stopped midstream.

A slim elegant woman with blonde hair opened the door. She looked Raynes and Carlisle up and down. "It's you!" she said. "You'd better come in."

Raynes followed Mrs Hayman down a narrow hallway, passed the telephone and entered a room at the back of the house which was obviously her study. From floor to ceiling there was shelf upon shelf of books, all most neatly arranged. There was a fine leather-topped desk sporting only a decanter of whisky and a paper knife in the shape of a dagger.

Mrs Hayman sat down behind the desk which was placed sideways on to the window. She crossed her legs. Raynes and Carlisle sat in two easy chairs beside the fire. Raynes noticed that he was obliged to look up to Mrs Hayman. Round One to Rosalind!

He looked at all the books.

"You are a writer, Mrs Hayman?"

"Horror stories."

"I see. Have you been doing this for a long time?"

"For the past four years."

"There must be quite a market?"

"There is."

Carlisle noted how controlled she was. What a contrast with the harridan they had heard screaming down the telephone!

"We've been to see Commander Kenworth," said Raynes, stating the obvious. "So you'll know why we've called. We're investigating the death of Mrs Sophie Jack who died last year. I believe you were the Commander's alibi?"

Mrs Hayman nodded.

"I also believe that you had every reason to hate Mrs Jack. She seduced your husband and she was also an old friend of

95

the Commander?"

Mrs Hayman's eyes narrowed.

"She was just a cheap, money-grubbing whore. She'd do anything for a tenner. She had no principles. No morals. She didn't care what she did – or whom she used."

"Your husband became infatuated with her?"

"We met at one or two … social evenings. He got carried away. He was stupid. Easily led. She arranged to see him behind my back, but I wasn't having that. I told him he had to choose …"

"And he chose her?"

Raynes tried to sound sympathetic.

"Well, he said he wanted to be free."

"How long had you been married?"

"Seven years."

"No children?"

"No."

"These social evenings? Would they be wife-swapping parties? I believe such things do happen in University circles?"

"They happen in all sorts of circles!"

"I suppose they do," said Raynes thoughtfully. "Two or three couples come together for an evening, have a few drinks, play a few party games and then pair off for the night? Is that the way it goes?"

"Usually."

Mrs Hayman replied quite naturally to Raynes' question and then realized that she had been led into a trap. She had as good as admitted that she had been to many such parties. As of course she had. But she was annoyed with herself for allowing this stranger to look into her soul too closely. She shut her lips tight.

"So Mrs Jack came to one of these parties? Who brought her?"

"I think it was one of the Biochemistry lecturers. I thought she was his wife – or his girlfriend. But Gordon didn't get her that night. It was at the next one that she got her claws into him."

Raynes thought that this was a bit like the pot calling the

kettle black. Mrs Hayman had long nails painted a savage shade of pink. He looked at them. Mrs Hayman noticed – and laughed. "Yes," she said, "it's the law of the jungle."

"Sounds like it," said Raynes. "So your husband took to seeing more of Mrs Jack? And you both had a bust-up?"

"Several!"

"And he moved out?"

"Yes."

"Where did he go?"

"He got a flat in Riverside Drive."

"Near Sophie?"

"About one hundred yards down the road."

"And she visited him there?"

Mrs Hayman nodded.

"But now, I'm told, he's left the country? Gone off to Canada and got a job there?"

"Vancouver."

"And that was last summer as well?"

"The beginning of July."

"Did he go alone?"

Mrs Hayman picked up her paper knife and twisted it round in her hands. "No," she said. "No, he didn't. He went off with one of his post-grad students. She'd been seeing him on and off for about six months, and when he went, she went too. Her parents were most upset about the whole business."

"Is that the girl you attacked?"

Mrs Hayman noted that the Inspector had been well-briefed about her background. "No," she said grimly, "that was another one he had. She used to go to the parties as well … She was a real Jezebel!"

"You make your husband sound quite a Casanova!"

Mrs Hayman continued to twist the knife angrily but said nothing.

"I think you were charged with assault? Twice?"

She nodded.

"And I think you also put petrol through the letter-box of Gordon's flat? Tried to set it on fire?"

Mrs Hayman's big eyes shed a couple of tears.

"That was when I still loved him," she said. "I was so angry. So hurt. I didn't know what I was doing."

"You knew perfectly well what you were doing!" said Raynes – but with a kindly voice. Mrs Hayman looked at him thoughtfully.

"Yes, I suppose I did. I wanted to shock him. Make him realize the strength of my feelings. To make him understand what he was doing to me. I wanted some reaction. I couldn't bear him just ignoring me!"

"So, instead, you decided to attack his women?"

"Yes. I thought that'd make him do something."

"But it didn't?"

"No. He just left the country to get away from me."

"That was when you turned to the Commander for help?"

"Well, I'd known him for some time …"

"You met him at one or two of these wife-swapping parties?"

"How did you guess!" She was sarcastic. "He was very kind. The perfect gentleman. He knew how to treat a woman. So when things got rough, I turned to him."

Raynes was surprised. "I thought Commander Kenworth had a rather violent reputation where women are concerned?"

Rosalind shook her head.

"Not really. It's just games that people play. He has fantasies. Don't we all? He likes to play-act. To feel he's a strong, masterful male. But, inside, he's just a softie … all heart."

"I thought he had a reputation for tying people up … bondage, whips, chaining people to the bed. That sort of thing!"

Mrs Hayman smiled ever so sweetly.

"He may do such things with people like Sophie – but not with me! I get him to talk about his fantasies – rather than actually do them. He gets just as much fun talking about them. Saying what he'd like to do. But, at his age, he can't afford to get too … physical."

Raynes thought of the afternoon shift so recently departed and wondered what the fair Rosalind would make of that.

"Doesn't it work both ways?" he asked.

"I beg your pardon?"

"Doesn't he try to get you to talk out your fantasies with

98

him? Do you, perhaps, discuss the plots of your horror stories with him?"

There was a short silence whilst Mrs Hayman tried to decide which way the conversation was going and whether she was in any danger from the Inspector's questions. Eventually she replied: "Now and again."

"So," said Raynes, "you were quite likely to have discussed with Commander Kenworth your feelings about Sophie Jack and your husband, Gordon?"

There was another pause.

"Quite possibly."

"It's not just 'possible'," said Raynes. "It's absolutely certain. The Commander has just told us that you regularly discussed ways and means of bumping her off. Poison. Strangulation. Where you were going to burn the body ..."

"Not strangulation!"

"Are you sure about that?"

"Quite sure!"

"How can you be so sure?"

"Well, it's a very crude method, isn't it?"

"You would prefer something with a little more sophistication and imagination?"

"Wouldn't you, Inspector?"

Raynes found himself enjoying his interview with the fair Rosalind. She had been expecting a tooth-and-nail fight to the death, but he had been gently playing with her like a fisherman drawing in his first salmon. He decided to change tack.

"What do you do when you are not writing – or going to wife-swapping parties?" he asked.

"Do you mean what I do for a living?"

Raynes nodded.

"I teach – part-time."

"And in your spare time?"

She looked at Carlisle. "I drink. I drink a lot. I cook. I enjoy cooking. I like going out for nice meals. I do crossword puzzles. Take photographs. And I occasionally take part in amateur dramatics ..."

"I believe that you are also a member of St Benedict's?"

"That's where we do the dramatics."

"I see. And I believe you're on their management committee? Their P.C.C.?"

"I used to be. But after all the trouble with Gordon, I had to resign. It was a great pity because I like the Church and Canon Murray's a very good man."

"So I believe," said Raynes who was quite unwilling to believe anything good he had heard about the incumbent. "Did he make a pass at you?" he asked mischievously.

"Certainly not! He's a very saintly man. He had a lovely wife."

Raynes smiled in a friendly fashion.

"You must have been on the P.C.C. when they were discussing whether they should rebuild the organ?"

Rosalind grimaced. "Don't mention it. It's something we've been thinking about – and arguing about – for a number of years. It was so expensive. It's not something you rush into. I had no idea what such things cost. And the Treasurer wasn't very keen. He and Derek – Derek Coates-Smythe – the lawyer – they were at daggers drawn for years over it. But eventually, we all agreed it had to be done. Canon Murray insisted. Derek called his bluff. And the Treasurer … well, he just collapsed like a pack of cards."

"And now it's being done?"

"At long last! I shall be glad to see it finished."

The mention of "cards" set Raynes thinking about visiting cards.

"You must know Derek Coates-Smythe quite well?"

"Very well."

"Is he your lawyer?"

She smiled. "Among other things!"

"And he is also interested in photography?"

"Yes. But not in the same kind as me."

She was clearly aware of the lawyer's taste in pictures.

"And he was also a client of Sophie?"

"If you'd seen his first wife, you'd know why! She was a cow! No other word for it. Anyone would have been an improvement on her. Even The Jack!"

Raynes nodded thoughtfully. Mrs Hayman was undoubtedly a woman of strong passions. Strong likes and dislikes. He wondered how she would react to the picture he was about to paint.

"Mrs Hayman," he said slowly. "I have no strong feelings one way or the other about Mrs Jack, but I want to see this case cleared up. Justice has got to be done and I'm here to see it's done." He paused.

"Now, we've been told a lot of lies by your friend, the Commander. He said at first that he was in London on the Saturday evening with a Miss Joanne Ritchie, who wasn't even in the country at the time. Later he admitted he was with you. He claims that you were both at the restaurant together on the night in question. But the people in the restaurant have said that they think you were there on the Friday night. Commander Kenworth explicitly said that, during the meal, you discussed ways of killing Mrs Jack. It seems clear to me that, of all the suspects in this case, you and the Commander have the best motive – and the worst alibi."

Mrs Hayman said nothing.

Raynes continued: "Both you and Kenworth have a track record for violence. When you have been drinking, I am told that you can become extremely violent – even dangerous. You were anxious to get your revenge on Sophie for the way she pinched your husband. The Commander says that you were determined to humiliate her in public. From what I have read in your case notes, I can well believe it."

"You were also unhappy about the amount of time the Commander spent with Mrs Jack. 'A cheap money-grubbing whore' you called her. You didn't like the things he did with her nor the money he spent on her. Frankly, you were jealous! I have been told that you and the Commander have been thinking about getting married and that this possibility has increased since Gordon went off to Canada. So you had as good a reason as any for wanting Sophie out of the way and her death was something we know you talked about – and plotted – in the weeks before the murder."

"From the evidence we have, it is very clear that whoever killed Sophie knew her extremely well. She went to meet her murderer quite happily – without the slightest anxiety – wearing her best dress. So it must have been someone she trusted. The Commander had been a good friend to her for almost ten years – but you had already tried to kill her when she was spending the night with Gordon."

"So, could it not be that whilst the Commander innocently lured her to the Meadows, you could have been lurking in the background? And, once he had done his bit – blindfolded her, tied her up to the tree – you came in and delivered the *coup de grace*? The Commander says that he saw nothing – and I'm half inclined to believe him. But that does not mean he was not a party to the murder. He knew what was going to happen …"

Raynes pointed to the paper knife which was now lying on the leather-topped desk. "You are rather partial to sharp instruments … and we know that you had already used a knife to slash the tyres on Sophie's car. Why should you not have dealt a couple of amateur slashes to her stomach as a final gesture of contempt?"

Mrs Hayman still said nothing – but Raynes could sense that she was registering his every word. She was sitting like a statue behind her desk. Her hands had not moved an inch. Nor had her lips. Raynes had watched in vain for any reaction.

"Finally," he said, "it seems that the death of the Commander's first wife was pretty tragic – and not entirely accidental – and that he was also thinking of remarrying at the time she died. Now he is thinking once more of wedding bells – and we have another murder. I must tell you this. The Commander emerged from my interview as a proven liar – and even as a possible murderer. If you've done it once, it's not hard to do it again. But I think that if he was planning to do in Sophie, he'd have needed an accomplice. And that accomplice was you!"

Mrs Hayman's reply was short and concise.

"Inspector, you have painted a very interesting picture, but your evidence is wholly circumstantial. If the Commander cannot prove his alibi, then neither can I. How his first wife came to die has nothing to do with me. But although I hated Sophie Jack – I admit it; I do not deny it – I hated her … in fact, I still hate her … but I did not kill her. I will also admit to you that I thought about killing her. The Commander and I certainly discussed ways and means and it is quite possible that we discussed it in the restaurant that night."

"I cannot deny that I am a violent person – especially when I have been drinking. I have done some pretty stupid things under the influence. But neither I nor the Commander were in the Meadows that night. That is my word, whether you believe me or not. The Commander may be a liar, but I was brought up to tell the truth. If anything, it seems that I have been too honest … too open … for my own good."

Raynes listened to her every word with the greatest of care. She sounded sincere but he had to remember that she was an actress. She was capable of acting a part. Which one was the real Rosalind? The bitch screaming down the telephone? Or the calm, sensible woman telling him that she had never broken the ninth commandment? Clearly she was very much a Jekyll and Hyde. Should he tear into her and make her explode? Or would it be better to lull her into a false sense of security?

It was after 5.00 pm.

Raynes stood up.

Mrs Hayman looked surprised – and relieved.

"Are you going?" she asked.

"Is there anything more you wish to say?"

She looked at him.

"Not really."

Raynes walked out to the porch. There he stopped. He turned back and looked at her. "Are you still thinking of marrying the Commander?"

She seemed surprised.

"Why? Yes. We've been talking about it for ages."

"I think it would be a mistake," said Raynes. "A great mistake!"

15 *An Event in Hampshire*

"You gave her a very easy ride," said Carlisle, as they got back into the car.

"I'm not always rude," said Raynes. "There's something to be said for tact and diplomacy – especially with a woman like her. She's the sort that'd probably have enjoyed a blazing row. Because she was treated nicely – and with respect, she'll be worried: frightened about what she might have given away; wondering if she might have said something incriminating. She'll talk to the Commander, of course – and he'll say all the wrong things. Then she'll explode – all over the sitting room carpet. Should be quite fun!" He smiled to himself. "Great fun!" he said. "At times like this, I wish I could be a fly on the wall." He laughed. "Amateur dramatics!" he said. "Now there's an idea! Imagine our dear Rosalind as Lady Macbeth! She'd play the part to perfection."

"Why did you tell her not to marry Kenworth?"

Raynes said that he'd been thinking about the girl Carlisle had caught creeping down the stairs. It seemed obvious that the Commander was completely promiscuous. Wanted to have his cookie – and eat it. He reckoned that Kenworth had no intention of marrying Mrs Hayman; he was just stringing her along. It was his opinion that the more trouble one could cause between these two – the better. "Anyway," he asked, "who was that girl? Do we know her?"

"Well, I know her," said Carlisle. "She's not on our records or anything like that. She used to be married to a policeman but it broke up. I think there was a divorce. A couple, perhaps? Anyway, she now hangs round the bars of the better class hotels like the *Grosvenor* or *The Green Man* – Fiona Brown, her name is."

Raynes was hard put to keep a straight face. But for a simple matter of choice – a better-looking bottom – he might have been sharing Kenworth's mistress. And that would have been quite catastrophic. He swallowed twice. "Well," he replied, "that at least ties up one loose end. I shall spend the evening tying up a few more." No more visits to the cocktail bar – not at least till this case was over!

Raynes dropped Carlisle off at his home on the outskirts of Grasshallows and drove back thoughtfully to the police station. There he collected his own car. The incident with Fiona Brown reminded him of his promise to buy Debbie a case of champagne. Should he keep that promise? What would happen if Mrs May were to tell her friend Fiona that she had entertained a police inspector and that he had gone as far as to give her six bottles of Moet & Chandon? Would Fiona tell the Commander on her next visit? Would the Commander tell Mrs Hayman? It was a bit dodgy! Should he rather trust Mrs May's discretion? After all, she had given him a great night – and a good breakfast. She had kept her side of the bargain. Should he not keep his? Raynes was not always at his best where women were concerned – but he liked to keep his promises. He decided to be rash and buy her two cases of bubbly. He would deliver it in person early on Wednesday morning. He turned on the ignition and drove out to a supermarket he had seen near Mrs Hayman's home. He put the cases in the boot and locked it. He then decided to avoid the dining room at *The Green Man* and submitted himself once again to the spartan pleasures of the police canteen.

* * *

Raynes returned to his office at 7.00 pm, having had a leisurely meal and two cups of black coffee. He had read the evening paper and felt refreshed. He had listened to a report on the sheep-stealers and was briefed about two burglaries, an attempted rape and another accident involving a car from the Reid brothers. He gave the necessary instructions and then returned to the case which had occupied his first two days in Grasshallows.

He spent another half-hour going through Sophie's diary and address book. He thought about the smooth Derek Coates-Smythe. Was he villain or victim? Surely he had too much to lose? And then the Commander? A foolish man – easily led, as Mrs Hayman had so wisely observed. Why had he told so many lies … unless he really had something to hide? Why had they all told him lies? One after the other … not forgetting Lady Macbeth! That cool, calculating actress with a drink problem and a vicious streak; a lady not averse to wielding a dagger.

Two days ago, these people were just names on a list. Now that they had acquired flesh and blood, the case had become more complicated. He thought of the barriers and the false alibis which had been laid across his path. The Reid brothers certainly had something to hide. Canon Murray was a liar. So was the Commander. Perhaps even Ernie McCulloch was stringing him along? His story was so beautifully pat. He knew all Sophie's movements. Had watched her for years ... And there was more to come.

Whilst he had been out, the telephone lines had been busy. Paul Brown had been tracked down to a new address in Derby. He was working as a sales assistant in an evangelical book-shop. Raynes picked up the phone and told the duty officer to get in touch and summon him down to Grasshallows for an interview on Thursday morning at 9.00 am.

Emilio Zaposito was in jail. He had been in Wormwood Scrubs since December after a particularly horrible rape in Brighton the previous September. Raynes put through another call and arranged for an interview on Wednesday afternoon. This little bird might not talk – but neither could it walk.

John and Linda Jack were even closer to hand. They were living in Army quarters in North London. Raynes personally contacted their Commanding Officer and made sure that he would be able to have separate meetings with John and Linda on Wednesday morning. He expected to be there by about 11.00 am. He asked the Commanding Officer not to let them know who was coming or what the interview would be about. The Commanding Officer seemed co-operative and friendly.

Raynes put down the phone and picked up the final sheet of information on his desk. It concerned George Erskine Murray. Archives had been most thorough. Seven traffic offences had been libelled against him over the years – five for speeding and two for going through red traffic lights. During his time at school, he had been accused of embezzling common-room funds. The police had been called in but the matter had been settled internally. Whilst he was at the Theological College, he had twice been charged with drunk and disorderly behaviour. The first time, he had been admonished; the second time, he was fined £5.

But what interested Raynes most was an episode from his army career. There had been an unpopular sergeant at a training camp in Wales. He was the sort of tin-pot tyrant who regarded it as his self-appointed duty to make the life of a young recruit sheer hell. Nothing had happened to him in Wales but, later, their paths had crossed once more in Hampshire. The artillery company had recognized their tormentor and the mood was one of revenge. It was after a particularly rowdy night at the NAAFI that the incident occurred. The hated sergeant had been waylaid, hustled into the nearby woods, stripped stark naked and tied up to a tree. The soldiers had then subjected their victim to every possible indignity. He had been drenched with the contents of a fire extinguisher and a can of red paint had been poured over his head. The sergeant had been left there overnight – a chilly, damp, November night. Nobody had taken pity on him and it was not until noon the following day that he had been found.

Not surprisingly, he had suffered from exposure; he had a severe attack of pneumonia and was in the military hospital for nearly two months. Then he had a nervous breakdown and had had to be pensioned out of the Army. From the safety of his sick-bed, he was only too willing to name his persecutors. Eighteen soldiers were charged with assault and five of them were court-martialled. George Erskine Murray was not one of the ring-leaders but he was one of the eighteen men involved.

Detective-Inspector Raynes was fascinated by the story and its undoubted similarities with the case of Sophie Jack. No wonder the elderly Canon had been so reticent about divulging his past! With a record like that, even Detective-Inspector Parkinson would have marked him down as a prime suspect.

Raynes looked at his watch. 9.10 pm. Was it too late to go round to St Benedict's Rectory and have a word with Canon Murray? He thought not. He phoned up the Traffic Department and asked whether the Granada was available. It was – so he went.

16 *The Canon's Lament*

When Raynes arrived at Canon Murray's home, a canary-coloured Fiesta caught his eye. It was parked right outside the front gate – beside the Rector's rather battered Volvo. He felt he had seen the car somewhere before. Certainly within the last forty-eight hours. Whose could it be?

He walked up the steep path slowly trying to cast his mind back. But the answer was swift in coming. The front door of the Rectory opened and there was Mrs Hayman in a blue track-suit saying goodnight to the Vicar. Raynes paused to watch and listen.

"I wouldn't worry too much," said Canon Murray. "If you have a clear conscience, you have nothing to hide. You mustn't let yourself be bullied by such a pompous little upstart."

"But I thought the whole thing was over and done with long ago. It's most unpleasant, things being raked up again."

"I know ..." Canon Murray suddenly realized that they were not alone in their conversation. "Why! It's ..."

"... that pompous little upstart!" said Raynes.

Mrs Hayman looked at him with cold hatred in her eyes.

"I'm going," she said. "I've had quite enough of you for one day!"

"Goodnight!" said Raynes politely. "And may your God go with you!"

Canon Murray did not seem any more pleased than Mrs Hayman to find the Inspector on his doorstep so late at night. He was tired. He had slight indigestion. Mrs Hayman's visit had troubled him deeply. And beyond that, he had already conceived a deep antipathy for Raynes. Reluctantly, he invited him into his house.

Raynes did not engage in any pleasantries.

"When I spoke to you yesterday afternoon, Mr Murray, I asked you whether you had a criminal record. If I remember rightly, you refused to answer my question. Now I see why. It's not a very pretty story, is it? Embezzlement ..."

"Embezzlement?"

"At school, when you were a prefect? A small amount of cash going amiss? All hushed up?"

Canon Murray took off his spectacles. "Good heavens!" he said. "Talk about the long arm of the law! I'd quite forgotten about all that. It's nearly fifty years ago. And, anyway, it wasn't embezzled. Every penny was repaid!"

"Embezzlement is what it says," said Raynes. "And drunkenness. Two charges, I believe."

Canon Murray was clearly shaken.

"I'd forgotten that too. So long ago …"

Raynes raised a third finger.

"Seven traffic offences. You've probably forgotten those too!"

"I couldn't have told you how many – but I know there were a few. I normally plead guilty by letter. They were all minor things. Nothing serious. We all do them."

Raynes delivered his final blow.

"Well, I hope you haven't forgotten a little event down in Hampshire. A certain Sergeant Kaye? No? I didn't think you had …"

Canon Murray put his head in his hands and let his glasses fall to the floor.

"… Tied to a tree all night. Covered in red paint. A brush attached to his private parts. A fire extinguisher let off in his face. Left to freeze to death on a cold winter's night. I should have thought a good practising Christian like yourself might have crept back later and set him free?"

Raynes paused but the Canon said nothing.

"Not surprising he almost died of pneumonia, is it? And had a nervous breakdown? A youthful prank perhaps?"

The Canon seemed lost for words.

Eventually, he spoke: "He was a very cruel man … A very spiteful man. Of course, that's no excuse. He didn't deserve such … such treatment. But the lads were very angry … they were out to get him … and it just happened."

"But you were there!" persisted Raynes.

"I was there."

"And you were almost thrown out of the Army because of what you did?"

There was silence.

A long silence.

Finally, the Canon sat up. His eyes were red. His skin looked very grey and haggard. He wiped his face with his handkerchief. He looked around for his spectacles.

"They're on the floor," said Raynes.

The Canon murmured apologetically: "A lot of water's flowed under the bridge since then. I can't say I've forgotten it ... but I've tried hard to forget it. To make amends. It was a bad business and there's no denying it. I'm heartily sorry for what I did."

"I'm not interested in your apologies," said Raynes. "I'm interested in why you tried to bamboozle me yesterday afternoon. When you tried to pretend you were such a sweet, kindly, bumbling old clergyman who wouldn't hurt a fly – whilst in your heart of hearts you know that you are a cold-hearted bastard who'd think nothing of leaving a man strung up on a tree – on a cold November night – leaving him to freeze to bloody death ... That's the sort of man you are!" Raynes paused. "It's no use hiding things from me. I may be 'a pompous little upstart', but I've never done anything like that to anyone. *I* have a *clean* record."

The Canon drew a deep breath.

"I'm sorry for what I said. I'm equally sorry for what I've done. I was punished for what I did. Punished quite severely. And ever since, I've done my best to be kind to people. I even went to see Sergeant Kaye and apologized to him personally ..." Canon Murray remembered the psychiatric hospital and the broken figure slumped in a wheelchair staring blankly out of the window. "I did everything I could ..."

"I think," said Raynes, "that you've missed my point. Again! The point is that if you've tied up one person to a tree; why should you not be suspected of doing it again? Mrs Jack, you knew, was leaving you a very handsome and useful legacy in her will. St Benedict's needed the money. Churches always do. So why not accelerate the process a little? No one would expect the Vicar to be a murderer. Not even Mrs Hayman! So why not meet Sophie down in the Meadows and let history repeat itself? Don't tell the police what you once did down in Hampshire! They might get nasty ideas!" Raynes shook his head. "I'm not surprised that you wanted such things kept dark. I'm afraid, Canon Murray, that you are busted – wide-open!"

The clergyman looked at Raynes with utter horror.

"That's a lie!" he snapped. "An absolute lie!"

"So was much of what you told me yesterday afternoon," said Raynes. "Everyone round here seems to have an idyllic picture of you as their Rector. But it's false. And you know it as well as me!"

"I never killed Sophie!"

"What's your alibi?"

There was a short silence.

"I haven't got one. I can't remember what I was doing this time last year. I never saw any need to think about an alibi. When you're innocent, your mind doesn't think of such things."

"Innocent?" exclaimed Raynes. "Innocent? Then tell me, why does your name appear in Mrs Jack's address book as one of her customers?"

"Mrs Jack's address book?"

Raynes nodded.

"I know nothing about her address book!"

"No, I didn't think you did. Or her diary. But your name's there …"

"Well, I am her Rector …"

"… but it also has a tick beside it. All the people in that diary who were her customers have a tick beside their name. Your Treasurer, Mr Bridges, his name's there, but he doesn't have a tick. So he wasn't one of her clients. But you do. So what am I to think? Why should her address book lie? You … innocent!" Raynes sneered at the elderly cleric.

Canon Murray appeared very upset.

"I was never – as you put it – one of Mrs Jack's customers. I have never paid her a penny. I can promise you that. And I never killed her. Despite what you may think, Inspector, I have never tied anyone to a tree. Not even Sergeant Kaye. I took part in that disgusting business – certainly – but it put me off violence for life. I promise you; I'm telling the truth!"

Raynes looked at him.

"I'm sorry," he said, "I still don't believe you. There's …"

The sentence was never completed.

From outside on the road, there was a tremendous crash, a

sound of tearing metal and a tinkle of cascading glass.

"It's a crash," said the Canon. "Quick! Someone may have been killed!"

Raynes needed no urging. In a few seconds, he had reached the front door, flung it open and run down the steps. There, at the roadside, stood the police Granada, bent broken and twisted. A complete write-off. Something had struck the car a monstrous blow midway between the two offside doors. That side was completely stoved in to the depth of about two to three feet and the roof was buckled in waves like a child's plastic toy. Most of the glass had gone and there was a strong smell of leaking petrol.

But what had hit it? Raynes looked up and down the road. There was no other vehicle in sight but in the quiet of the evening he could hear the distant sound of a heavy motor accelerating in low gear. Realization began to dawn. Some heavy vehicle had deliberately reversed into the Granada. It had been no accident.

Once he had recovered from his surprise, he raced back up the Rectory path, ignoring Canon Murray's pathetic condolences. He seized the phone, dialled 999 and got through to the duty officer at Grasshallows police station.

"Raynes here. Yes, Raynes. Someone has smashed up my Granada. Yes, smashed it up completely. Get a car out straightaway to Reid's garage. Reid's! You know 'em. If you're quick, you might just catch them. And send a car here. To St Benedict's Rectory, as quickly as possible!"

It was perhaps understandable that his message took several minutes to sink in. A kamikaze attack on the police Granada! Such things had never been heard of in Grasshallows! But as Raynes had begun to poke and probe, he had touched some very tender nerves. And now the enemy had begun to strike back!

17 *The Soldier*

"But what hit it?" asked Carlisle.

They were driving down to London in Raynes' own car.

"I fancy it was the metal-framed towing bar of the recovery lorry from Reid's garage. It has a good solid chassis. It wouldn't take much to make mincemeat of a modern car. I think they just stopped about thirty yards down the road, angled themselves up properly for maximum impact and then reversed as fast as they could. A quick change of gear and off they went."

"Been a bit sticky if they'd got stuck?"

"I expect they'd simply pass it off as an accident. Inexperienced driver – not familiar with the gears … A mistake anyone could make!"

"Did they find the Reid brothers?"

"In the local – been there for two hours! Perfect alibi. As usual."

"And the recovery lorry?"

"Found in a lay-by outside the town."

"A joy-rider?"

"Yep. Must have left the keys in the cab. Always handy in an emergency …"

"So nobody can be charged?"

"No. Another perfect crime!"

"I think Jim and Eddie are chancing their luck?"

"Undoubtedly. But why go to such lengths unless you have something to hide? Someone must have been stalking me last night. How else would they know I was at Canon Murray's? It's a nasty thought."

They drove on in silence.

* * *

At the Army barracks, they interviewed John first.

"I believe you were in Aldershot on the night of the murder?"

"Yes, sir. I was watching a video."

"You were on your own? Your wife and family were away?"

"That's right."

"They'd been away for some time?"

John nodded. He'd been through all this so many times he was word-perfect.

"You realize that, without an alibi, you remain a prime suspect in your mother's murder?"

"Yes, sir."

"I believe that you hated her pretty strongly?"

"Well, I didn't approve of her ... way of life, sir."

"But you were quite prepared to profit by it?"

"Not much, sir. She was always very tight with her money. Parted with it like gold dust. You had to wring it out of her ... and even then, you only got a hundred or two. Me and Linda have had some pretty hard times, sir – what with the kids and so on – and we both felt she could have done more to help. It made us pretty bitter, sir. Pretty damn bitter."

"I thought the chief cause of your money problems was your gambling? But I'm told you're now a reformed character?"

"Well, that's what she said, sir. But most of it went on the kids. And Linda. It hasn't been easy for her."

Raynes looked at the healthy, bronzed young soldier in front of him, his arms covered in tattoos, his body radiating fitness and health.

"Did you have access to a car that weekend?"

John paused.

"Yes, sir."

"What kind of car would that be?"

"It's a clapped-out red Escort, sir. It belongs to my mate, but he lets me drive it."

"So you could have driven up to Grasshallows that night?"

"I could, sir, but I didn't."

"Did you use that car on your previous visits? When you beat your mother up; when you stole £200?"

"I didn't really beat her up. I grabbed her by the hair. She hit me – so I hit her back."

"More than once, I believe?"

"It may have been, sir, but I was bloody angry. We were in real trouble. She didn't seem to understand. 'Independence' she called it! It was all right for her! Too bloody independent if you ask me!"

"But on these occasions, you travelled up in your mate's Escort?"

"When I could afford the petrol."

Raynes paused.

"When did you pay your last visit to your mother?"

114

"The Sunday before she died."

"And did you get a warm welcome?"

"No, sir."

"I think the Army padre had spoken to you …?"

"Warned me off, sir. Told me to cool it; so I did."

"You were feeling a bit low at that time?"

"Well, sir, I was. Linda had left me – gone to stay with her mum and dad. She did that from time to time."

"Had you been rough with her?"

"Well, I'm a bit easy on the fists, sir. Lose my temper too quickly. Lash out, you know. Bit short-tempered with the kids, but Linda knows how to handle me. Most times, any rate. She's a good lass, sir. Been a good wife. We've got a lovely pair of kids."

"I'm glad to hear it," said Raynes, thinking what a good witness John would make in court. He was friendly, open, rough as they come – yet with a certain charm and an infectious smile. He was undoubtedly a rogue, a tough customer in a fight, but Raynes felt it was unlikely that he would have killed his mother in such a sophisticated and humiliating way. Had he done the job, he would have beaten her over the head with a bottle or a blunt instrument. There would have been blood everywhere. Or perhaps he would have broken her neck with one savage blow. John was not a plotter. He was a man who burned on a very short fuse.

Raynes continued: "You must have been pretty angry about the contents of her will?"

"You mean her money, sir? I was but there was nothing I could do. I knew the score. She told me long ago. But while she was still alive, sir, I hoped. Hoped she might change her mind. Thought she might leave a thousand or two to the kids. I think she would have done so too, sir, given time."

"I think I agree with you," said Raynes, "but the atmosphere was pretty poisonous."

"Very poisonous, sir."

"I think your wife, Linda, hated her even more than you?"

"Strong views, Linda has. Very strong. Comes from a strict home. Didn't tangle with the likes of mum. She was against

115

her from the word 'go'. Mum did try. I'll give her that. But Linda put her back up. Said some pretty nasty things to her …"

"But she still tried to screw money out of her?"

"For the kids, sir. For the kids."

Raynes felt that he had got all that he was likely to get out of John Jack. He had a large file on him back at Grasshallows. There was only one more question he wanted to ask: "Who do you think was responsible for your mother's death – if it wasn't you?"

"It wasn't me, sir. That's for certain. One of them perverts she went about with …"

"Male or female?"

"Male, of course!"

"You don't think a woman would be capable of doing such a thing to your mother?"

"No, sir."

"You don't think your wife, Linda, would have done such a thing – knowing how much she hated her? Divine punishment, so to speak?"

"Linda? No, sir. She's not violent. Wouldn't hurt a fly. Besides, she was with her aunt that night. She wasn't out, sir. And she wouldn't have gone to her anyway. Her parents keep her pretty well, sir – and the kids."

Everything seemed to come back to "the kids". Clearly, they were the apple of John's eye. Raynes asked a few more questions about his family and then sounded him out on his pet theory.

"One final question, John. All your mother's money has gone to the Church. Do you think that the vicar, Canon Murray, could in any way be responsible for her death? I know he looks like a nice old guy – but some people will do anything for £100,000. What do you think about him?"

John raised his eyebrows and laughed.

"Well, I know they were pretty close, him and her; they worked hand-in-glove so to speak. He used to write letters for her. Things like that. But I can't see him murdering her. No."

"When you say 'close', what do you mean?"

"Very close, sir."

116

"You think he was one of her customers – on the side?"

"Very likely, sir. Very likely, I should say. My mum would corrupt anyone, sir. She had a way with men. Could wrap 'em round her little finger. Still, the old Canon's been pretty kind to me. He gave her a nice funeral. Said some nice things about her. And he sent me a couple of thousand ..."

"Did he?"

"Yes, sir."

"That's very interesting," said Raynes. "But you think there was something between them?"

"Can't prove it, sir. But it stands to reason, doesn't it? She wouldn't leave all that money to him if there weren't a bit of dirty work at the crossroads, would she? Where your 'eart is and all that!"

Raynes smiled.

"Thank you, John," he said, "you've been most helpful."

John rose to his feet and saluted smartly.

"Thank you, sir. I hope you get the bastard, sir."

"So do I," said Raynes, "so do I."

18 *The Soldier's Wife*

Ten minutes later, Linda was brought in by the Army padre. She looked pale, drawn and on the verge of collapse. He helped her into a chair and said to Raynes and Carlisle: "Go easy on her. She's very distressed!" He seemed inclined to stay but Raynes bid him a brusque farewell and waited till the sound of his feet reached the end of the passage. In the meantime, he looked at Linda.

She was one of those unfortunate women, slim but utterly unattractive. A mere bag of bones. No hips. No bust. No dress sense. Long blonde hair which hung drearily round her shoulders. Her skin was plain and lacked lustre. But she had large grey eyes – like a dead fish, thought Raynes.

"Mrs Jack," he said, "do you know why we're here?"

"I can guess," she said, and burst into tears.

"Shut up!" said Raynes, "and stop play-acting!"

He waited till she had recovered some composure.

"We're here in connection with the death of your mother-in-law in Grasshallows a year ago. The case has been re-opened and it's my job to go through the facts with you. That's what I'm here to do. And provided I have your fullest co-operation, this meeting need not last long."

Linda looked happier – and managed a smile.

"Good!" said Raynes. "Now I expect you will recognize Detective Carlisle. He was here with Detective-Inspector Parkinson last year and he has given me most of the details. I would just like to check them over with you. Now I believe that at the time of your mother-in-law's death, you were staying with your aunt and your children were with your parents. Is that correct?"

She nodded.

"Now your parents live in Ongar and your aunt lives in Leytonstone. Is that correct?"

She nodded again.

"Please answer my questions properly," said Raynes. "Yes or no. Don't nod your head. You're not a donkey." He gave her a vague smile. "Now on the night in question, I believe that you were at a disco. Where was this disco?"

"In the east end of London."

"Whereabouts?"

"In Leyton."

"Did you go to this disco alone?"

"Yes."

"And it was good?"

She smiled. "Yes."

Now you told Detective-Inspector Parkinson that you didn't come home that night. Didn't come home to your aunt's. You spent the night with the DJ. Is that correct?"

Linda looked very upset.

"You won't say anything to John, will you? He doesn't know anything about it. I haven't told him."

"If you are honest with me," said Raynes, "I shall respect your privacy." He looked at her. "Who was he then?"

"I don't know."

"Oh, come on! You can't sleep with a bloke without know-

118

ing his name! You must have called him something. Was he English, African, Spanish, American or what?"

There was a long pause.

"I think he was Italian."

"Why d'you think he was Italian?"

"He looked Italian."

"Had you ever met him before?"

"No."

As she replied, Raynes knew that she was lying.

"Are you aware," Carlisle intervened, "that the DJ of the place where you said you went for the disco is Irish? They call themselves the 'Begorra Brothers'?"

Linda looked surprised.

"We've checked up on your story," said Carlisle.

"Your alibi's up the spout!" said Raynes. "You may have been able to fool Detective-Inspector Parkinson but you don't fool me!"

Linda said nothing.

"You spent the night with this Italian? Is that true?"

"Yes."

"Where?"

"In his flat. And it's no use asking me where – because I don't know. It was the top flat in a long street."

"Have you been out with him since?"

"No."

Another lie. Raynes wondered how he could break through her fragile defences without unleashing another avalanche of tears.

"Your parents knew nothing about this bloke?"

"Nothing."

"They would have been upset?"

"Very upset!"

"Why? Because he was an Italian?"

"No. Because he was a Roman Catholic!"

"Does that matter?"

"The Catholics are the Anti-Christ!"

Raynes raised his eyebrows at such bigotry.

"You mean that'd upset them more than you committing adultery with a bloke you didn't know?"

119

"Probably."

Raynes shook his head in disbelief.

"But I thought adultery was one of the things you held against John's mother? And she was a Protestant."

"Oh, she was a bitch! It wasn't just adultery. It was everything. The constant stream of men. The perversions. The life of the gutter. It was disgusting. She deserved everything she got!" A rare streak of passion lit up her face.

"What did you dislike most about her?"

"Her job, of course! It was dreadful. Fancy John being brought up in that atmosphere! Knowing that your mother was a common tart. And she had no shame about it. She flaunted it. She revelled in it. She was proud of how much she earned in a night. She taunted me that I couldn't earn that sort of money. Me – a mother of two children! 'When you can earn a couple of hundred a night', she used to say, 'then you'll be able to stand on your own two feet'. What a disgusting thing to say! Trying to drag me down to her level ..."

"Yes, yes," said Raynes, "but you were happy enough to sponge money off her. You and John."

"Only for the sake of the children."

"That was because your husband was gambling away most of his pay?"

There was a silence.

"Yes."

"And if you asked for money or put pressure on him, he would hit you and the children?"

"Yes. Sometimes."

"And then you decamped with the children? You went home to your parents ... till things got better?"

"Yes."

"Which they have?"

"Yes. Things are much better now."

"The money from Canon Murray?"

"It helps."

"Who's looking after it – you or him?"

"The padre."

"I see."

Raynes felt he was getting nowhere fast.

"Did you ever wish your mother-in-law dead?"

She thought about that one.

"Yes."

"Quite often?"

"I prayed about it."

"Did you ever think about killing her yourself?"

Her reply was surprisingly honest.

"No. John talked about it now and then – but there would have been no point. She wasn't leaving us a penny. She told us that long ago. So, even if he had killed her, it wouldn't have done us any good."

"So it was a question of begging or threatening?"

"Mostly."

"You knew she was very fond of her grandchildren?"

"I wouldn't let her go anywhere near them. I didn't want her polluting their minds. She sent them presents of course. Expensive presents. But that didn't feed them. She was no mother to John. Twice divorced. Living on the streets. Selling herself to anyone ..." She shuddered at the thought of such a person being in contact with *her* children.

"Did the Italian pay you anything for your night of passion?"

She was silent.

"Well, did he?"

"I'm not going to answer that question."

She looked angry.

"We'll assume that he did!" said Raynes.

"He gave me my taxi money home."

"Every woman has her price," said Raynes.

Linda burst into tears again.

Raynes looked at Carlisle despairingly. He was by this time feeling remarkably unsympathetic. "If you go on crying," he said, "and keep interrupting me, I shall take you into custody – and we can continue this conversation elsewhere."

The crying stopped immediately.

"You can't take me away from my children!"

"I most certainly can; and, if necessary, I will. Unless you conduct yourself like a grown-up woman. Stop behaving like

121

a spoilt child and pull yourself together!"

It was a long time since anyone had spoken to Linda with such absolute authority. She didn't know whether to cry or not. Raynes said: "Despite your good background and your high Christian principles, you have told me two lies – possibly more. First of all, you said that you had never met this Italian before – and then you said that you had never seen him again. Both those statements were untrue."

She faltered.

"How did you know?"

"Because I'm old in sin. When people tell me lies, I know. I have no desire, no desire whatsoever, to pry into your sordid past – but this man is your alibi! How can I be sure that you were not in Grasshallows that night, getting your revenge on your mother-in-law?"

Her shoulders shook.

"I couldn't do a thing like that."

Raynes was firm: "Neither you nor your husband has an alibi for the night in question. There is no reason why the two of you could not have borrowed the red Escort and sailed up to Grasshallows, done her in and been back home by midnight. There is a considerable question mark against John and, until you come clean about this Italian, there's an even bigger question mark over you. Can't you see?"

"I wouldn't kill anyone." It was a whine.

More tears were on the way.

Raynes finally lost his temper: "You can decide one way or the other. Either you come clean and tell us who it was – or I take you away now and hold you in custody in Grasshallows police station till you decide to make a statement." He sat back and looked at Carlisle.

Linda Jack continued weeping.

"Have you got the handcuffs?" Raynes asked.

"In the car."

"Get 'em."

"I'll tell you!" screamed Linda. "His name was Emilio ..."

"Emilio Zaposito?"

"Well, if you knew, why did you bother asking?"

122

Raynes looked at Carlisle with amazement.

Linda's voice had now reached the higher decibels – she was howling: "I won't leave my children! I won't, I won't, I won't!" – when the door suddenly crashed open and the Army padre rushed to her side.

"I must protest," he said, "at this treatment. I warned you that she was in a very delicate condition. I must insist that you stop this questioning now – and give her time to calm down!" He put a protective arm round her shoulders.

Raynes looked at Carlisle before he replied.

"Mrs Jack is suspected of complicity in the murder of her mother-in-law. She tells us nothing but lies – then weeps. It's all an act. I'm afraid screaming is no defence in a court of law." He looked without the slightest pity at the woman sobbing and wailing in front of him. He said: "We shall be going to Wormwood Scrubs to see this man, Emilio Zaposito, and when we come back, I shall want a full statement from Mrs Jack. Failing that, she will have to be taken immediately into custody. If you have any respect for the law of the land, you'll do your best to make sure she co-operates. And you'd better make sure she doesn't try to commit suicide."

Raynes picked up his keys and stormed out of the room.

19 *The Italian Connection*

After a cup of coffee and a sandwich, they arrived at the prison. Like most people, they found the atmosphere somewhat oppressive. The rattle of keys. The crash of metal gates. The measured tread of prison officers. The smell of disinfectant and the all pervading lemon-coloured walls. They followed the warder through a labyrinth of passages till they reached the small room where the interview was to take place. They waited for five minutes whilst Zaposito was brought from his cell.

Emilio was a swarthy, thick-set man of moderate height, about forty years old. He had rather bulging eyes, thick lips and, as Linda had said, he looked "Italian". His hairline was receding and he had a very broad forehead. His eyes were lazy and suspicious but his manner was cowed and submissive. He sat down and folded his arms. A prison officer stood about four feet behind him.

Once Emilio was sitting comfortably, Raynes began:

"Mr Zaposito," he said, "you may remember Detective-Constable Carlisle. He came to see you this time last year in connection with the death of Sophie Jack – Sophie Luccione. He took a statement from you."

Emilio smiled.

"I see too many policemen. I forgetta their names."

"I'm sure you do. But at least you should remember Sophie?"

Emilio did not smile.

"I don't forget her!"

"No, I thought not. You worked with her in London?"

"She worked for me."

"And she also shopped you to the police for that knifing in Hammersmith. How long did you get?"

"Ten years. But I only served six."

"That's a long time!"

"Too long."

"Did you see Sophie again when you came out?"

"Yes."

"Did you threaten her?"

Emilio thought for a while.

"Yes. I threatened her. I said: 'You pay me £5000 or I slash your double-crossing face.'"

"Did she pay up?"

"She paid £1000. Then I was back in again. When I was out, I went to see her. She gave me £2000 – then I was lifted again. I let her off the last lot."

"Very generous of you," said Raynes sarcastically. "But surely she must have made you quite a packet when she was working for you?"

Emilio shrugged his shoulders. "She was good – but she cheated. She was too much her own boss. She was always looking to be her own boss. She was – very tight." He made a gesture with his fingers.

Raynes said: "I believe you have been up in Grasshallows to see her? When did you pay your last visit?"

Emilio shook his head.

"I do not know. Two or three years ago perhaps."

Raynes looked at Carlisle.

"That's what he said last year."

Raynes looked back to Emilio.

"I don't think that's entirely true, is it? I think you've been up to Grasshallows more recently. Just before Sophie died?"

Emilio had a pitying look in his eyes. It was the sort of look that said: 'It may be true but prove it'." Raynes decided to accept that challenge.

"Mr Zaposito, I think you know Linda Jack?"

The impact was instant.

Emilio's eyes which had been relaxed and friendly, suddenly narrowed. He looked like an animal at bay.

Raynes continued: "Linda Jack is Sophie's daughter-in-law. She's married to John, Sophie's son, who is a soldier."

Emilio said nothing.

"It's no use you denying it. She told me that you knew her; that you'd slept together in your flat – or someone's flat. In fact, you seem to have become quite pally!"

Raynes smiled encouragingly.

"You're not denying you know her? Tall, thin girl. Blonde hair. Grey eyes. Staying in Leytonstone with her aunt?"

There was a long silence.

"You know her?"

"May do."

"You're not very lucky with your women are you, Mr Zaposito? They always shop you to the police. First of all it was Sophie; now it's Linda. It's no use denying it. She told me all about you."

Emilio said nothing.

"You told Detective-Constable Carlisle last year that you were in a club in the East End on the night Sophie was murdered. It was a Saturday night and you were enjoying yourself with your chums. That was your story. But it seems it wasn't true! Linda has had second thoughts. Spilled the proverbial beans! She says you were with her that evening. True or false?"

Emilio still said nothing. He realized he was on very dangerous ground. Should he ask for a lawyer?

But Raynes decided to change the subject.

"How long are you in for this time?"

"Four years."

"So, with remission, you could be out just after Christmas?"

"Could be."

"That was for rape – this time?"

"It was a frame-up!"

"Of course! You were in the East End at the time!"

Emilio smiled.

"You guessed it!"

Raynes decided to appeal to the Italian's better nature.

"Look!" he said. "I know what you've been up to – but I want corroboration. Linda says that on the night Sophie died, you and she were up in Grasshallows to try and squeeze more money out of her ..."

He paused.

Most interestingly, Emilio did not deny the story.

"... You were going to split it 50/50. But, knowing you, more like 90/10. But you didn't get the money. You came back empty-handed. You spent the night in your flat – or someone's flat – and you gave her enough taxi money to get her home."

Raynes watched Emilio carefully. He had invented the story about Grasshallows because he thought it was a remote possibility. Linda was hiding something. Suppose she was terrified anyone might know she was in Grasshallows that night? Emilio had registered no emotion; uttered no denial. But the final detail about the taxi money visibly rattled him. It was the sort of fact that Raynes could only have got from Linda Jack – and if he had been told that much, what other aces was he holding up his sleeve?

Emilio said nothing. He was thinking hard.

Raynes continued: "I want to know exactly what you did that evening. I think that even you will remember a summer evening's drive with a pretty girl? If you killed Sophie, you might as well tell me now. If you hold out on me, I shall make sure that whether you murdered her or not, you will serve every day of the four years for the Brighton rap. If you have something to hide, you can remain silent. But if you are innocent, then you have nothing to lose by coming clean. Please think carefully before you speak."

Mr Zaposito had had long experience in dealing with policemen. There were some you could flannel and lie to. There were others whom one was obliged to meet half-way. When he had first seen Raynes he had known instinctively that he belonged to the second type. Holding his remission over him was blackmail – but as a long-term practitioner of the art himself, he knew when to give way. He conceded that Raynes had the cards well stacked against him.

Mr Zaposito spoke slowly.

He had indeed had a long-standing grudge against Sophie. He had felt particularly bitter about the way she had betrayed him over the Hammersmith affair. Things had never been quite the same since. During his long hours in captivity, he had plotted his revenge. For a start, he would screw her for £5000 – and then slowly tighten the screw. But when he came out of prison, Sophie had vanished. People said she had got married. Once, if not twice. It took him time to discover where she was living – and, by that time, he had other fish to fry.

But he'd given her a shock. Her face, when he appeared at the door! She had thought he was going to kill her! The sight of his knife with its razor-sharp blade! He had thought about killing her ... but a bird in the hand was worth two in the crematorium. He put it to her. £5000 was the price of her pretty face. If the money was not forthcoming, he would slash her face open from ear to ear. Sophie had delivered £1000 within two days. She promised a thousand a month for the next four months. It was easy money. Emilio was pleased.

What Emilio did not know was that to raise the rest of the money, Sophie had to go back on the game. She had raised the next two instalments but, by then, Emilio was back in jail for another long spell. But, unfortunately, her husband discovered what she had been doing and the marriage fell apart. Sophie never told her husband about Emilio.

127

By the time Mr Zaposito was once more in circulation, Sophie was living in Grasshallows looking after her mother. It took him a couple of months to track her down but the £2000 was there. He was so pleased by this windfall that he decided to be generous and waive the rest of the money. But every now and then, when he was in a tight corner, he paid a visit to Grasshallows and she gave him a cheque. He reckoned that she had paid out a further £2500. She was no longer as pretty as she had been so the threat to slash her face had lost its power. She had also warned him that the police had his name and if he laid a hand upon her, she would spill the beans. He reckoned that it was better to keep things the way they were.

But last June, he had been particularly desperate. He had just come out of jail and nothing was going right. No jobs were coming along – and cash was getting tight. He knew Linda Jack. He had met her once at Grasshallows and he had seen her again at a disco in Leyton a couple of years back. She had been living with her aunt at Leytonstone during one of her break-ups with John. He had had it off with her once or twice – but nothing serious.

Last June, he had phoned Linda. She was away from John. She thought she could spend a weekend with her aunt. She was as skint as he was – her parents didn't give her much pocket money. Emilio had suggested that as they were both hard-up, they should pay a visit to the "old lady". Linda had said that she was quite sure Sophie would give her nothing but Emilio fancied he might have more luck.

So they took his car – a friend's car – and set out on the Saturday for Grasshallows. They had meant to get there by lunchtime but the car was an old banger and had broken down outside Harlow. A kindly lorry-driver had towed them to a nearby garage but it had taken a couple of hours before they had found a mechanic willing to come out on a Saturday afternoon. Even when he'd come, his progress had been dismally slow and twice he had had to go off to get spare parts. It had cost Emilio £40. By 5.30 pm they were once more on the road and they had got to Grasshallows at about 8.00 pm. He thought.

They had parked in a cul-de-sac off Riverside Road. Linda had stayed in the car whilst he had approached the flat. There was no sign of Sophie's car but he imagined there was a light on in her flat. A table light, he thought; not the main light. But after he had gone up and banged on her door, the light had certainly gone off. He couldn't be sure if someone was in the flat or not. He had looked through the letter-box and even contemplated breaking in. But Sophie had taken precautions years before. Her front door had an iron frame, steel bracing and a strong mortice lock, so he had rejected the idea and waited for the lady herself to arrive.

He had returned to the car to tell Linda that she was not there. They had some fish and chips and then drove down to the Meadows. It was almost dusk. About 9.00 pm, he reckoned. They had seen her car. In fact, they had parked quite near it and spent about two hours waiting for her to appear. But nothing had happened so they had driven back to the flat to see if someone else had driven her home – but Sophie was nowhere to be seen.

Eventually, they had given up, gone back to London and spent a very unpleasant night in his friend's flat. He had suggested going up to Grasshallows on the Sunday but she was "frit". They had quarrelled and he had given her the taxi fare home. Next day it was in all the papers that Sophie had been murdered. They had met in a pub in Leyton and agreed that neither would mention the other – nor their visit to Grasshallows. Emilio was disgusted that Linda had squealed.

Raynes said: "Never trust a woman!"

Emilio shrugged his shoulders.

"Too late now!"

Raynes felt that Mr Zaposito had given him a fairly full picture … as far as it went. He had to remember that this story was remarkably different from the one he had told Detective-Constable Carlisle the year before and if he was capable of lying once, there was no reason to believe his most recent tale. The degree of trust he could put on Emilio's story depended on the extent to which Linda could corroborate the details he had given. The thought of returning to the Army barracks did not cheer him. He much preferred to grill a slippery rogue like Zaposito rather than endure the pathetic hysterics of a neurotic woman. Still, he had to admit, it was Linda who had given him the key to opening up the Italian.

There was just one final question that Raynes had to ask:

"Did you see anyone hanging round Sophie's car in the Meadows – or any strange bodies hanging round her flat?"

Emilio struggled to remember. Down in the Meadows he had thought there were quite a few punters hanging round Sophie's Marina

"Men – or women?" asked Raynes.

"Oh, men," said Emilio. "Of course, all men."

Could he remember any of them in detail?

No, he couldn't. He had been too busy watching out for Sophie. The punters had flitted back and forwards like ghosts. He remembered seeing the park attendant once or twice – but that was all.

"Had he at any point got out of his car?"

Once or twice to stretch his legs. But that was all.

Raynes thanked the Italian for being so honest with him. If a statement was required, Detective-Constable Carlisle would be back to take it. In the meantime, Mr Zaposito was encouraged to cast his mind back to June 27th and to try and remember any little details which might have escaped his attention. There was no mention of remission. Raynes reckoned that the longer Emilio was inside, the safer the great British public would be.

20 *Linda's Story*

"Did you believe him?" asked Carlisle.

"I don't know," said Raynes. "It's certainly an advance on his previous story. Getting him to admit that he and Linda were actually in Grasshallows that night was quite something. It puts a whole new light on the picture. But can you imagine that after all that effort to get to Grasshallows, they would leave without receiving a penny? Suppose they did see Sophie and she refused ... why shouldn't the two of them corner her in the wood and do a little ritual murder? Knives seem to be Emilio's favourite weapon …"

"So they do."

"The Hammersmith knifing. The way he threatened to slash Sophie's face open. That would certainly explain why her stomach was carved open. Emilio doesn't like women. He has complete contempt for them. I felt that in the way Sophie was treated there was evidence of contempt. Imagine what that scene might have done to Linda!"

"She'd have been absolutely terrified."

"Precisely. And that would go a long way to explaining why she refused to squeal."

"Do you think she'll admit to anything now?"

"No – not yet. I think we'll probably get a little further. I hope that bloody padre's done his bit and told her to come clean. These do-gooders are a bleeding nuisance!"

They arrived at the army barracks at about 5.15 pm, having been caught up in the rush hour traffic. Raynes' Rover had begun to overheat and there had been some anxious moments. However, they discovered that the Army padre had spent most of the afternoon with Linda and she was ready to talk.

"That's a blessing," said Raynes. "I thought we were in for another scene."

"She's feeling very vulnerable at the moment. Very raw. I think she and John are on the brink again."

"That's not what she said this morning."

"Well, you know how people cover up …"

In more ways than one, thought Raynes.

* * *

Linda was looking even paler and more washed out than she had at the morning session. She was twisting her handkerchief round and round and her dress was full of wet patches showing where she had cried. However, holding the padre's hand, she was willing to talk:

She and Emilio had met at her mother-in-law's flat in Grass-hallows several years before. Both of them had been touting for money. Emilio had given her a lift home. He had told her that if she should ever want a job, she should give him a ring.

131

He had given her a phone number where he could be contacted. She had kept the number – even though she regarded him as an out-and-out rogue. However, when things had been difficult between her and John, she had phoned him up and they had met. She had helped him in one or two small jobs – as look-out or carrying his tools. But she had refused outright his other suggestion that she might go on the game and earn really big money. She still had some principles.

Last June, Emilio had come out of prison and phoned her. Her parents had been rather suspicious but she had assured them that he was a man she had once worked for part-time and there might be a chance of another job. She had gone to meet him on the Friday night, slept at her aunt's and then gone round to his flat on the Saturday morning. It had been his suggestion that they might go up and see Sophie. Linda had no expectation of any favours and intended to keep in the background, but Emilio had been confident that he could wangle a cheque for £1000 or £1500. He told her: "Sophie's loaded."

Their journey north had been a chapter of accidents. First of all, one of the tyres had gone flat; then they had had trouble with the spare wheel because it was soft. Then the wheel bolts had been rusty and difficult to get off. Linda confirmed their long ordeal outside Harlow and their belated arrival in Grasshallows.

She knew that Sophie was usually on the job from 7.30 pm onwards and didn't think they would catch her at the flat. But Emilio said there was a light on. She had followed him at a distance but she hadn't seen any light. Emilio said it had been switched off. They had waited around for about five minutes and then decided to have some fish and chips because they were starving. She put their arrival at the flat at about 8.15 or 8.30 pm – a bit later than Emilio had said.

An hour or so later, they had reached the Meadows. They had not seen Sophie – but they had seen her car. She denied that either of them had ever left the car. They went back to the flat but no one was there. That was about 11.00 pm. After that, they had given up. Emilio wanted them to "kip up" together in the car and have another bash early on Sunday morning, but

Linda's conscience was troubling her. She was frightened of her parents questioning her movements and she must get home to her children. So they had driven back to London empty-handed. She had slept the night in his flat and he had told her she was a lousy lover. After that, it was merely a question of getting a taxi home. He had at least paid for that!

For a while, she had been frightened that perhaps she might be pregnant because they had taken no precautions. But far more worrying was the news of Sophie's murder. She had realized that it was whilst they were sitting in the car in Grass-hallows that she was being murdered. Linda was aware that, if the truth were known, she and Emilio would be prime suspects. The whole sordid story would be splashed across the gutter press. Her parents ... her children ... John ... What would they say? It was for that reason she had lied.

Raynes noted the differences between her story and Emilio's. He felt that they were of a minor nature and not really signi-ficant. What was really important was what he had *not* been told. He questioned her about the knife. Had the Italian been armed? She said not. Had he had a knife? She was silent for a long time after Raynes asked that question. She had known him to carry a knife on other occasions when he was "doing a job". What sort of knife? A German hunting knife – with a particularly vicious blade, razor-sharp. Was he carrying that knife with him on the day? She thought not. Had she seen it anywhere in the flat? No. Raynes made a mental note to ask Emilio where that knife was now – perhaps even to see whether it could be the murder weapon.

Raynes was well-pleased with his second interview with Linda, but he couldn't resist trying out his new pet theory that Emilio might have gashed Sophie with his knife. Hard as he tried to push this idea, the more worked up she became and denied loudly and tearfully that Emilio had never got out of the car – let alone entered the woods. Since Raynes knew this to be a lie, he was inclined to push at the already creaking door, but he caught the padre's eye. Enough was enough, for one day at least.

He thanked Linda for her help, promised her that he would

say nothing to her parents or John and asked her to think over her evidence in case a full statement would have to be made. Carlisle had taken full notes of this and every interview and on the basis of these notes a statement would be drawn up. But if she had anything to add … Linda said that she had nothing to add and again broke into tears.

Raynes thanked the padre for his help. He nodded to Carlisle and they slipped out of the room. They let themselves out of the front door and there encountered another problem. An angry husband. John was in a highly menacing mood.

"Is my wife in there?" he shouted.

"She is."

"And what have you two pigs been doing to her? She's been in there all day."

"I think you'll have to ask her that."

"She hasn't done nothing. She was with her parents."

"So I believe."

"If you've done anything to hurt her, you bastards!" He put his fist under Raynes' chin; "I'll smash your bloody guts in!"

Raynes looked him in the eye.

"Most of the time," he said coldly, "she's been defending you. Accounting for your movements. Telling us about your relationship with your mother. It's not a nice story. A bit more colourful than the story you told us. But she's a good girl is Linda. You ought to be proud of her. She defended you to the hilt."

John slowly lowered his fist.

"Did she?"

"She did. I don't know why, but she did. If you want to help your wife, young man, I would suggest that you say *nothing* – ask *no* questions – and go home quietly. In fact, I would take her out for a nice dinner. Or buy her a new dress. You're a very lucky man and you should be thankful that your wife is so loyal."

John smiled.

"You mean that?"

"I do. Go in there. Thank the padre for his help. Take her home. Give her a big hug. Tell her that the police are complete

134

bastards. Ask her no questions. Just put your arm around her and take her out for a good steak."

John grinned.

"Sounds like a good idea!"

Raynes and Carlisle escaped. As he climbed into the car, Raynes said: "Light the blue touch paper and stand clear …"

21 *Evans and Co.*

During the journey home, Raynes and Carlisle discussed the different tales they had heard. Raynes told him about Canon Murray's youthful exploits and Carlisle whistled with amazement.

"That puts him in a totally different light!"

"So it does. But you can see now why he was holding out."

"But I still can't see him murdering Sophie."

"Suppose," said Raynes, "suppose that he had been knocking her off – on the quiet. Suddenly he has a crisis of conscience – decides to stop. And Sophie threatened to tell. Even worse, if she decided to change her will. St Benedict's will lose £100,000! That's quite a blow! Canon Murray will have to act quickly. Or before Sophie tells. Imagine what Grasshallows will think when they discover their Rector has been having a little on the side! His ministry would end in shame and scandal …"

"I still can't see Canon Murray wielding a knife."

"Until ten minutes ago, you would hardly have believed he could tie up some poor sod to a tree. But it's true."

"It's hard to believe," said Carlisle, "I'm far more inclined to point the finger at the Commander or Mrs Hayman. They were lying through their teeth. And even more at the Reids – especially after what happened last night. They must be quite desperate to do a thing like that!"

"I'm afraid we've stirred up quite a hornets' nest," said Raynes. "I think there'll be quite a few daggers flying. We shall have to watch out."

* * *

That evening, Raynes endured another miserable meal in the police canteen; but his mind was not on food. It was on murder.

Who could have killed Sophie? How? And why?

The more enquiries he made, the more muddy the water became. Motives multiplied. Alibis crumbled. Fresh revelations suggested a whole host of different scenarios. Once upon a time (Monday lunchtime, in fact) – how long ago it seemed! – things had looked so simple and straightforward. But three days on (God! It was still only Wednesday) he was getting muddled and mixed up.

Worst of all, he couldn't be sure that the suspects presently lined up were the only ones to be considered. Important people had been left out. What about Gordon Hayman? How could he do anything about him now he was in Vancouver? And what about the rest of the clients whom Detective-Inspector Parkinson in his infinite wisdom had passed over. What about Ralph, Beaver, Cecil and Wynn? He had taken over Carlisle's list as being the most likely. But suppose it was faulty and incomplete? And what about his own first instincts? Did they still hold water?

What made it so infuriating was that his fellow officers were all buzzing with excitement. Everyone was anxious to help. People smiled at him hopefully. Asked how he was getting on. Junior members of the CID kept remembering little details from last year's investigations which they hoped would not be overlooked. Unsolicited memoranda were constantly piling up on his desk. When he came home on Wednesday night, he read them all – and filed them as "Useless". In the canteen, people were saying to him things like: "You won't forget Briggs?" Whoever Briggs was! At the back of his mind, there lay that irritating question from another famous murder: "Why didn't they ask Evans?" But had he even got "Evans" on his list?

With these unhappy thoughts seething around in his mind, Raynes listened to the latest reports on the sheep stealers. It now appeared more than likely that they came from Wales. Raynes said that it didn't surprise him one bit. "Why didn't they ask Evans?"

And then there was the Reid brothers and their blasted recovery lorry. No evidence of course! Raynes decided that just as they had frightened him, he would frighten them. "Pull them in for questioning," he said. "Jim tonight. Eddie tomorrow. Throw the book at them! Everything you've got! Put on the most savage and unsympathetic officer you can find!"

"That'll be Evans, sir!"

Of course it would have to be Evans! It was that sort of day!

* * *

After clearing his desk, Raynes went for a long walk beside the river to refresh his soul. He had hardly looked at the city of Grasshallows but tonight he tried to absorb the wholesome atmosphere of his new home town.

He walked past the University, past the boat-sheds and laboratories, out past the weeping willows and people exercising their dogs. He kept well away from the Meadows and followed the towpath as it meandered towards the next village. There he had a pint of lager and lime and a chicken in the basket. After all, he had had no lunch!

Feeling more cheerful, he whistled as he walked home. Through his mind, he ran over what he knew about each suspect. It was quicker than any computer. He balanced their statements against what he had read in their files. It was possible that he was wrong in his guesswork – after all, there were two people still to be seen – but, on balance, he felt sure he had cracked it. He still needed hard proof but his instincts were rarely at fault. It must be! Surely there was no alternative? It was clever. Damnably clever. But that must be the solution. He felt elated but he told himself: "Don't plunge in too quick ... Don't make a move till you're absolutely sure." He'd done that once and regretted it. The woman had escaped. This time ... there must be no mistake.

He returned to *The Green Man* at about 11.45 pm. It was deserted. He was about to walk up the stairs to his room when the porter called out: "There's a letter for you!"

Raynes was surprised. He wasn't expecting any letters. Not even bills. He took the letter and looked at the handwriting. He didn't recognize it. But it was local and had been delivered by hand. There was a whiff of Rive-Gauche. Of course; it was from she!

He thanked the porter and took the letter up to his room. He stripped off his clothes and had a shower. Then, comfortably settled in his warm bed, he tore open the envelope:

DEAR SIR (it said)

WHAT A LOVELY SURPRISE! TWO CASES! SOMEBODY MUST HAVE BEEN *REAL* SATISFIED! LOOK AFTER YOURSELF! YOUR SECRET IS SAFE WITH ME! CALL ROUND ANYTIME – FOR BREAKFAST – OR ANYTHING!

MUCH LOVE,
D.

with twelve little crosses and a telephone number.

Raynes smiled to himself. He had the beginning of an idea … but he had had enough ideas for one day. And as he shut his eyes, he went straight to sleep.

22 *The Brown Man*

Raynes arrived late at the office the following morning. He had had a leisurely breakfast and it was well after 9.30 am before he rolled in. He was told: "Mr Jim Reid has had a very unpleasant night in the cells."

"I'm delighted," said Raynes. "I shall see him later."

"And there's a young man been waiting to see you. He said he had an appointment for 9.00 am."

"That's right. I'll see him now. Where's Carlisle?"

"Down in Records."

"Send him up."

Paul Brown was a small, insignificant figure wearing a brown Harris-tweed jacket, a pair of grey flannels and brown suede shoes. He had rather shiny brown hair, a narrow face and sad, watchful brown eyes. Raynes instinctively felt sorry for him.

"I'm sorry we had to bring you down here at such short notice, Mr Brown, but we've re-opened the case on Mrs Jack. I believe you were seen by Detective-Inspector Parkinson last year – and everyone involved then is being seen once more. I believe you were friendly with Sophie?"

"We got to know each other through the University."

Raynes smiled.

"What's a respectable fellow like you doing with the likes of Sophie?"

Paul Brown looked serious.

"We were doing a special series of in-depth encounters called: 'Face to Face with Sin'. We had a chap from Ladbrokes to tell us about gambling; we had a police officer to tell us about theft and crime; we had the publican from *The King's Head* on the evils of drink, and Sophie came to talk about sex and prostitution."

"How did you get in touch with her?"

"I asked my lecturer, Dr Hayman, and he said he'd heard people mention her as a good sort."

"Heard it on the grapevine, I suppose?"

"I suppose so."

Raynes was amused to think of Gordon Hayman recommending Sophie to a bunch of Christian Union students. But he managed to keep a straight face.

"So you phoned her up?"

"Yes. She seemed quite willing to come."

"Was she any good?"

"Well, she told us a lot about her work with the handicapped and people who had obsessions. She said that it was perhaps better those sort of people going to her rather than attacking other people. She spoke about people with marital problems suffering from frustration. She said that there were more perverts going about than people realized. The power of evil is very strong."

"She's right there," said Raynes.

"Some of the people didn't like her. They felt she seemed to enjoy her work. They said she was corrupt and decadent, the devil's angel and that her feet went down unto hell ..."

"What did Sophie say about that?"

"Well, she was quite good really. She said that some people had to do the dirty jobs in life. The refuse collectors and the lavatory cleaners. It was a dirty job – and sometimes a dangerous job – but it had to be done. She said that some of the people she had to work with, regarded her with such ... revulsion

139

(that's not the word she used) that they wore gloves – even to take photos. Presumably in case they caught something? Others seemed to revel in squalor like pigs."

"It takes all sorts," said Raynes, wondering which of her customers had worn gloves. Derek Coates-Smythe perhaps? Surely not the Commander? "What did you think of her?" he asked.

Paul Brown considered.

"I thought she was quite a nice person to talk to. She was quite open and friendly. Didn't take offence … one or two people walked out … but most people found what she said helpful and interesting."

"When did all this happen?"

"Last February or March. It was my last year at Grass-hallows."

"And how come you kept in touch?"

"Well, I took her for a coffee after the meeting and she told me to come round and see her some time."

Shades of Mae West!

"Which you did?"

"Yes. I phoned her up and she invited me round to tea. She was an unrepentant sinner of course, but I felt there were grounds for hope. I thought she might see the error of her ways and turn to the Lord."

"I'm sure there's hope for us all!" said Raynes hypocriti-cally. He looked at Carlisle who had looked up from his notes and was grinning broadly. "Even for you, Carlisle!" he said.

That knocked the grin off his face!

"So you went round quite often?"

"Mostly for tea. Sometimes for lunch. She said she looked on me as a second son. Her first one hadn't been much use to her. I gather he was in the Army … a bit of a waster …"

Raynes nodded.

"… and I think she was glad to talk to someone who wasn't going to use her. She needed to talk. We talked about her family, my family, about the students, about her work. I tried to make her give it all up, but she said it was her bread and butter … she couldn't afford to take a day off. She always started her evening shift at 7.00 pm."

"That's right," said Raynes.

Carlisle intervened:

"Wasn't there something about birds?"

"Oh, yes, of course. She liked birds. She had several books about them. In fact, she gave me one of them when I left Grass-hallows. I used to show her my photos. I even had one of an osprey. She liked that."

"She belonged to the RSPB, didn't she?"

"She did."

Raynes listened to Paul rambling on about Sophie's love for her feathered friends. After listening to five minutes on peewits, lapwings and golden warblers, he felt he had had enough.

"You were, I think, the last person to see Sophie alive?"

It was not strictly true. Both Ernie McCulloch and the murderer had seen her later. But it made Paul even more serious.

"I suppose I was."

Raynes asked him what he was doing that afternoon.

"Well, I'd been packing. My parents were coming for me on Sunday. It was my last year, you see, and there were lots of books and things to be collected. I went round to see Sophie and say goodbye. We had tea and a nice chat. Then she said she must be getting ready ..."

"What time was that?"

"About 6.15 pm."

"And you left then?"

"About five minutes later. She gave me the book on birds."

"Were you expecting to see her again?"

"Well, I was hoping to be back in Grasshallows for the graduation about a fortnight later ... I thought I might see her then. But, of course, she was dead by then."

Raynes nodded.

"Did she give you any indication as to whom she might be seeing that night?"

Paul Brown shook his head.

"She never mentioned names. And I didn't ask her."

"I believe you told Detective-Inspector Parkinson that she had said the person she was meeting that night was 'a good one' – meaning a person who paid well but didn't want sex?"

Paul Brown looked hesitant as if expecting a trap.

"I think it was this detective I spoke to." He indicated Carlisle.

Raynes said: "It doesn't matter which of us it was, but is it true that she said it was 'a good one'? Why should she have told you that?"

"Because I was urging her not to go. There was a special meeting on that night at the Baptist Church and I hoped she might come along to it. But she didn't. If she had come, she wouldn't have been killed. If you disobey the Lord's will, you're always punished."

Raynes ignored the theology.

"Who d'you think killed her?"

Paul Brown did not hesitate.

"One of those disgusting perverts she met down in the Meadows … I read about what they did to her in the papers … It was horrible!" The words were emotional but Paul Brown did not shed a single tear.

"But surely," said Raynes. "Surely it was the person she was going to meet at 7.00 pm who killed her? And he was 'a good one'. He wasn't a sex maniac. We've been thinking he might have been a photographer? Someone who merely wanted her to model for an artistic pose?"

"It's still very sinful."

"Yes, I know it is. But the police are not interested in moral judgements We're here to find the killer. You are a photographer. You had, I am told, a large knife. What was to stop you going down to the Meadows and carving her up?"

"Why should I do a thing like that?"

"Because she rejected your advice to go straight. You wanted her to get a job in a shop – or be a waitress. You had spent four months trying to make her forsake her evil ways. And she had just laughed at you. So you were angry. Very angry. It was your last night in Grasshallows. Many of the students had already gone. By Sunday lunchtime, you'd be a couple of hundred miles away. What was to stop you creeping down to the Meadows and carving her up?"

"I'd never dream of doing a thing like that. You don't reward evil for evil …"

142

"But there's nothing wrong in punishing the unrighteous?"

"No. But you don't kill them!"

"Don't you?"

"No, of course you don't! And anyway, I went back to the college for dinner." It was Paul Brown's first sign of anger. His eyes blazed.

"What time was that?"

"6.30 pm."

"And what did you do after that?"

"I went to the meeting at the Baptist Church."

"And after that?"

"I went home and wrote Sophie a letter."

"A letter?"

"To say thank you for the book."

"Did you post it that night?"

"No. I delivered it."

Raynes raised his eyebrows. Carlisle looked up – surprised.

"You delivered it?"

"Yes."

"What time was that?"

"About 10.15 pm."

"Did you see anyone round the flat at that time?"

Paul Brown was silent, deep in thought.

"I'm not sure."

"What d'you mean, you're not sure?"

"Well, just as I was arriving at her flat in Riverside Road – you approach the flat through an alleyway and up some stairs at the back – well, I think I saw this woman coming out of the alleyway. But I can't be sure."

"What did she look like?"

"Oh, elderly … about medium height. She had a grey coat, a grey hat – and spectacles. I remember the spectacles. But I'm not sure if she was coming out of the alleyway beside the bookies or not."

"Was she there when you came down?"

"I think so. I think she was talking to a man on the other side of the road. It was getting dark at the time."

"What did the man look like?"

143

"Well, as I say, it was getting dark. But I would say he was rather common. Baggy trousers. Dark jacket. Black hair …"

"Young or old?"

"Youngish, I should say. He had spectacles too!"

"Why should you have noticed them?"

"Well, because I thought they were looking at me."

"Perhaps they were? Perhaps they had seen you go into the alleyway? If so, they must have guessed you'd been up to her flat?"

"I suppose so. That might explain the tin."

"What tin?"

"Well, there was a small tin – container, I suppose – plastic, blue plastic with a red stopper, sitting near the front door. The sort of thing you carry petrol in …"

"Did you touch it?"

"No."

"Was there any smell of petrol?"

"No. I don't think so. It was just sitting there."

"So you just posted your letter and came down the stairs and saw these two people chatting on the other side of the road?"

"They were about fifty yards up the road. But I couldn't post my letter …"

"Why not?"

"… because the letter-box was barred."

Carlisle intervened: "That was another of her safety measures. Along with the iron frame and the reinforced door. After what happened to her that night …"

"Quite so!" said Raynes butting in quickly lest Carlisle should mention Gordon Hayman. He returned to Paul Brown: "Did you leave your letter?"

"On the doormat. So that she'd find it when she came back. But of course she didn't."

Raynes turned to Carlisle. "Did they find the letter?"

"I think they must have done. That's probably why Paul was put on the list of suspects."

"Was there any sign of this plastic container?"

"No."

Raynes turned back to the young man. "Thank you for coming to see me. I'm very grateful for your information. If there's anything else you remember, you must let me know – immediately." He paused, thinking ahead. "I'm afraid I must ask you to stay in Grasshallows over the weekend. I shall want to see you on Monday – or Tuesday evening. Please notify the duty officer where you are staying. I shall see that the bill is paid."

Paul Brown brightened up.

"That's very kind of you. I should be glad to have a few days back in the old place. Just like old times!"

"But without Mrs Jack?"

He nodded sadly. "Yes. Without Mrs Jack."

When he had gone, Raynes looked at Carlisle with a broad smile. "The plot thickens," he said. "Were you aware of the petrol can?"

"No. It's news to me."

"And two elderly people wandering round in spectacles – heavily disguised?"

"The Commander and Mrs Hayman?"

"Why not? About to do a little arson job on Sophie's flat?"

"But they didn't."

"No. Either because they were seen. Or because the letter-box was barred."

"Which it wasn't when Mr Zaposito called."

"No. He told us that he shouted through the letter-box. So it must have been barred later; between 8.30 and 10.15 pm."

"Someone must have been inside. Someone with a key."

"Precisely. But who? And was the letter-box barred to keep the petrol out – or the fire in? Did the mysterious couple have the key to the flat or not? Did Mr Zaposito and Linda see them when they came back to the flat at 11.15 pm?" Raynes smiled. "This case is getting very interesting. Very interesting." He looked at Carlisle. "But I didn't like Paul Brown. Nasty piece of work. A snake in the grass. He had no feelings for Sophie. None at all. All he's interested in is Paul Brown. I'd like to see that report on his knife. Could it have been the knife used to slash open her stomach?"

Carlisle nodded. "It's possible."

"Well, dig it out then we'll have a few words with Mr Reid."

23 *A Red Car*

Mr James Reid had had a singularly unpleasant night in the police cells. It was not his first visit – nor was it likely to be his last. But the atmosphere, he felt, was different.

In the past, he had been bundled in and out of the police van roughly – but kindly. He had been offered a cup of tea and a police doctor had attended to his wounds. He'd been given a bowl of hot water and a towel to freshen himself up and, during the night, he had been allowed to go to the toilet as often as he wanted. In the morning, he had received a good breakfast, had a further wash and shave and been transported in a fairly civilized manner to Grasshallows Police Court where he had invariably pleaded not guilty and been released in time for lunch. By the time the case was heard – normally two months later – his case had been thoroughly prepared by a competent lawyer and very often he had had the pleasure of seeing the jury – confused and bewildered – returning a verdict in his favour. Now and again things had gone wrong but, on the whole, Jim Reid had found the British system of justice very much to his advantage.

On Wednesday night, Jim and his brother had been drinking peacefully at *The Royal Oak* – one of their favourite hostelries. They had played several games of darts and had had a bar supper to soak up any excess of alcohol that might possibly have lingered on in the system. Eddie had chatted up the new barmaid and Jim had had a quick grope with a middle-aged woman, who had been one of his "ex-es", in the passage outside the toilets. They had had three minutes of undisturbed fun and after a little blackmail she had agreed to meet him the following lunchtime for a more relaxed encounter. So, all-in-all, it had been a good evening and as he came out of *The Royal Oak,* Jim Reid was feeling charitably disposed towards all mankind – especially womankind.

However, at that point, things began to take a turn for the

worse. A police van was sitting round the corner from the pub and six pigs were waiting to pounce. He was rapidly surrounded and frogmarched to the back of the van. Purely accidentally, his head had twice made contact with the steel handle on the van door and when he had climbed in, he had stumbled, grazing both his shins in a very painful manner. It was his belief that he had been shoved, pushed or kicked in the back. Instead of being invited to sit on the bench, he had been left on the floor. Someone had trodden heavily on his right hand; he had been booted viciously in the ear and another unkind person had grabbed him by the hair and rammed his face three times against the floor, breaking his nose and causing much blood to be spilt. It would be explained later that Mr James Reid had actively resisted arrest.

In the police cell, he had fared little better. He had literally been thrown into the cell and his knees had been added to the sum of his injuries. No police doctor had ministered to his needs. He had not been allowed to go to the toilet and had therefore wet himself most unpleasantly. He had not slept very well and for breakfast he had received merely a cup of weak tea into which some mistaken orderly had placed two spoonfuls of salt rather than the usual sugar. All this had depressed Jim's natural optimism. He had been allowed to wash himself in cold soapy water but his clothes were badly stained and smelt foul. He discovered that there was no move afoot to take him to court for his usual charity performance. In fact, he was being kept very much in the dark. It appeared that he was being charged with a variety of offences, ranging from murder to grievous bodily harm with malicious damage, assault, indecent assault and drunk-driving flung in for good measure.

Not unnaturally, Mr James Reid decided it was high time for him to see his lawyer.

* * *

Mr Derek Coates-Smythe did not exactly relish having the Reid brothers as his clients but since they regularly needed a good lawyer and were invariably a lucrative source of income – natural common interest brought them both together.

At 11.00 am, the elegant lawyer visited Mr Reid and was surprised to hear that he had not yet been charged. He observed the injuries his client had received and detected behind them the iron hand of Detective-Inspector Raynes. He therefore listened to Jim Reid's protestations of innocence for twenty minutes before moving upstairs to face Raynes in his office.

The contrast between the two rooms – one occupied by the lawyer and the other by the policeman – could not have been greater. Raynes' office had by now acquired more comfortable chairs, a new map, a more interesting calendar and an in-and-out tray, but it could still not be called anything other than spartan. Mr Derek Coates-Smythe faced the inspector across the battered old green-topped desk. He found Raynes far from co-operative.

No. Mr Reid had not yet been formally charged. He had been pulled in for questioning about damage to police property. He did not need to say more. The whole of Grasshallows had now heard what had happened to the police Granada on Tuesday night. Jim Reid had also been guilty of selling a Rover car to a Mr and Mrs Birchwood which had recently crashed and seriously injured the couple. Police evidence showed that the car was totally unfit to be on the road. He was awaiting a full statement from the couple when they left hospital. Jim Reid had also been accused of sexually assaulting a middle-aged woman in *The Roal Oak* and had been arrested as he was on the point of entering his car when he was too drunk to drive. On all these counts, Raynes felt more than justified in pulling him in. He would be interviewing him shortly. Charges would follow.

Mr Coates-Smythe asked cautiously:

"So this has nothing to do with the Sophie Jack case?"

"No. Why should it?"

"I thought the Reid brothers were prime suspects?"

"No more than you. I am still investigating that case and once I have sufficient evidence, arrests will follow. The law is no respecter of persons, Mr Coates-Smythe. It is, you know, still quite possible that you may very soon be joining Mr Reid downstairs!"

The lawyer bristled with anger.

"That was a very offensive remark!"

"It was meant to be," said Raynes. "I've been reviewing your evidence very carefully and I discovered you told me at least one lie. You said that when you were returning from your teatime sauna with young Hilary in Picton Dale, you were nowhere near the place in the Meadows where Sophie was killed. You said that you were travelling home to Newton St Mary's on the A193."

"That is correct."

"But you also said that this road was about two miles away from the murder scene across the fields. Being a stranger to Grasshallows, I took your word for it." Raynes smiled. "But I also double-checked your word on our excellent new map" – he waved his hand towards the new addition on his office wall – "and I discovered that, as the crow flies, the distance between the A193 and the actual tree where Sophie was murdered is just under half a mile ..."

Mr Coates-Smythe's bushy eyebrows narrowed.

"... Now that's a very different picture. Suppose you left your golf club at Skipper's Hill at 5.00 pm, you could have been in your office by 5.15 pm. Two letters do not take long to post. By 5.30 pm you could have been out at Picton Dale tumbling your beloved Hilary. If you left Hilary at about 6.45 pm – rather than the 7.00 or 7.15 pm you suggested – then there is no reason why you could not have stopped off on the A193, crossed the fields – which were not muddy ... and for which you would not have required wellingtons – you could have done the deed, retraced your steps to the car and still have been home by 7.35 pm. Hilary is hardly likely to have remembered the exact time her lover left ... she was probably still sleeping off her lust between gold satin sheets." Raynes paused. "Would you not say, Mr Smythe, that such a picture is entirely plausible?"

"It is entirely plausible. But you seem to forget I had no motive. No motive whatsoever. And what is more, I fought a court case last year to clear my name. And that case depended utterly and completely on the timing of my movements between Picton Dale and Newton St Mary's."

149

"I have looked at that evidence too, Mr Coates-Smythe. The suggestion was that you would not have had the time to return to the Meadows and enter by the conventional route. There seems to be no mention of the A193 in your evidence. So why throw dust in my eyes by suggesting that the distance across the fields is four times more than it is?"

"I have never measured the distance ..."

Mr Coates-Smythe began to speak – then stopped.

There was a silence.

"... Inspector," he said, "you have just jogged my memory. I have just remembered something which I did not tell Detective-Inspector Parkinson last year. Something that I had completely forgotten – because it did not seem relevant at the time ..."

"And what was that?"

"I saw a red car parked in a lay-by on that road on the night of the murder. At about 7.25 pm."

Raynes asked: "How can you be sure that it was on the actual night? You must often have sped along the A193 from Picton Dale?"

Derek Coates-Smythe ignored the insult.

"I hadn't thought of it till now. But when you accused me of leaping through the fields, I built up a picture in my mind. And then I suddenly remembered that red car."

"You can't remember what make it was?"

"Something ordinary," said the lawyer. "An Escort or a Fiesta ..."

"Not a Marina?"

"No."

"It was a Ford of some sort. And it wasn't a local car. I can remember thinking what an unusual number plate it had. A London number, I think. But it was certainly there."

Raynes looked at the lawyer with an appreciative smile. If true, this could be a most useful addition to his jigsaw. If untrue, a further nail in the lawyer's coffin. A mystery car! In just the place where one might expect to find it. A place where the murderer could approach the Meadows unseen by Ernie McCulloch and then escape quickly. Of course, the car might very well be a red herring. Mr Coates-Smythe might himself

150

have parked his car in the same lay-by and have invented the phantom Ford as an alibi.

"What kind of car were you driving this time last year, Mr Smythe?"

"Same one as I do now – a red Citroen."

"No confusing the two?"

"Certainly not!"

"And certainly not bought from Jim Reid!"

They both laughed.

The conversation ended politely with a little more warmth than the first interview. But Derek Coates-Smythe still felt very doubtful about Raynes' methods of conducting a case. There was a ruthlessness and a brutality which constantly surfaced in his conversation. Detective-Inspector Parkinson had been a very tough nut, but he had been a much kinder and more gentle man. Whatever the case ... whoever the person ... he had treated people with respect. Raynes was different.

The lawyer had not the slightest doubt that his client had been brought in and roughed up on Raynes' personal orders. But that was not the way things were done in Grasshallows. Derek Coates-Smythe felt that Raynes was taking short-cuts and that any mistake on his part would lead to his speedy departure. He decided that he would lodge an official complaint over the treatment meted out to his client. That should give Raynes something to think about. A little something to compensate for the humiliation he and others had endured. Mr Coates-Smythe was therefore dignified and polite. He requested that charges should be preferred against Mr Reid as soon as possible, but Raynes would make no promises.

24 *The Prisoner*

After another wholesome lunch at the *Grosvenor*, Raynes decided that Jim Reid would now be sufficiently sober to answer a few questions. He had been cleaned up, seen his lawyer and hopefully would now be a little more co-operative. Raynes and Carlisle therefore descended to the "dungeons" – and waited in a small basement room whilst Reid was brought from his cell.

He was not a pretty sight. His trousers were torn and stained with blood and urine. His hand was bandaged and his face badly cut and bruised. Despite the sweet odour of pine disinfectant, Mr Reid smelt as repulsive as he looked.

The sight of Raynes and Carlisle sitting calmly on the other side of the table did nothing to help the atmosphere. First of all, Jim Reid kicked the table violently and then lunged out at Raynes with his bandaged hand. Two officers grabbed his arms and dragged him into a chair which was bolted to the floor. He was handcuffed to the chair. But this did not stop Jim Reid. For a full five minutes, he ranted steadily against all police-men – especially Raynes and Carlisle. They were shits; they were bastards; they were turds; and if he ever met them on a dark night, they would be "goners".

When the tirade was over, Raynes pointed out that it was precisely because of such threats – against Sophie Jack – that he had become a leading suspect in her murder. Now he had made similar threats against the police, he would of necessity have to be remanded in custody. There was no way he could be released on bail whilst he was threatening murder and revenge.

"You can't say I didn't warn you," said Raynes.

"You gave me till Monday!"

"You smashed up my car."

Jim Reid denied all knowledge of how the police Granada came to be destroyed but in his eyes there was a quiet gleam of pride that he had scored at least one blow against authority.

As for the other charges, he was equally adamant of his innocence. No way had he indecently assaulted Mrs Gibson. She was an old flame of his. She had consented to a bit of slap and tickle. She had agreed willingly to meet him that afternoon for a little bit more. All talk of blackmail was a frame-up. When he got out, he would give Nellie Gibson a bloody good thrash-ing for telling lies.

Raynes raised his eyebrows.

"Can't you ever stop threatening people?" he asked.

"Not if they bloody cross me!"

Raynes shook his head.

"But what about all the people you've hurt? The Birchwoods, for instance …? They bought a car from you – in perfectly good faith – as so many others have done. They didn't deserve to end up in hospital with a fractured skull and broken ribs. You can't get out of that one! You sold them a car with defective steering, with a bogus MOT and we have the evidence to prove it."

Jim Reid was silent and looked at the ground.

Raynes continued: "You did precisely the same to Sophie Jack. You sold her a lousy car. You diddled her – and she objected. She warned people what you and your brother were like. She heard from your mechanic, Mr Mitchell, what you were up to and she quite rightly reported the matter to the police. You can't go round killing people. Diddling people. Screwing people. Smashing up cars and stealing. The time comes when decent people have to say 'stop'. Think what you'd feel like if some maniac killed your brother or one of your children? You'd be the first to demand action from the police. You'd never rest till justice was done. Now that the law has caught up with you – you don't like it. But quite a lot of decent people will be very glad to see you lifted and out of harm's way."

Jim Reid remained silent.

At least he was listening.

"Last night," said Raynes, "you had a taste of your own medicine. You felt what it was like when a load of bastards set to work on you. That was just an appetizer. There are quite a few other people in the force who would be only too delighted to put the boot in and I don't think anyone will complain when they read your track record. Once you've been kneed in the groin a couple of times, even you will talk! I want the truth out of you, Mr Reid, and I want it quickly. I want to know precisely what you were doing on the night Sophie died. I want to know if you took out a contract for her killing or whether you did it yourselves. If you don't give me a full confession by Monday 5.00 pm I'll pull in your brother and give him the full works. I'm sure one of you will squeal!"

For most of this monologue, Jim Reid continued to stare

fixedly at the ground showing no reaction, no emotion. But when Raynes mentioned his brother, Eddie, he looked up. For a moment, there was a flash of anxiety.

"Don't you do anything to my brother, copper!"

Raynes realized he had touched a raw nerve.

He looked at Jim Reid.

"The order is already signed. He was due to be brought in tonight. But I'm willing to stay my hand till Monday. If you come clean with me – well and good. If not, Eddie will get the full works on Monday night. It's up to you."

As there was nothing else to say, Raynes and Carlisle left the "dungeon" and were glad to be back in the general office upstairs.

"Do you think he'll break?" asked Carlisle.

"I should think so," said Raynes. "He's obviously very sensitive about his brother. I hadn't realized that. Anyway, he has three days to think it all over. I reckon he'll talk. If he doesn't …"

Raynes smiled.

"… Even if he doesn't, I think we might still pull it off. But a confession would be helpful."

He looked at his watch.

"Now," he said, "we've got about four hours before we see the Church treasurer. So you go home and see your wife and I'll have another bash at these cattle rustlers. I'll pick you up about seven."

However, when he got back into his office, Raynes picked up the file on Paul Brown and read it through most carefully.

25 The Banker

Peter Bridges opened the front door and gave the two policemen a warm, open and friendly welcome – something which Raynes instantly regarded with the utmost suspicion.

In his experience, bank managers were nearly always rather miserable people, except when they called you in to question your overdraft. At such moments, they suddenly and positively radiated with glee at your unhappy plight. If, however, it was a question of mortgages or loans – anything which involved getting money out of the bank – then they were invariably sombre, serious and thoughtful people whose responsibilities bore heavily upon them and where mirth or the more light-hearted symptoms of humanity seldom travelled the length of their tightly-buttoned lips.

Peter Bridges was obviously an exception to the general rule. So Raynes responded in an equally friendly fashion and even went as far as to accept the hospitality of a large gin-and-tonic – something he had stoutly resisted during his previous visits.

Whilst Mr Bridges was coming and going between the cocktail cabinet and his guests, Raynes gave his host the once over. He was tall – about six foot or just over – well-built but not fat; with a balding head and twinkling, deep brown eyes. He was wearing a thick white woollen cardigan and a pair of dull green tweed trousers – but relaxation went no further than that. Underneath his cardigan, he still sported his white office shirt and dark blue golf club tie.

"Have you chaps been here before?" he asked as he settled down with his glass of whisky and soda. "Or is this your first call?"

"Well, Canon Murray said you wouldn't be back before Wednesday so there wasn't much point in coming earlier. You've been away at the Bank's annual conference, I hear?"

"Go every year; never miss it. Amazing how easy it is to lose touch with old friends. Some of my young trainees are now managers in their own right. It's grand seeing them getting on so well."

"The conference was in Bournemouth, I believe?"

"Yes. It's always in one of the major seaside resorts. Brighton, Bournemouth or Blackpool. It gives the whole thing a much more relaxed holiday atmosphere. We manage to get the business despatched so much better – and so much quicker!"

"Does your wife go with you on these trips?"

"I don't think she'd enjoy it all that much. She has her interests; I have mine. Mostly, it's an all-male do. Far too much shop-talk for the ladies."

"And the wrong kind of shops? I imagine the bars are the chief object of pilgrimage – like our own police conferences?"

"Precisely. Can't afford to lose our sense of priority!" He laughed cheerfully and took another sip of his whisky. "But you didn't come here to talk about bankers letting their hair down – not that I have much to let down," he added, rubbing the crown of his head with a delicate white hand.

"Not really," said Raynes. "I'm sure Canon Murray will have told you that we've re-opened the file on Sophie Jack who was murdered last year. You will perhaps remember that the case fizzled out sometime last November with nothing really solved. There were a lot of loose ends needing to be tidied up and since I was a bit of a new boy round here, I thought that would be a useful way of getting into the swing of things."

"When did you arrive in Grasshallows?"

"Sunday past."

Raynes felt sure Canon Murray had told him all this – and more – over the telephone before he arrived, so he exchanged pleasantries for a few more minutes before coming to the point.

"What I came to ask you about was this legacy which Mrs Jack left to the Church."

"Oh, yes. An amazing windfall!"

"First of all, I wanted to ask you how much it actually was?"

"Well, I should need to go and check my file on that, but it was around £86,000 when all the legal expenses had been deducted and her flat finally sold. It's taken quite a bit of time for all the figures to be finalized but the last instalment came in about a month ago. I'll just go and check."

He went off to his study and came back with a box file prominently marked "St Benedict's Finances 1987-88". He put on a pair of horn-rimmed spectacles and examined a small red book. "£86,881 it was. Not quite so much as we originally expected, but these lawyers are absolute rogues!"

"That's Derek Coates-Smythe, isn't it? I thought he was a friend of yours?"

"Yes, that's the fellow! Nothing wrong with him as a chap. Nothing at all. In fact, we play golf together at least once a week. But once these people put on their legal hats and get their hands on a nice, juicy legacy, the costs mount astronomically."

156

"How much were you expecting?"

"Well, I wasn't expecting anything at all. Thing came completely out of the blue. I was counting up the church's pennies to see if we'd have enough to do that blasted organ ... cursing the PCC for taking such an expensive decision. I'm sure it could have waited another four or five years. I'm sure it could." He smiled broadly. "I'd dearly have loved to have bequeathed that problem to my successor! Given him something to get his teeth into ... But whilst I was cursing the cruel fates, Canon Murray suddenly phoned me up and told me we had struck lucky. Of course I was very sorry to hear about the poor woman dying – and in such a horrible way – but if the money had to go to anyone, the Church is certainly the best place. No jealousy. No squabbling over who gets what. St Benedict's is such a beautiful church – one of the real beauties of Grasshallows. Have you seen it yet, Inspector?"

"Only from the outside," said Raynes. "I've had a very busy week so far but I shall find time to pop in."

"You must. Of course, it's a terrible mess at the moment. The organ builders are hard at it. Pipes and soundboards all over the place. But the windows are still beautiful and the high altar ... magnificent!"

"How long have you been Treasurer of St Benedict's?"

"Seventeen years this September. I told the Rector last Christmas, I'd do another three years in harness then he must get someone else. Twenty years is enough for anyone!"

"And how old are you now?" asked Raynes.

"58. Only another couple of years to retirement."

"Looking forward to it?"

Peter Bridges shrugged his shoulders. "In one way, yes. But I shall miss the company – and the staff. I've been in the Bank ever since I left school."

"But you'll have your golf?"

"Yes. I shall be out at Skipper's Hill every morning."

"Do you have any other hobbies – photography perhaps?"

Peter Bridges looked surprised.

"I think I can say with all honesty, Inspector, that I haven't put a spool into a camera for over twenty years. Not since

157

the children grew up. Gardening – yes. Photography – no."
He looked across at Raynes' glass which was almost empty.
"Another drink?"

"No thanks," said Raynes. "I'm still trying to get the facts
straight about this legacy. How much did Mrs Jack actually
leave in her estate?"

"Well, I can't tell you exactly. You'll have to ask Mr Coates-
Smythe about that. I believe there were two or three minor bene-
ficiaries. But at a rough guess, her flat must have gone for about
£38,000 – quite a good price considering it's above the bookies.
Her personal effects must have brought in a couple of thousands
and her bank account must have been something over £60,000.
It's amazing! I never realized that prostitution was quite so
profitable."

"She wasn't one of your customers at the Midland?"

"No, dear boy, no! I believe Canon Murray said she had
most of it with the building societies. She'd have done better
if she'd had it in equities with the Stock Market on the up and
up. But she didn't. Properly invested, she could have doubled
that £60,000. No doubt about it."

"Would that have made you happier?"

"Well, I must confess that I'm pretty satisfied with what we
got. It's a long time since the Church received such a handsome
legacy. Every year, we get piddling little hundreds and two
hundreds but they get swallowed up in routine expenditure. It
must be over twenty years since we had a really good legacy
in five figures."

Raynes thought for a few moments before he put his next
question. "Does St Benedict's make a surplus – I can't call it
a profit, can I, it being a church?"

"Call it what you like! We make a small surplus most years
on the current account. Five hundred pounds or so. Last year,
we ended up £834 to the good. A mild winter, you see? It's
amazing how the weather plays havoc with your budget. Fuel
bills can rocket up. But it's not the current account which
causes the problem. It's the repairs – that has to come out of
our capital reserves. New gutters, slates, dry-rot in the kitchen,
new timbers in the bell-tower, woodworm in the ladies' toilet

… it's never-ending. Now I'm a great admirer of Canon Murray, don't get me wrong. He's done a splendid job for the Church over these past 25 years, but he's always spending. New this – new that. I reckon that in the past ten years, we must have spent nearly £50,000 on the building alone."

Raynes showed suitable surprise. He had always thought churches – like all historic buildings – were a hideous waste of money. They looked good but whether they were worth all the expenditure on upkeep – that was something he very much doubted.

But Peter Bridges wouldn't hear of it.

"Of course it's worth it! Beautiful old place! Rich in history. Founded by Sir Thomas More – before he lost his head of course!" Mr Bridges laughed heartily. "We couldn't let it go. It's part of our heritage! Part of Grasshallows! I'm not the most ardent Christian but I do love the place. Canon Murray will probably have told you."

"So how much has St Benedict's got in the kitty – apart from Mrs Jack's legacy?"

Mr Bridges crossed his legs and looked thoughtful. "That's a difficult one. So much of our money is in shares and government securities that it's difficult to say exactly how much we're worth at any given point. At the end of our last financial year – that's November – our book figure was about £118,000, but that was after Black Monday – the Stock Exchange crash. Before that, we might have been worth about £135-140,000."

"So that without Sophie's legacy you'd have had to dig deep into your reserves to pay for the organ?"

"We would indeed. I think we could have managed the initial cost. That was £60,000 plus VAT. But when it started creeping up, I really began to get a little anxious. You never know what more they are going to find and add on to the bill. There's contracts. Then supplementary contracts. Then all the extras – transport, electrical work, insurance. Fortunately, Mrs Jack's legacy has taken all the anxiety out of the situation. We would have managed – no doubt about that – but it made our task much simpler."

"So your reserves will hardly be touched?"

"Hardly at all. About £12,000 for the initial down-payment when the contract was signed."

"And when was that?"

"About a year ago. April it was."

"So it's taken about a year for things to start happening?"

"Well, they had a lot of preparation work to do at their factory." Peter Bridges suddenly looked very serious. "The only thing that really worries me … and I'm being honest with you, Inspector … is that the Canon might start having other bright ideas. I thought this organ business might be his last fling – but now I'm not so sure! I believe he's thinking about re-casting the bells!"

"But you haven't paid for the organ yet?"

"Three instalments so far."

"And Sophie's money will be earning interest?"

"I jolly well hope so!"

"So you should manage to pull through?"

"I suppose so. A Treasurer's lot is never a very happy one. He gets a lot of abuse. A lot of brickbats. But it's not so bad. I must enjoy it if I keep doing it …"

"It always helps if you have a sympathetic auditor."

"You're right there, Inspector."

"Do you have your accounts audited locally?"

"No. I go to a good London firm. Nothing but the best for St Benedict's!"

Raynes levered himself out of his comfortable armchair.

"Well," he said, "we must be going."

He stood looking out of the window over the garden where Mrs Bridges was weeding the rose-bed.

"Thank you very much for filling me in, Mr Bridges. I sometimes get quite lost with all this high finance."

The three men walked towards the hall.

"Did you ever meet Sophie, Mr Bridges?"

"Only once to my knowledge. My wife and I were introduced to her at a charity dance in the University. Not quite the person one expects to meet at that sort of function."

"No," Raynes paused. "You never met her at the Church?"

"I don't think so. She may have been at the Annual General

160

Meetings but I'm not a great mixer. I go to the early service."

"But you enjoy socializing at your conference?"

"Oh, that's different."

Raynes asked: "Is your conference always the same week-end every year?"

"Yes. Always the last weekend in June."

"So you were away when it all happened?"

"I suppose I was. Yes, I remember reading all about it in the Monday papers. It was a horrible business. Quite revolting."

Raynes nodded.

He turned to the front door – and then turned back as if he had forgotten something. "Oh, by the way, Bridges, could you send me a complete set of the Church accounts for the past five years. Just drop them in at the station tomorrow morning. I'd like to see them. Just for the record. Might even give you a tenner for the Organ Fund!"

With that, Raynes bid the Church Treasurer a hearty fare-well and returned to his car.

26 *Champagne Charlie*

By Friday morning, all the suspects had been interviewed – some more than once. There were ten suspects selected by Detective-Inspector Parkinson and two others which Raynes had added himself.

Now was the time to analyze the statements they had made; to cross-check on all the information received. Either Sophie Jack's murderer was one of the twelve. Or one of the other 288. Or else, someone completely unknown.

Raynes had set himself a limited objective – and a limited amount of time. The case must either be solved quickly – or abandoned. There was no way he was going to interview 288 people. Either he had the murderer within his net – or the murderer would escape justice altogether. Raynes had his suspicions – a mere hunch – but a lot of spadework would be needed if he was to be proved right. He had given himself till Tuesday night. Surely, by then, the Reid brothers would have spilt the beans?

First of all, he considered the case of Paul Brown. It was profoundly unsatisfactory. Young Paul had been one of the last two people to see Sophie alive. He was with her till 6.20 pm, and as far as Raynes could see, there was no corroboration for his movements thereafter. Certainly he had said that he had gone back to his college for dinner at 6.30 pm and had then gone to that meeting at Grasshallows' Baptist Church. But, hunt as he might through Paul Brown's file, he could find no evidence to confirm that he had been seen in either place.

Raynes shook his head at such shoddy detective work.

It was quite conceivable that, incensed by her unrepentant sinfulness, Brown might have decided to punish her once and for all. He could have arranged the "date" for 7.00 pm and then slipped off to the Meadows to lie in wait for her. It was Paul Brown who had mentioned that the "date" was "a good one" – i.e. not involving sex – and a great deal of interpretation had been laid on those words. He was the one who had mentioned gloves. Could Paul have persuaded her to do him one last favour – bizarre in the extreme – and then killed her? Sophie might have been willing to humour him on his last night in Grasshallows? For all Raynes knew, Sophie could have been fully clad when tied up to the tree. The stripping and the knifing could have come later.

Then there was the admission that he had come back to the flat. Emilio Zaposito had spoken of a light being on in the house at about 8.00 pm. Could that have been Paul, newly returned from his work of divine punishment – raking over her sordid past? Raynes did not trust religious fanatics of any creed or colour.

And then there was that letter delivered at 10.15 pm. There is a saying that murderers cannot keep away from the scene of their crime. Suppose Paul had dropped by at the end of the meeting in the Baptist Church, mingled with the redeemed and then come back to Sophie's house – leaving a letter on the doormat which would immediately bring him to the attention of the police? It seemed strange and naive but Paul was a peculiar person. He held very strong views on sin and judgement. He was a photographer and he had a hunting knife in his room at the University. Not the murder weapon, it was said, but who could say whether or not he might have had a second knife?

Raynes read through all the notes in Paul Brown's file and wondered why he had told him a different story about how he and Sophie came to meet. One version had them meeting in the Meadows; the other in the University. Which was true?

Raynes felt so annoyed with all the inconsistencies that he sent Carlisle off immediately to track down Paul Brown and get some answers to these questions. In the meantime, he decided to have a strong black coffee with two spoonfuls of sugar.

* * *

When he got back to his office, he found that Peter Bridges had sent over the copies of the accounts for St Benedict's Church. Raynes ran through them whilst he drank his coffee. They seemed to be very straightforward but Raynes was taking no chances. He picked up the phone and rang his friend who was a bank manager in Manchester.

He asked him if he knew Peter Bridges and how he was regarded by his peers. He asked where the Bank had held its Conference in 1987 and did his friend know anything about Messrs Coulter, Veal and Blyth, the Church's accountants who appeared to be based in Croydon? Raynes' friend in Manchester confirmed that Peter Bridges was a popular and well-liked member of the banking fraternity. He was regarded as a dry wit and a keen golfer. As a ladies' man, he was a non-starter but he was occasionally reported to have gone a little overboard with the whisky.

Whisky reminded Raynes of champagne – and Debbie. So whilst he was on the phone, he decided to give her a call.

"Hello? Grasshallows 815267?"

Raynes put on his best Scottish accent.

"Is that my very dear friend, Mrs May?"

The accent clearly fooled her.

"Yes. But who's speaking?"

"It's the mon with the tartan trews and the eight inch caber!"

Debbie chuckled.

"I've never known a Scotsman with such a small caber! Come on! Who is it?"

"Champagne Charlie," said Raynes.

"Oh, great!" she said. "You must have got my letter?"

"It was a very nice letter."

"Well, what can I do for you this morning?"

"I was wondering if I could tempt you to take a night or two off and come away for a disgusting weekend …?"

"That sounds horribly expensive!" said Debbie.

"It's a mixture of business and pleasure."

"Whose business?" she asked. "And whose pleasure?"

"My business," said Raynes. "Your pleasure."

"I think I'd prefer it the other way round!"

"I'm sure you would," said Raynes. "Saturday afternoon to Monday lunchtime?"

"Paris?" she asked optimistically.

"No," said Raynes, "Rye."

It was the one bright spot in an otherwise boring morning.

* * *

Later on had come the news that Jim Reid had been remanded in custody for a week. His brother and their two wives had made a great scene in court and been ordered out. Eddie Reid had been charged with assault. Mr Derek Coates-Smythe had publicly stated that the police had used excessive force in detaining his client. An official complaint was to be made.

Raynes uttered a silent curse on all members of the legal profession. He had no time to do more. At that moment, he was busy phoning round all the building societies in which Sophie had placed her money. He double-checked on all the figures given to him and found that she was indeed worth over £60,000. He phoned the local estate agent and checked on the sale price of her flat.

After that, he phoned up several car hire firms trying to kill two birds with one stone. What price would they quote for a Ford Granada to replace the shattered wreck now lying in the station yard? And could they identify a red car which had been seen on the A193 one Saturday night over a year ago? The quotations offered for a Granada were pricey – far beyond what he could legitimately claim on expenses. But his search for the red car proved more fruitful. Raynes selected two firms that he thought might know the answer. Within ten minutes, the red car was no longer a mystery.

* * *

At 12.30 pm Carlisle returned. He was in low spirits. The Paul Brown case remained unsatisfactory. There was no one whom he could provide as an alibi before 9.00 pm.

Raynes told Carlisle that Mr Coates-Smythe had decided to put the boot in. Carlisle agreed that things looked pretty grim.

To round off the morning's misery, Raynes and Carlisle went along to the canteen for fish, chips and processed peas, rhubarb crumble and watery custard. It tasted like cardboard. Both men were conscious that the atmosphere had changed. Gone was the early enthusiasm for the master sleuth hunting down Sophie's killer. In its place had come a certain chilly disapproval of Raynes' methods. For all his faults, Jim Reid deserved better treatment than he had received. One did not give an eye for an eye or a tooth for a tooth – at least not in Grasshallows! A city which had a large following in Amnesty International was not amused. Members of the police, finely tuned to the slightest nuance, scented trouble.

27 *The Actress and the Flower Lady*

After lunch, Raynes felt in need of a breath of fresh air. So, taking Peter Bridges' advice, he decided to pay a visit to St Benedict's Church and see where all Sophie's money had gone. It was a very hot July afternoon and the sun beat down on Grasshallows High Street with a fierce heat.

By contrast, the interior of the Church was cool and dark. The grey stone walls felt cold to the touch and the only evidence of the summer sun was the pink, gold and blue reflections from the stained glass windows which flecked the plain oak pews with a gentle light.

As the Treasurer had said, this was not the ideal moment to appreciate St Benedict's. Two huge black soundboards occupied the south aisle and great rolls of grey trunking filled the north aisle. Heaps of wooden box pipes marked "Oboe 8'" or "Vox Dulciana 4'" littered the pews. Boxes of tools, tins of paint and electrical cable polluted the floor and made it essential to watch one's step. The organ chamber itself looked very bare – like a jeweller's window after a smash-and-grab. Raynes stood and looked at the debris for several minutes.

In the middle of all the mess, a tall lady was doing the flowers. She was working on a large display with lots of greenery already in position. She was looking at the arrangement thoughtfully, trying to decide which flower she should put first into the oasis. She tried a pink gladioli – then a white one. Raynes watched her repeat the action several times. He then walked over to the chancel step and complimented her on the delicate art. He asked her if she had been doing it for a long time.

"For twenty years," she said with a sad sort of smile. "It's almost second nature to me now."

"Do you do it every week?"

"Just when it's my turn."

Raynes indicated all the mess around the church.

"Doesn't that discourage you?"

"One tries to ignore it."

Raynes observed – as a stranger might – that the whole operation must be costing a lot of money. The flower lady looked even sadder.

"A huge amount. Almost £100,000. And it's all so unnecessary! The organ sounded perfectly all right, but apparently it's over fifty years since anything was done and the Rector said that if we delayed, it would end up costing even more. I suppose he's right – but I can't help wishing they'd just left it. It's cost my husband so many sleepless nights."

For once, Raynes was taken aback.

"You must be Mrs Bridges?"

"That's right. How did you know?"

"I was seeing your husband last night. You were out in the garden weeding the rose bed."

"So you must be Inspector Raynes?"

"That's right."

166

The ice having been broken, Mrs Bridges talked more freely. She said that in her opinion the PCC had bullied her husband shamelessly into agreeing to the decision. "I told him to resign," she said. "To stick to his principles – and let them do all the worrying. But he's so fond of St Benedict's he wouldn't give up. He fought them every inch of the way – but it was no use. They won. And now we have this huge bill."

"But you have the money?"

"Of course we do – but it's never-ending. Spend, spend, spend! One gets so tired of it. One does think the church should set an example."

As a change from such sordid matters, Mrs Bridges showed Raynes round the church, pointing out all the interesting features. Clearly, she had done it many times before. Raynes was shown the shields, the plaques, the carving on the reredos behind the high altar and the wooden stalls in the choir. They entered the Lady Chapel but someone was praying so Mrs Bridges withdrew.

Raynes was thoughtful.

"Wasn't that Mrs Hayman?"

"Yes. Dreadful woman! She's one of those harpies who badgered my husband. When you think of her reputation and all the horrible things she's done, it's a wonder she dares to put a foot inside the place!"

Raynes observed that the Church was supposed to exist for the benefit of sinners, but Mrs Bridges felt differently.

"There's sinners – and sinners! And she's one of those!"

Raynes said that there were one or two questions he wanted to ask Mrs Hayman. Would she mind if he left her for a few minutes?

"Grill her long and hard!" was Mrs Bridges final shaft. "She deserves it!"

Raynes walked slowly – and almost silently – down the aisle of the Lady Chapel. He sat down in a chair three rows behind Rosalind and looked at her golden hair. It must be dyed, he thought, but she does it rather well. He meditated quietly on the case which had now occupied his attention for a whole week, wondering how quickly he could tie it all up. Just a few more pieces to go – and this was one of them.

Mrs Hayman had been praying for about twenty minutes. But she gradually became conscious that she was not alone. She had heard steps. They had stopped. There had been the creak of a chair. Then silence. But the person was still there. She continued her devotions, crossed herself and got up.

Behind her ... watching her ... was that wretched policeman with a mocking smile on his stupid face.

"Praying for forgiveness?" he asked.

"What would you know about it?" she said.

"I'm sorry I seem to call at the wrong moments," said Raynes, "but I just happened to be passing, saw you and decided to drop in. Can we have a chat?"

Rosalind sat down on the wicker-bottomed chair.

"I thought that this would be one place where I would be spared your sordid attentions."

Raynes raised his eyebrows.

"I thought this was where you performed some of your greatest dramatic roles?"

"In the Church hall. Not here."

"I see. Have you ever played Lady Macbeth?"

Mrs Hayman visibly jumped.

"Yes. Why?"

"I just wondered."

"I played it at school – in an abridged version. Why?"

"I was just thinking about you – and daggers. Daggers were very much Lady Macbeth's weapon. She reminded me of you." He smiled at her. "I was just wondering where you bought your dagger?"

"It wasn't mine. It was Gordon's. He bought it when he was on holiday – as a scout. He bought it in Whitby or Scarborough or somewhere ..."

"I see. But you kept it?"

"For defensive purposes."

"Of course. But you didn't use it for defensive purposes?"

"No. I slashed her tyres. I admitted that."

"I know you did. But what happened to the knife?"

"The police took it away."

"Did you get it back?"

"No."

"Did you ask for it back?"

"No."

"Did you buy another?"

Rosalind paused.

"If you want an honest answer, Inspector, I did think of it. I decided that if I was ever in Whitby or Scarborough or any of those places, I would buy another. For defensive purposes … if you live alone …"

Raynes nodded.

"I understand. But the trouble is, Mrs Hayman, that the police think that it was precisely that sort of knife which was used to carve up Mrs Jack. If you handed over your knife – then obviously it cannot be the murder weapon. But there's no reason why you couldn't have gone and bought a similar model – which you have just said you were thinking of doing."

"I was being honest with you."

"I appreciate your honesty," said Raynes.

"I didn't buy one."

"Perhaps you would care to be honest with me on another matter? Your alibi?"

Mrs Hayman shook her head.

"The Commander and I have already told you …"

"… and I don't believe you."

"You can't prove anything!"

"That's true. But we can always grill you most unpleasantly." (As Mrs Bridges would prefer, thought Raynes.)

"Like that poor garage man your thugs beat up last night!"

"News travels fast in Grasshallows!"

"It certainly does. Everyone was talking about it this morning. You beat him up and broke his nose. When the Beaver hears about it, he'll be furious!"

"I didn't beat him up personally," said Raynes. "Quite a lot of people have strong feelings about the Reid brothers. I imagine that, given the opportunity …"

"But the police aren't supposed to do things like that!"

"Christians aren't supposed to tell lies – but they do!"

Touché.

169

But the fair Rosalind did not bat an eyelid.

Raynes decided to change tack.

"Mrs Hayman," he said, "suppose you were writing a novel about all this? About Sophie being murdered? Whom would you choose as the murderer? Assuming of course that it was not yourself?"

Mrs Hayman looked at the decorated tiles on the floor.

"I've thought about that. Several times. I thought about the Reid brothers. They seemed the most likely suspects. They've done some pretty dreadful things in their time. But," she said, looking up, "that's no excuse for beating them up ..."

Raynes said nothing.

"... Still I think they would have to be the No. 1 suspects. They said they were going to string her up and they did."

"You don't think the rope and the blindfold were a little sophisticated for the likes of the Reid brothers? I should have thought they'd have been far more likely to biff her over the head one dark night?"

Rosalind shrugged her shoulders.

"Did you see the scarf?"

"The one they used on her?"

Raynes noted with interest the use of the plural. Mrs Hayman clearly believed there were two people involved. She continued:

"Yes ... The police brought it round to me."

"What did you think of it?"

"Cheap," she said. "And nasty."

"I believe it was quite expensive material?"

"Yes. But it wasn't the sort of thing a woman would buy for herself."

"Why not?"

"It was too ... too flashy. It was the sort of thing a man would buy his mistress. The sort of thing a man buys for his wife at Christmas. Black nighties and lingerie. And then the wife goes back to the shop and changes it for something more sensible. It was that sort of thing."

Raynes thought her views were interesting – and probably sound. Women often understood such things better then men.

"So you don't think it belonged to Sophie?"

"It might have belonged to her – but I don't think she'd have bought it for herself. She had plenty of adoring men to buy her such rubbish."

"So you think that one of them ...?"

"Who knows?"

"Could it have been your husband, Gordon?"

He knew from his first interview that she was very sensitive about her ex-husband. Once again, tears came into her eyes.

"No. My Gordon would not have murdered her."

"Well, what about a strange couple who were seen near Sophie's flat at about 10.00 pm on the Saturday night?"

The ghost of a smile flickered over Rosalind's face.

"There are a lot of strange couples wandering around Grass-hallows on a Saturday night."

"All carrying blue cans full of petrol and wearing fancy dress?"

Mrs Hayman smiled sweetly.

"You forget, Inspector, the Commander and I were in London that night."

She rose to her feet.

"I must be going."

"One final question," said Raynes. "I notice that your Fiesta was bought since last August. What kind of car were you driving before then?"

Mrs Hayman looked surprised.

"Another Fiesta. I quite like them."

"And what colour?"

"Red."

A look of triumph appeared in Raynes' eyes.

"Just as I thought!"

Mrs Hayman wondered what she had said that could possibly have made the Inspector so excited. Yes, she had had a red car. Yes, she had seen the black scarf. Yes, she had possessed – and used – a savage hunting knife. Yes, she even had one or two thoughts about the mysterious couple ... But the combined significance of these isolated facts was lost on her. She felt herself being enclosed by some invisible net. Raynes was drawing it closer and closer. He could see it but she could not. Once

171

again she was frightened that she might have given something away. Incriminated herself without realizing it. The Inspector knew what he was after and she and the Commander had their secrets. But she hated this feeling of being entrapped. He had crept up on her and invaded her sanctuary. Now he was smiling at her. She wanted to hit him – to hurt him – violently. But she had no weapon to hand. Instead, she suddenly burst into tears – and ran crying from the church.

* * *

Raynes returned thoughtfully to Mrs Bridges.

"Did you get rid of her?"

"Yes. She burst into tears and ran away."

"A guilty conscience!"

"I expect so."

"Far too highly strung – and the drink doesn't help! She was a perfect nuisance at the Amateur Dramatic Society; had the morals of an alley cat and always demanded the best parts. I remember her a couple of years ago when we did Shaw's 'St Joan'. She was tied up to the stake and set fire to. It was very dramatic. I rather hoped that they'd tie her a little more securely to the stake and she'd go up in smoke – like the real St Joan. But she didn't …"

"And she's still around to plague you?"

"I'm afraid so."

Raynes pondered on the significance of the St Joan episode. Could there be a lead here? Was this perhaps the connection between the killing and the petrol can? Had the final scene of the drama been aborted? And if so, why? More prosaically, Raynes found himself asking Mrs Bridges whether her husband involved himself in amateur dramatics?

"Good heavens, no!" she said. "He would never dream of such a thing! He comes along to watch all our shows – but his only true love is golf. Golf, golf, golf-mad! And dinner parties with his golfing cronies. I've told him that when he dies, I shall see that he is buried at Skipper's Hill."

"He doesn't do any photography?"

"No! What a curious question! He doesn't paint. He doesn't dance. He doesn't play any musical instrument. In fact, the only thing he seems to enjoy – apart from golf – is a glass of whisky."

"I was just wondering," said Raynes innocently, "whether he photographs things like the organ or the church spire? Or whether he keeps an album of all the work done on St Benedict's?"

Mrs Bridges shook her head. "It's not that we don't have a camera. In fact, we've got two or three that belong to the children. But they just sit in a drawer. They're nothing like the ones Derek Coates-Smythe has – with all the extra lenses and things. He's gone into it in a big way. Spends a great deal. Peter once showed me one of Derek's cameras which he had collected from Munns. It was an absolute beauty."

"So his only other relaxation is this annual binge at the end of June?"

"Yes. He's gone off every year for the past fifteen years. He seems to enjoy it …"

"Meeting all his old friends? But you don't go with him?"

"No. The garden needs me at the end of June. Besides, it's good for all the men to get together once in a while. I've got my flowers and the amateur dramatics; he's got his golf and his work. We have a very happy marriage, Peter and I."

Raynes watched her place the final flowers in the display.

"So what's he going to do when he retires – in two or three year's time?"

Mrs Bridges looked round the church. "I should think he'd rather enjoy being the official guide to St Benedict's. He'd be able to tell them how much everything cost. After all the time he's spent worrying about the place, I think he'd rather enjoy it."

* * *

Raynes walked back to the police station across the hot baking pavements, still thinking about Mrs Hayman and St Joan. It was yet another twist to an otherwise complicated plot. Why the rope? Why the blindfold? Why the knife wounds? Why fire? Was there some ritual element in the murder? Or was it a piece of play-acting that went terribly, terribly wrong?

Raynes called into Munns, the leading photographers in

Grasshallows, to ask them about Derek Coates-Smythe's cameras. How much did they cost? Who did his developing? Apparently he did most of it himself. Raynes asked about the photographic activities of his other suspects. He learnt that Ernie McCulloch had bought himself a fine new camera about two years before. Raynes was most grateful for the information he received.

* * *

Once he was back in his office, he spent the final part of the afternoon dealing with the cattle rustlers who had been back twice and stolen more sheep from the nearby farms. Raynes listened to all the reports and doubled the number of officers involved in the investigation.

For the sake of completion, he asked Carlisle to check over the colour, make and registration numbers of all the cars owned by the suspects in June 1987. He said that he hoped they would not all be driving red Fiestas or Escorts!

On that final cheerful note, Raynes concluded his first week at Grasshallows. He felt that it had been very constructive and interesting. He had risen to great heights of popularity within seventy-two hours. Now he was under a bit of a cloud because of Jim Reid. It would clear. He was was looking forward to a splendid two days away with Debbie. She would be expensive but it would be fun. That night, Friday, he had been invited to dinner by Detective-Constable Carlisle and his long-suffering wife. Raynes rehearsed all the apologies he would make for her husband's long hours at work and he prepared himself to appear as the most suitable godparent any couple could wish for their son or daughter. Atheist or no – he rather liked the idea of being a godfather; but he fancied that Canon Murray would regard the choice as positively satanic!

28 *A Smuggler's Tale*

Raynes picked up Debbie on Saturday after lunch. She was wearing a dark blue blouse and a white pleated skirt. He thought she looked most unprofessional.

"Good afternoon, Inspector!" she said almost demurely, as

Raynes put her red leather suitcase into the boot of his car.

He looked at her.

"That's a little mystery I still want to clear up. How did you find out I was a policeman?"

Debbie laughed as she climbed into the front seat of the Rover. "Fancy you not working that one out! You surprise me, Inspector."

Raynes accelerated down the London road.

"Well, it can't be my feet," he said, "because they're small. And there's nothing in my car that could have told you. I had nothing in my wallet to identify me. (Not that you would have gone through my wallet!) All my official papers are locked up in the hotel. You didn't speak to anyone that I remember. Perhaps I talked in my sleep ...?"

Debbie smiled and shook her head.

"Alimentary, my dear Holmes! You have a mirror in your car – as one would expect. When I got into your car at *The Green Man,* I flicked down your sun visor to have a quick look at my make-up. Surprise, surprise, that is where you keep your AA card. It says: 'Mr R. Raynes'. You take off your watch. On the back, it says: 'To Richard ...' Therefore I know you are Richard Raynes!"

"Fair enough. But that didn't tell you I was a policeman?"

"Of course not," said Debbie. "But people talk. People are always talking. People tell me that good old Detective-Inspector Parkinson is leaving. Everyone knew Detective-Inspector Parkinson. He's been around for years. He didn't manage to find out who killed Sophie – but he was well-liked. So people say: 'Who's going to get his job then? Will it be a local guy? No,' they say, 'it's some chap from up north called Raynes.' So, put two and two together – I must be screwing the new Inspector! What a surprise!"

Raynes smiled.

"That was clever. I'd forgotten about the watch but I knew there was nothing in the car to connect me with the police. I cleaned out the car last Friday."

He looked at Debbie more seriously.

"You understand now why I was asking you about Sophie?"

"You were wondering who killed her?"

Raynes shook his head.

"No. I know who killed her. But I'm looking for proof."

"Is that why we're going to this place – Rye?"

"Yes."

"Is it on the expense account?"

"I should think so."

Debbie curled up like a contented kitten and smiled at Raynes. "I shall make sure it's a very expensive weekend," she said.

* * *

The old smugglers' town of Rye does not boast of any large hotels. Perched on top of a small hill, surrounded by meandering walls, there is scarcely room for a Hilton. But what hotels there are have colour and charm. Raynes had chosen to stay in an hotel on a steep cobbled street leading down to a stone wall from which one could look over the harbour and Romney Marsh. Their bedroom had low, dark beams, latticed windows and a four-poster bed which Debbie was anxious to sample.

Raynes shook his head.

"Work first! Then dinner."

They walked down the narrow winding streets, each house with its name painted on a ceramic tile embellished with spring flowers. They came to the river beside the windmill and walked along the cobbled quay looking at the boats.

Eventually they arrived at a studio which had been converted out of an old cottage and a boathouse. The artist was an old friend of Raynes; they had been at University together. Consequently, Debbie received a rapturous welcome. The artist waxed poetic over Debbie's body and insisted that she would make a wonderful model. Even though it was early July, they ended up sitting round a wood-burning stove drinking several glasses of very fine French brandy.

Raynes spelt out his problem.

He was looking for Canon Murray's *pied-à-terre*. It did not appear in the telephone directory and might well be under some other name. The painter who had friends all over the town promised to have an answer within twenty-four hours.

176

Debbie could hardly wait till they were walking home.

"Do you think Canon Murray murdered Sophie?"

"He's one of the leading suspects."

"And you think he was having it off with her?"

"I'm sure of it."

"I'd never have thought it of him. I really wouldn't. He seems such a nice old guy."

Raynes looked at her. "I thought you were the one who said that you could never tell what a person was like till you got them in private? Then they come out in their true colours. That was what you said."

"You've got a good memory!"

"I have to. I'm constantly being given little snippets of information. It's like a huge jigsaw. It's my job to put all the pieces together. So everything gets sorted and put away in the memory box."

"But how can you be sure you've got the right person?" asked Debbie. "I mean, what would happen if you made a mistake?"

"Absolute disaster!" said Raynes. "But you don't make mistakes. You don't pounce till you've got every piece linked up to every other piece. There's always a chance that what you thought went in one way – goes in upside down …"

"I know the feeling!"

"So the picture changes – sometimes dramatically – at the last minute."

"So Canon Murray might still be innocent?"

"Innocent till proved guilty. Like you!"

Debbie smiled. She was thinking of the little black velvet dress she was going to wear for dinner. Black ribbed stockings. A suspender belt. Nothing else. And that new perfume. Mm! She was looking forward to a glass of champagne … two glasses of champagne … prawn cocktail … a lovely steak, well done – and, of course, the dessert!

She sighed contentedly and looked up at the little town perched on its hill with all the lights shining like stars.

"Do you think, Inspector, that there are still smugglers round here?"

Raynes marvelled at her innocence.

"Of course there are still smugglers round here," he said. "Where d'you think that brandy came from?"

* * *

By eleven o'clock next morning, Raynes was outside the door of a first floor flat in a large Victorian house which had been converted into four or five holiday homes. This was No. 3. Raynes was busy with plastic and wire. The artist had other tools in a small bag.

"Don't worry about damaging the paintwork," he said. "I can always come back later and touch it up." He looked at Debbie. "This is great fun, isn't it? I've always wanted to do a spot of burglary!" He kept looking at her shapely figure. "Are you sure you won't let me do a quick oil? You'd look terrific! Green velvet? Like Bourchier. Green and gold. It'd be a sensation!"

"She's not in your price range!" said Raynes grumpily. "She charges artists about £240 an hour!"

"Good gracious! How selfish! To keep such beauty to oneself!"

"I'm not exactly a sweet young thing. I am 31!"

"Ah, but you have the full bloom of womanhood. I can see exactly what Dick sees in you."

"And what exactly is that?" asked Mrs May.

The door finally clicked open.

Raynes looked at her.

"Availability. Mobility. Good lubrication and, of course, customer satisfaction."

"Sounds more like a hired car than a woman!"

They entered the flat.

It was plain and simply furnished, but it smelt slightly musty as if it was a long time since anyone had opened a window and let fresh air flow through. Raynes looked into all the rooms and then settled himself at a large roll-top bureau.

"What are we looking for?" asked Debbie.

"Letters, pictures, photos, black underwear …"

"Canon Murray's?"

"Who knows?"

Debbie and the artist explored the kitchen and the bedroom.

178

Debbie discovered a photograph album and several packs of prints. Raynes' artist friend went through the bookcases and cupboards. There were very few places where things could be hidden.

Raynes worked his way through the drawers of the bureau – and was rewarded. In the bottom drawer on the right, he found a brown envelope among several other brown envelopes. But this one was sealed. Raynes inserted a paper knife and cut it open. Out came several pictures of Sophie Jack. They had been taken in or around Rye – and were not very good. There were a few postcards and letters signed "S". A nice picture of her in a studio taken many years before. A dedication in biro on the back.

Raynes read through the letters and was amazed that any-one should bother to keep such rubbish. The terms of endearment were slushy and maternal. But Canon Murray was, he supposed, a sentimental old soul. Couldn't bear to part with a thing. Raynes looked at a couple of theatre tickets and four or five restaurant bills. He checked the dates. It seemed that they had had two or three short holidays in Rye. It was all he needed to know.

He flung down the envelope on the desk.

"Success!"

"You found them?"

Debbie had been too busy looking at the photos to notice what Raynes was doing.

"Jolly good show!" said the artist who was trying to mend a picture which had fallen off the wall and broken its cord. "What shall we do to celebrate?"

"More champagne!" said Debbie enthusiastically. She reached out a hand for the envelope. "Can I have a look?"

"Sure."

Debbie looked at the pictures and read one or two of the letters. "It's sad really," she said, "to think of them together down here. Being happy and all that. And now she's dead. And Canon Murray's about to walk the plank. How did you know they'd been here?"

"Instinct," said Raynes. "Just instinct."

"And what good will these letters and things do?"

"They'll stop him lying to me."

Debbie May looked at Raynes thoughtfully. He did not look happy even though he had found what he was looking for.

But the artist was pleased Raynes had found something. "Great stuff, Dick!" he kept saying. His contacts had told him that Mr Murray had had a couple of holidays in the flat with an anonymous blonde. "A quiet couple. Kept themselves to themselves." It was remarkable that anyone remembered them after all this time.

"Well," he said. "I propose that we go and drink the very best champagne in town. I propose that you treat us to a splendid lunch. And then, if the young lady is agreeable, I propose that we go back to my place for coffee and brandy, and I shall knock off a stunning picture of Debbie for you to hang over the fireplace in your new home. 'A Prospect of Rye.' Your colleagues will be queuing up for invitations to dinner!"

Debbie blushed.

"He's very persuasive."

Raynes said: "He's also a very good artist. Though it grieves my heart to say it. If he says he can do a good picture, he will. But it's up to you. If you want this rake leering over you, slobbering over you, lusting after every inch of your body – it's up to you. But I shall be there. I'm not letting you out of my sight. After all, it's my expense account you're on!"

Debbie smiled broadly.

"Inspector," she said. "I do believe you're jealous! But I've decided. I shall be immortalized in oil!"

"Thank heavens for that," said the artist. "At least it's cheaper than champagne!"

* * *

By Monday lunchtime, the holiday was over and Raynes and Debbie were back in Grasshallows. On his way home, Raynes had paid two visits. First of all, he had called in to Croydon to see Messrs Coulter, Veal & Blyth to clarify one or two points in the church accounts and thereafter he had paid a second visit to Wormwood Scrubs to see Emilio Zaposito for the second time.

It was a fairly brief visit. Raynes wanted to know what sort of car it was that he and Linda had used on their visit to Grasshallows. It was an old Viva – a red Viva. (Raynes groaned inwardly at the thought of all these red cars.)

Next, he wanted to confirm that there had been a light on in Sophie's flat on his first visit at 8.00 pm. The Italian was hesitant but after some thought said he was not sure. If there was a light on, it was a small light. But he would not swear to it. From that, Raynes moved to the letter-box. Raynes asked him whether it was locked or open? Emilio was quite certain that it was open. He had shouted through the letter-box. The detective then asked him whether he thought there was anyone in the flat at the time? That would explain why the light had suddenly been extinguished. Emilio suddenly became quite co-operative. He realized that if the Inspector was suggesting that someone else was in Sophie's flat then it was no longer he who was chief suspect.

The Italian was happy to confirm that he had seen no sign of any blue plastic container on either of his visits. Nor had he seen any strange people wandering round in the vicinity of the flat. In fact, the only peculiar person he had seen that night was the park-keeper down in the Meadows. What had been strange about him?

"Well," said Emilio, "he had been carrying a knife. There was blood on it." The park-keeper had told Emilio that he had killed an Alsatian which had been troubling his geese. It was a stray – so he had cut its throat and buried it. To a man used to using many weapons, a knife seemed inappropriate. Emilio wondered why the park-keeper had not shot the dog, or hit it on the head with a spade or – more simply – phoned up the RSPCA and got them to deal with it? Raynes agreed that it was a bit odd and made a mental note to have a few extra words with Ernie McCulloch.

However, nothing would persuade Mr Zaposito to say that he had strayed more than a few feet from his car whilst it was parked in the Meadows. He had said on Wednesday that he had got out of the car to stretch his legs but he had not entered the woods – not even for a moment.

Raynes thought his denial was strange and touched with fear. He remembered the anxiety on Linda's face when she denied that Emilio had ever left the car. Raynes was sure both Linda and the Italian were lying. They had entered the woods. They had either done the murder – or seen the body tied to the tree. For that reason, they had fled from the Meadows as quickly as possible and rushed back to London. Raynes tried to find out whether Emilio was carrying his own knife with him that night but the Italian swore on the life of his sister's grand-daughter that he had travelled to Grasshallows unarmed that night.

Raynes made one final attempt to get Mr Zaposito to tell the truth but fear or guilt predominated and Emilio would say nothing more.

29 *Thespians Anonymous*

On Monday afternoon, Raynes and Carlisle once more disturbed Commander Kenworth's siesta – this time with the fair Rosalind. Once more, the aged housekeeper proved no obstacle to the Inspector's forceful charm.

"It's us again!" he said cheerfully and swept into the hall. "We'll wait in the sitting room!" he added.

However, it was unfortunately in the sitting room – and not the bedroom – that Mrs Hayman and the Commander had been enjoying their siesta. The thump of the knocker had given them some warning but they had never expected that Raynes and Carlisle would simply barge in. Mrs Hayman was in a black slip and the Commander in a pair of red and white striped boxer shorts

"Oh, my God!" cried Mrs Hayman.

"Wrong one!" said Raynes. "It's just your friendly local detective!"

With that, he shut the door quickly and retraced his steps to the front door, trying not to laugh. Carlisle thought the situation was hilarious but was worried that the housekeeper might lose her job. Very wisely, she had disappeared downstairs to the basement.

The Commander was mortified.

"Inspector! Have you no respect for the privacy of a man's home? Dammit, Raynes! An Englishman's home is his castle. You don't just walk in on a chap …!"

Raynes looked him coldly in the eye.

"When you tell me the truth, I shall respect you. Not before! Come clean with me on what you were doing on the night Sophie died, and I might even give you an apology. But after the lies you and this trollop have told me …"

Mrs Hayman had been sitting on the sofa nearest to the fireplace with a half-empty glass in her left hand – ignoring both policemen. However, at Raynes' calculated insult she turned and glared and screamed: "Trollop? You bastard!" And flung her glass hard and accurately in the Inspector's direction. Raynes ducked and the glass shattered violently against the wall.

She then burst into tears and the Commander rushed over to comfort her. Raynes sat down calmly on one of the sofas and waited for the storm to pass. Comforting the fair Rosalind took all of five minutes.

When peace was restored, Raynes began: "Commander, I've only one question today. Were you or were you not in the vicinity of Sophie Jack's flat on the night she died – at about 10 pm? Yes or no?"

The Commander looked flabbergasted at the directness of Raynes' attack. "I … I …" he stumbled, looking appealingly to Rosalind for help.

"You weren't here!" she said forcibly. "You were in London!"

"I wasn't here …" the Commander began.

"You were here," said Raynes. "I have a witness. You were dressed as a woman. Grey coat, grey hat and spectacles. When I first came here, I had no idea you had thespian tendencies! Now I find you carrying round plastic containers full of petrol and wearing fancy dress. Why?"

The Commander was speechless.

Raynes turned to Mrs Hayman.

"And a man with baggy trousers, a green jacket – also with spectacles and black hair?"

Rosalind could not avoid the shadow of a smile.

"You should join our Drama Club, Inspector; you would be a great hit!"

"As Brutus?"

"I was thinking more of Julius Caesar on the Ides of March!"

It was clear that Mrs Hayman was slowly recovering her nerve. Raynes was determined to shatter it.

"Do you get all your ideas at the Drama Club?"

"I'm afraid I don't follow you, Inspector?"

"Shaw's 'St Joan'? I believe you had the star role? You were tied to the stake and set on fire?"

"Who on earth told you that?"

"One of your admirers. They think you might have got your idea there for killing Sophie. A truly splendid public humiliation! A most dramatic act of revenge! Tied to a tree. Strangled, stabbed, burned. Only you didn't get as far as burning the body, did you? You were going to do the flat in first. But a young man saw you!"

The Commander intervened.

"Inspector, this is a preposterous suggestion!"

"I'm afraid it is," said Raynes, "but it comes very near to the truth. You went upstairs with that blue plastic container. You found the letter-box blocked. (Sophie knew what Mrs Hayman was capable of doing.) So you left the container on the landing and came downstairs to ask your colleague what you should do. As you walked out of the alleyway, you met this young man coming in with a white envelope. You were surprised and hurried across the road to be with Mrs Hayman. You watched him come out. You realized you had been seen. You went back for the petrol – well, one of you did – and left in a hurry. To construct a decent alibi which would fox the police. But you can't fool me! I know what you were doing down Riverside Road and I want to know what you were doing earlier?"

The Commander fell for Raynes' trick.

He turned to Rosalind

"What were we doing earlier?"

"You fool!" shrieked Rosalind. "We were in London!"

Raynes watched the tensions between them with interest. He felt that the Commander wanted to speak but was terrified of Mrs Hayman. He dared not speak.

Raynes continued: "We know it was Mrs Hayman's red Fiesta which was parked in a lay-by on the A193 on the far side of the Meadows that Saturday night. We know it was Mrs Hayman who supplied Derek Coates-Smythe's visiting card. Shopped her old lover as, one day, Commander, she will shop you!"

The look of horror on Rosalind's face was priceless. She was struck dumb by Raynes' presentation of the facts. The Commander rallied to her defence.

"Inspector," he said, "there's been a great mistake. Rosalind hasn't killed anyone …"

"The biggest mistake," said Raynes, "is that neither of you is capable of telling the truth. Tomorrow night at 7.00 pm a police car will come and collect both of you and bring you to a special meeting where the facts will be made public. If you should wish to plead guilty beforehand, that's up to you. But I would strongly advise you to tell me the truth – however horrible it is. And that is my last word!"

As he pushed himself up from his seat, he encountered a small handful of black silk. He looked at it, dangled it with two fingers and dropped it on the ground. He glanced at Mrs Hayman: "Your knickers, I believe?"

* * *

"She'll never forgive you for that," said Carlisle.

"What? For walking in on them?"

"She won't forgive you for any of it. Specially not for being called a trollop. Women hate that word. I've never seen anyone so wound up. If I were you, I'd block your letter-box and wear armour plating under your suit!"

"You may be right,"'said Raynes thoughtfully. "But let's go and see this man about a dog."

* * *

Ernie McCulloch confirmed the Italian's story. He had indeed killed a dog that Saturday night. It had been seen in the Meadows on two consecutive nights and had killed three of his Canadian geese. He had trapped it earlier in the day by offering it some food. Once the park had been cleared of people, he had taken it out, slit its throat and buried it. He offered to show Raynes the burial site. Raynes was more interested in the knife. Where was it? Ernie told the Inspector that the police had taken it away for tests. It had not been a hunting knife, merely a cut-throat razor. If he could have it back, it would be nice. Raynes promised to check Ernie's story at the station.

"About this Italian," said Raynes, "would he look like this?"

He showed him a photograph of Emilio Zaposito.

Ernie exclaimed with delight: "That's the guy!"

Raynes said: "I thought you said to me that you saw no suspicious characters around that night? This man has been guilty of at least one murder, several robberies with violence, white slavery and assault! He came here specifically looking for Sophie. And you say you didn't think he was a suspicious character."

Ernie looked a bit shocked.

"But, Inspector, he had his girlfriend with him. And she was such a frightened wee thing. Hanging on to his arm and crying. He couldn't have done nothing to Sophie with the likes of her hanging around. Besides that, it was much later, sir. Much later. It was about 8.30 pm when I was burying that dog. That's why I didn't tell either you or Detective-Inspector Parkinson about 'im. He said 7.00 to 7.30 pm. They didn't go into the woods till later."

"They went into the woods?"

"Must have done. That's where I saw them."

"What were they doing?"

"What d'you think?" Ernie laughed. "They weren't worried about rum, sodomy or the lash, sir! Not them! Nothing but a good, honest bit of all right. I saw 'em. Ernie sees everyone."

"He didn't see the murderer!" said Raynes.

"If I hadn't been talking to that bloke about the dog," said Ernie, "I might have caught that chap sneaking into her car. Stands to reason, they can't both be murderers. It's one or the other."

30 *The Blackmailer*

Canon Murray opened his front door and discovered – to his horror – that he was about to have a third visit from Inspector Raynes. "Come in," he said – with no great enthusiasm.

Raynes and Carlisle made their way into the sitting room and sat down. Canon Murray offered them coffee but his offer was refused.

"I have been to Rye," said Raynes. "I have been to your flat. I have examined the contents of your desk. And in that desk, I found a brown sealed envelope containing photographs of Mrs Jack together with cards, letters and restaurant bills. What do you say about that, Murray?"

The elderly Canon looked thunderstruck.

"You broke into my flat!"

"No. We were let in by a friendly local."

"But I'm the only person who has a key!"

Raynes looked at him with undisguised contempt.

"I don't think that keys are the main point at issue. What is important is that you seem to have been cohabiting with Mrs Jack on at least two or three occasions since your wife's death."

"Inspector, really! Your behaviour is quite unacceptable!"

"I should have thought that cohabiting with a known prostitute was even less acceptable, Canon Murray! And lying …"

"I have never lied to you!"

Raynes raised his eyebrows.

"Canon Murray, you explicitly said to me in our first interview that you had had no dealings with Mrs Jack in her professional capacity."

"That was true."

Raynes paused to think.

"Oh, I see. You didn't pay her? That's what you meant? She felt sorry for you? Gave you your nookie for nothing?" Raynes was as offensive as possible.

Canon Murray's eyes blazed with anger.

"Inspector, I will not tolerate your rudeness for another

minute! Get out of my house – now! This very minute!"

"This is not a social call," said Raynes. "This is a police investigation into a very serious act of murder. This is my third visit. On each visit, we have had to squeeze the truth out of you drop-by-drop. You may not have lied to me, but you have in no way been honest or straightforward. In fact, you have been totally unhelpful. If you continue to put up a smoke-screen, I shall take you into custody – immediately – tonight! Try explaining that to your congregation!"

Canon Murray sat miserably in his chair. His face crumpled. Tears poured down his cheeks. Carlisle felt like going over and wiping his face with a handkerchief.

There was a long silence.

For several minutes.

Then the Canon began to speak.

"It was just as you said, Inspector. Sophie was sorry for me. When my wife died, it was a terrible loss. You see, I'd been nursing her at home – for several months – and then she was taken into hospital. We all hoped they might be able to do something – but it was hopeless. When she died, I just broke down – completely. It knocked all the stuffing out of me. But people were very kind. They had me out for meals. They sent flowers. They prayed for me. And it made things a little easier to bear. Sophie was one of the kindest. She was a gem. She came round and made tea for me. She used to drop in with a bottle and we'd have a glass or two. One night, I broke right down in front of her. And she was tremendous. She comforted me, put an arm round me, kissed me. I suppose we could have ended up in bed that night – but we didn't. I wouldn't do anything like that here in Grasshallows; you never know who's watching. So I said: 'Not here!' And she said: 'Shall we go away somewhere? Have a little holiday? Blow away the cobwebs?' And I said: 'Well, I've got this little place down in Rye.' So she said: 'Well, let's go there!' So we did. She was very kind … Of course, I knew it was wrong. Very wrong. Especially for a man in my position. But I was so lonely, I was just desperate. I needed a woman's love. She didn't push herself forward. Didn't ask for any money. She just helped to build me up – and then withdrew. Went back to being a normal member of the congregation; and we never mentioned it again. That's how it was, Inspector."

It had the ring of truth – even to Raynes' prejudiced ears. But was it the whole story?

"Did anyone else know about this?" he asked. "Anyone apart from you and Sophie?"

Canon Murray looked wary.

"You might as well tell me," said Raynes.

"Her son, John. He knew. He read her diary."

"I see. So that was why you paid him a couple of thousand after the funeral?"

"How did you know that?"

"He told me."

"The rat! The poisonous little rat! It was meant to be a secret!"

"He said that he knew you and his mother were pretty close. 'Hand-in-glove' ... those were the words he used ... 'Hand-in-glove'. He said you used to write her letters for her. He said she could wrap men round her little finger and you were no exception. He seemed to think that she had left all her money to St Benedict's out of personal affection for you ..."

"I don't believe that was the real reason."

"... and that you felt a bit guilty about it. So you gave him £2000."

"Well, it came out of her legacy."

"Did it? I didn't see that in the accounts?"

"I asked Peter Bridges to make sure the young man got something. I knew he and Linda were having a pretty rough time."

"Kindness?" said Raynes, "or blackmail?"

The Canon looked at the Inspector.

It was impossible to lie to him.

"Blackmail!" he said. "He's been quietly milking me for three or four years. I thought about going to the police. But ... well ... if it had gone to court – or got into the papers – that'd be the end. There was too much at stake."

"The end of a distinguished career?" said Raynes. "Public humiliation? Shame and embarrassment for your son and

189

daughter? So you paid up? It's a wonder you didn't think of bumping him off!"

"I did."

The Canon spoke very bitterly.

Raynes looked at Carlisle thoughtfully. This was the man who said he would never think of murdering anyone. He had lied. It seemed that the mask was slipping.

"Blackmail's a nasty business," said Raynes feelingly. "I sometimes think it's worse than murder. It's a sort of slow torture. Real cruelty."

Canon Murray looked at Raynes.

"May I tell you something, Inspector?"

Raynes nodded.

"I promised to say nothing about it. Nothing ever. But since John has spoken to you, I don't see why I should keep silent any more. You might as well know that John was up here in Grasshallows the night his mother died ..."

Raynes' eyes lit up.

"... He came up to get some money from her – as he often did. He came up from Aldershot at about 5.00 pm and went up to her house. At least, that's what he told me. But she was busy. He heard voices. So he thought he'd call back later. He came round to see me and asked me for £50."

"Did you give it to him?"

"I had no money in the house but I gave him a cheque."

"And he went off quite happily?"

"Well, he said he was hoping to catch his mother 'in between calls' – that was how he put it. He said he was going down to the Meadows and he hoped to see her there. I told him not to go. If he went down there and disturbed her, she would be sure to put the police on to him – again! And that would be the end of his Army career. But he laughed. He laughed and said there wouldn't be any violence, not this time anyway."

"What time was this?"

"About 5.30 pm. Just before I went off to Evensong."

"He had a car?"

"I suppose so. I didn't see it. I was glad to see the back of him. He was a nasty type. I didn't see him again till after the funeral. I was glad to get him out of the house, I can tell you."

"And you told none of this to Detective-Inspector Parkinson?"

"No."

"Why not?"

"Because, Inspector, if John knew I'd split on him, he'd split on me. And I had too much to lose."

"So you made a pact?"

"We had a few words over the phone. He told me he'd taken my advice and gone straight home."

"Did you believe him?"

"I don't know. When he came to see me after the funeral, he told me it wasn't he who murdered his mother. He promised me on the Bible – that one on the table. He said he'd gone down to the Meadows and waited around for about ten minutes. Then he had decided to go home. He swore blind that he hadn't seen her – let alone touched her."

"And you promised him £2000?"

"He asked for five."

"But the Treasurer wouldn't play ball?"

"No."

"I'm glad about that," said Raynes. "I'm glad that someone at least has had the guts to stand up to that young man and say 'No'."

Canon Murray stared at the floor.

"It's a rotten business, isn't it?"

"That's what I tried to tell you on my first visit but you wouldn't come clean. You could have saved me a lot of time if you'd been a bit more honest."

"I'm very sorry, Inspector, but it's all so humiliating and sordid."

Raynes said nothing. He was thinking of how much Canon Murray had already hidden from him. First of all, there was his behaviour in the army. That was pretty damning! Then there was the visit of Sophie's son to Grasshallows on the actual night she was murdered. And John was the one suspect who had no alibi. Now there was a suggestion of blackmail. If he had not been ruthless with the Canon, not one of these juicy pieces of information would have come to light. Only after relentless pressure had Canon Murray begun to talk. How much more was still hidden away?

He looked at Canon Murray long and hard.

John Jack was so obviously a swine – such an obvious suspect – that had his guilt been provable, he would surely have broken down under questioning the previous year. He had not broken down ... so he was either a formidable liar or he was innocent. But if Canon Murray was correct, John Jack had lied to him. He had denied being in Grasshallows on the night of the murder. Raynes had doubted his statement but had not picked up a direct lie on his sensitive antennae. So was there more to be dug up?

He looked at Carlisle.

"Pull him in tomorrow morning. First thing!"

To the clergyman he said:

"Tomorrow night, I'm having a little meeting at about 7.30 pm to which you are invited. You can either come under your own steam or I shall send a police car to fetch you. I'm determined to get all the facts out on the table once and for all. So I should like you – and your Treasurer – to come along and represent St Benedict's. It'll last about an hour and a half. I shall not accept any excuses. You've wasted a lot of my time. I shall now waste yours!"

Canon Murray looked very anxious.

"You won't mention anything about Sophie and me?"

Raynes smiled to himself.

Here was Canon Murray asking to be blackmailed. How splendid!

"Well," said Raynes, "I can't promise absolutely. But I can assure you that I shall not raise the issue. Your secret is safe with me. But if John Jack should say anything then it'll be his word against yours."

"It sounds a most unpleasant evening."

"I suppose it does. But you might like to remember that Sophie also had rather an unpleasant evening. Fortunately, your suffering will be nothing compared with hers! If you lose face, think what she lost! If you can do something to clear up this case, then I think you owe it to her to do your

192

best. If you have anything more to tell me, you have only to phone. Failing that, we shall see each other tomorrow night!"

31 *The Chief Constable*

When Raynes arrived in his office on Tuesday morning, there was a note waiting for him: "See Chief Constable, 9.30 am". For the past two weeks the Chief Constable had been away on holiday. Raynes had expected that at some point the Chief Constable would ask to see him but, as far as he was concerned, such a meeting was a mere formality. Although he had met the Chief Constable at his interview, all that he could remember was that he was a nice old buffer with a moustache and a dark brown face. Clearly, he had come back from holiday and was anxious to extend a few words of welcome, to ask Raynes how he was settling in to Grasshallows and wanted to know what had been going on whilst he was away. From Raynes' point of view, such pleasantries were a complete waste of time, but he adjusted his tie, brushed his hair and headed for the Chief Constable's office on the second floor of the building, quite unaware that most of the staff in the police station knew he was heading for a first-class row and one of the most unpleasant and stormy meetings of an already turbulent career.

The Chief Constable was furious.

"Never," he said, "have I come back to Grasshallows to find such a complete and utter shambles! I have received a whole string of complaints from all sorts of distinguished people in our community – lawyers, bankers, clergymen, retired folk – all complaining about the brutal and unpleasant way they have been treated. The farmers are up in arms because someone has been pinching their livestock and they say the police are doing nothing about it. This morning, I hear that a formal complaint has been made to the Home Secretary about the treatment of a police suspect – something that has never happened before – ever! I come back to find the newest and most recent addition to the car fleet – the car which was bought for my own personal use – smashed to smithereens and the whole criminal community stirred up like a hornets' nest."

193

"Then I am told you are using the telephone for private calls of a frivolous nature and fixing up disgusting weekends. I believe you have been consorting with a known prostitute and, what is worse, you have been wasting your time – and everybody else's – trying to dig up an old case which has long since been buried, stirring over the coals and making a thundering nuisance of yourself to one and all."

"I know your reputation, Raynes! And that you were only sent here as a special favour – to give you one last chance. But I must confess, your behaviour during the past week has been quite disgraceful. Quite inexcusable. The whole station is talking about it and what the Police Committee will say, I just do not know! I realize you have this desire to prove yourself – but you are not doing it at my expense! If you are not capable of conducting yourself as a Detective-Inspector – like your distinguished predecessor, Detective-Inspector Parkinson – then I think it is better that you leave us sooner rather than later so that the reputation of this force is not damaged or destroyed any further."

The attack took Raynes completely by surprise. For once, his brain was slow to find an answer to such a catalogue of woes. He spoke slowly – still trying to think clearly.

"I'm very sorry that you should have come back to such an unhappy picture, sir. But I'm afraid it looks a little different from my angle ..."

"I don't care a damn about your angle, Raynes. Just consider the people you've upset – the Rector of St Benedict's, his Treasurer, the chief partner of Logan, Smythe and Smythe, Commander Kenworth, people in the University. These sort of people carry great weight round here. They're members of my golf club. In fact, many of them are friends of mine. When they tell me what you've been up to, I just can't ignore them."

"I believe that several of them were suspected last year of being involved in Mrs Jack's murder?"

"Suspected, Inspector, suspected ... but not guilty. Detective-Inspector Parkinson knew the background. He handled the whole thing with great tact and diplomacy. But you have been going round bullying these people. Accusing them. Threaten-

194

ing them. I don't know how we will ever live it down! I think the best thing is for you to go – to go as soon as possible!"

Raynes' eyes narrowed.

"Chief Constable," he said, "I've been investigating a murder …"

"On whose authority I might ask? Who told you to get involved in a case that was thoroughly investigated by Detective-Inspector Parkinson? What business was it of yours?"

"Unfinished business, sir. I had nothing to do on my first morning and I discovered that this case had never been solved."

"Who told you that?"

"Detective-Constable Carlisle. In fact, early last week, the whole station seemed particularly glad that the matter was being reconsidered. They felt very unhappy that the case had been shelved. They told me so."

The Chief Constable said nothing so Raynes continued:

"Having nothing else to do, I read through the files. I re-interviewed the chief suspects. I have not ignored the farmers. I've had two officers following up all available leads and, every night, I've gone through the case with them. Whoever told you I had been ignoring the case, is lying. I'm quite capable of handling two cases at once and everything that could be done has been done. You have my word on that."

"Your word!" sneered the Chief Constable.

"As for the murder case," Raynes continued, "I have worked long hours of overtime …"

"With Mrs May?"

"You shouldn't believe everything the switchboard girl tells you, sir! I am a senior serving officer … and, as I say, I have worked long hours in overtime – which I shall *not* be claiming. As a result of my investigations, I have brought the case to a successful conclusion. There will be an arrest and a formal charge tonight."

"Not Canon Murray or Mr Coates-Smythe, I hope? That would really put the cat among the pigeons!"

"No one is above the law, sir. Canon Murray has proved to have a quite appalling record. He has lied consistently. He has been involved in blackmail, torture, theft and – what is more to the point – he spent no less than three weeks cohabiting with Mrs Jack in his flat down in Rye."

"What absolute rubbish! A man of his reputation …!"

"It's all perfectly true, I'm afraid. There's a great deal my worthy predecessor, Detective-Inspector Parkinson, did not dig up. And as for the other gentry whom you mentioned, they may be your friends and golfing cronies, but they're a pretty sordid lot … wife-swapping, taking dirty photographs, tying women up and beating them. To me, they're all *prima facie* suspects in a particularly brutal murder and if you are going to defend them – because they are your friends – then I shall go straight down to the *Echo* and give them the full story. I hardly think you'd like to see your face splashed over the front page of the evening newspaper!"

As Raynes said these words, a headline flashed through his mind: "Beaver hushes up scandal!"

Now why should that thought have suddenly come to him? Who had told him that the Chief Constable was nicknamed "The Beaver"? Of course, it was Mrs Hayman! "When the Beaver hears about it, he'll be furious." Now where else had he seen that name? In a little book, with a tick and a telephone number?

Raynes felt an inner glow of triumph.

It all tied up. Beautifully and simply. The Chief Constable was one of Derek Coates-Smythe's golfing partners – along with Ralph, Cecil and Wynn. He too had appeared on Sophie's list. She was one of his crowd. No wonder Detective-Inspector Parkinson had had to tread with such tact and diplomacy. His own boss had been one of the 288 possible suspects. How embarrassing! How splendid!

Raynes grinned happily.

"Take that stupid smile off your face," said the Chief Constable. "You're finished. You're fired … as from this moment. Clear out your desk and go!"

Raynes shook his head.

"If I'm fired – so will you be. I don't think you quite understand, Chief Constable. Quite a lot of people have seen Mrs Jack's address book. Quite a few people have seen the names contained in that book … all Sophie's customers. Quite a few people also know who the Beaver is. It doesn't take much to put two and two together. If the Beaver is seen to be trying to hush things up, the Press might quite reasonably think there is a cover-up and start to investigate. I should of course be perfectly happy to help them. I think, sir, you may very well be backing the wrong horse?"

The look of amazement – followed by horror – on the Chief Constable's face, told Raynes that his boss knew nothing about the address book.

"I'm afraid," he said, "that Detective-Inspector Parkinson was too kind to tell you that your name and telephone number appeared in Sophie's address book. All those whose names are ticked were her customers. I'm afraid there's not the slightest doubt that you were connected with her – in one way or another. If you insist on wielding the big stick, then so shall I. We shall both go down together. And your long and distinguished career will come to a very sticky end. I shall possibly be re-instated but you …" Raynes shook his head. "You're very lucky you weren't here last week," he added. "You might have ended up on my list as well!"

The Chief Constable was effectively silenced.

"You've made your point, Raynes."

"I take it, sir, that I may conclude this case in my own way?"

The Chief Constable nodded.

"… And that perhaps the switchboard girl might be moved to other duties?"

The interview which had begun with such fury and venom ended as sweetly as Raynes could have wished. Members of the station staff who had been expecting him to be packing his bags and clearing out his desk, were amazed to hear him whistling cheerfully as he walked back to his office.

* * *

After that, it was all downhill.

Having trounced the Chief Constable, Raynes issued a three-line whip for all the suspects to attend a meeting at 7.30 pm that night – including Mr Derek Coates-Smythe and Emilio Zaposito. This was how afficionados of the crime novel expected the story to end. Not in some hole-in-the-corner arrest, but in an elegant denouement in full technicolor. Who was he to disappoint them?

For his own convenience, he decided to hold the meeting in the smaller function suite at *The Green Man*. Free drinks would be laid on. He planned the scenario with a quiet smile on his lips.

* * *

Later in the morning, he had further cause for satisfaction. Jim Reid had signed a full confession of what he and his brother, Eddie, had been doing on the night of June 27th. Raynes read through the document with increasing interest. It amounted to an almost complete confession of murder – except for one small, significant detail. But Raynes could provide that detail! No wonder the brothers had kept so mum! Raynes asked Carlisle: "Did he make this confession of his own free will?"

"Yes and no," said Carlisle. "He didn't want to make it but he was so sure you'd drag in his brother and beat him up, that he apparently broke down yesterday afternoon. I'm told he'd made some promise to his mother on her deathbed that he'd always look after his younger brother. When it came to the crunch, he decided he had to keep that promise – even though he knew it'd put him back in jail."

"Good man!" said Raynes. "He'll feel much better now!"

"Will you be inviting him to the party?"

The Inspector looked thoughtful.

"No," he said. "I think not. His brother, Eddie, will be quite sufficient. We don't want a complete punch-up!"

Carlisle said: "Well, that's the good news then!"

"What's the bad news?"

"Mr Coates-Smythe is bringing two lawyers with him – just in case you malign him in public."

Raynes shook his head.

"That man just doesn't trust me one inch! Not one little inch! And yet, only this morning, he sent a little note round to my hotel to apologize …"

"To apologize?"

"He now feels he may have revealed the contents of Sophie's will at a rather intimate moment. He says to whom – but it's a bit late now. He could have saved me a lot of time and trouble last week."

Carlisle read the letter.

"It doesn't say much for his professional standards!"

"I don't think he's got any! And now he wants to turn up with his two legal rottweilers in case I bite him! It makes you sick …"

Raynes had a cup of black coffee.

Before he had finished measuring in the mandatory two spoonfuls of sugar, another confession had come his way. Commander Kenworth wished to tell Inspector Raynes the truth. Although he begged Raynes not to mention his call to Rosalind, he admitted that he had been nowhere near London on the night of the murder. It was a lie – as the Inspector had said. He also admitted that both he and Mrs Hayman had been intending to set fire to Sophie's flat that night. They had been planning to do it for some time. He was a most unwilling accomplice. It was a dreadful thing to do. But Rosalind had been at her most insistent. And as the Inspector knew by now, Mrs Hayman was not a lady to cross.

They had indeed turned up at the flat in Riverside Road – in disguise – but they had been thwarted in their attempt by the blocked letter-box and the sudden arrival of the young man. They had intended to do something very criminal – but their hand had been stayed. They had done nothing wrong. He begged the Inspector to believe him. And could he and Mrs Hayman be excused the meeting that evening? He did not think Rosalind could bear it. He feared she was on the verge of a nervous breakdown.

"Certainly not!" said Raynes. "This is a murder inquiry. Not a cocktail party! If you are not there by 7.15 pm, I shall immediately send two squad cars to bring you in!"

The Commander would not admit that he had been in the Meadows earlier that evening. He refused to account for Mrs Hayman's movements. She had come to him at about 8.00 pm and they had dressed up in their disguises before setting out for the flat. A conspiracy to commit arson was bad enough. The Inspector must understand …

"You're only telling me half the story," said Raynes angrily. "I want the full picture. You and Mrs Hayman have hatched this plot. Only you can unscramble it!"

He put down the phone.

"Those two drive me up the wall!"

Raynes drank the remains of his coffee.

Finally, there came news that John Jack was on his way from London to Grasshallows.

"We'll see him after lunch," said Raynes. "We'll get to the bottom of this business once and for all. Whatever he said or did, he's going to tell us this afternoon. I'm not enduring any more lies. Get out his file and I'll read it again before lunch."

* * *

To mark the conclusion of the case, Raynes had arranged that he and Carlisle should have another sumptuous lunch at the *Grosvenor*. At their first meal, it had been Carlisle who had done most of the talking as he outlined the case; but on this occasion it was Detective-Inspector Raynes who did most of the talking. Fitting together all the little pieces, he showed Carlisle how the whole picture had come together. He explained precisely what he wanted him to do at the evening meeting and how the exposition would be handled. "Nothing can go wrong," he said. "But I should like to round off the whole story in my own special way – with a little finesse!"

Carlisle agreed.

However, Raynes was seeking one final confession that afternoon.

"Why didn't you tell me," he said, "that The Beaver in Sophie's address book was the Chief Constable?"

"I thought you might have guessed it. Or someone might have told you."

Raynes shook his head.

"No one said a word. Except Mrs Hayman. If she hadn't blurted out that threat, this case would have been shelved – permanently – and I would be packing my bags. It was very close! As the Duke of Wellington would have said: 'Damned close'. Didn't Detective-Inspector Parkinson realize the connection?"

"He did. But he said the matter must be handled with the utmost tact and discretion. 'Dog doesn't eat dog'. That's what he said."

"Well, that advice almost cost this dog its day!" Raynes smiled. "However, that's all over now. Have another glass of champagne!"

He reached for the bottle in the silver bucket.

32 *The Black Sheep*

The company gathered in the smaller function suite at *The Green Man* at about 7.30 pm. Thirteen people had been invited but altogether eighteen people turned up to hear Raynes' exposition.

John and Linda Jack were the first to arrive. John went over to the bar and immediately ordered a pint of 80/- ale. Linda asked for a bitter lemon. Commander Kenworth and Mrs Hayman arrived next and contented themselves with a couple of large gin-and-tonics. Shortly behind them came Ernie McCulloch in his best suit. Following Inspector Raynes' advice, he modestly selected a glass of neat rum. Eddie Reid came in on his own but refused to drink anything. He sat on the edge of the party anxiously biting his nails and glaring with hatred at Raynes. Canon Murray and Peter Bridges came in together, smiling and relaxed. The Canon was in a fawn coloured suit with a faded grey shirt. Peter Bridges was wearing a smart grey suit with his golf club tie. The Canon had a cream sherry and the Treasurer had his usual whisky. Emilio Zaposito was escorted into the suite by two prison officers which caused a small stir. Linda Jack pointedly looked in the other direction. Mr Zaposito insisted on a rather elaborate cocktail for which he alone had the recipe. His order took some time to concoct. Paul Brown arrived, still wearing his tweed jacket and university tie; he was treated to an orange juice by Canon Murray. Last to arrive was Derek Coates-Smythe who had brought strong moral support in the shape of two lawyers and the Chief Constable himself. All four refused to accept any drinks and set up a cassette recorder very prominently on one of the bar tables.

Raynes watched their efforts with some amusement. He waited for ten minutes till his guests were sufficiently mellowed and then – in the best detective tradition – he called the meeting to order.

"Ladies and gentlemen," he said with a theatrical flourish, "I'm very glad to see you here this evening because I feel I owe you all a few words of explanation and – in some cases – a most sincere apology for the rough treatment you have received."

He was heard in total silence.

"I was first told about this case last Monday morning – my first day in Grasshallows – and I must confess to you that I was most intrigued. First of all, we have a truly appalling murder of a very popular person. Over three hundred people were at one time suspected of killing her – some suspected more than others. So when Detective-Constable Carlisle told me about Sophie's death, I decided to make it my business – my immediate business – to follow up the clues and see whether – even after the scent had long grown cold – any solution could be found."

"I would like to remind you of the facts. We are talking about the night of June 27th 1987. A Saturday night on the last weekend of June last year. Sophie Jack left her home at about 6.45 pm or just after. She reached the Meadows shortly before 7.00 pm, left her car in the car-park and walked into the woods wearing a red dress, gold belt and gold shoes, carrying a black handbag. She was in a happy frame of mind and was reportedly going to meet a customer who had pre-arranged to see her at about 7.15 pm. By 7.30 pm, she had been tied up to a tree in a distant corner of the 'forest' – as that part of the Meadows is called. She was naked, blindfolded, strangled with a piece of old rope. Her stomach had been gashed with three sharp amateurish blows – done, it is believed, with a German hunting knife."

The last two people to see Sophie alive were Mr Paul Brown who had tea with her. And Mr Ernie McCulloch, the park-keeper, who saw her going to her assignation. We have Mr McCulloch's word that he saw no one he recognized going in the same direction either before or after Sophie. There were of course plenty of couples and children still around at 7.00 pm but he did not see anyone we might call 'suspicious' hanging about. It is quite possible that the murderers – assuming there was more than one – might well have walked into the woods arm-in-arm without exciting the slightest suspicion. However, it seems to me more than likely that the murderer – male or female – single or a couple – was already in the woods waiting for Sophie to arrive."

"It also seems obvious to me that he or she may have approached the Meadows from a completely different direction – namely from the A193 which bypasses the city and runs no more than half a mile from the tree where Sophie died. This possibility was apparently not considered by Detective-Inspector Parkinson during his investigations last year. In fact, the question only arose because I suggested to Mr Derek Coates-Smythe that on his journey home from Picton Dale to Newton St Mary's he would have been very close to the murder scene. He thought the distance would have been about two miles – but, as I say, it is much nearer."

"Having made this bold suggestion, Mr Derek Coates-Smythe delved into the depths of his memory and came up with a curious fact which he had previously forgotten. He had seen a red car parked in the lay-by on the A193 on the night of the murder. I therefore set out to consider who might have been driving that red car. Mrs Hayman had a red Fiesta. Mr Emilio Zaposito had borrowed a red Viva. John Jack was driving a red Escort. The Reid brothers had a variety of cars at their disposal. The car could of course have been hired – or it could have been a red herring, a figment of Mr Coates-Smythe's imagination."

The lawyer shook his head.

"Anyway, the key point is that, however they got into the woods, the murderer – or murderers – were not seen. This may suggest to you, as it does to me, very careful planning. The murder was not done on the spur of the moment – or in the heat of passion – it was premeditated and very carefully carried out."

"The only clue that we do have is from Paul Brown. Sophie told him that her assignation that night was 'a good one'. From which he inferred that it did not involve sex as such. Knowing the scope of Sophie's activities, one might therefore assume that she was going for a photographic session with a person or persons unknown. This would explain the very isolated corner in which the body was found. You do not take nude poses in full view of the general public. You find a quiet little corner at the back of beyond. The corner where Sophie died is at the north end of the 'forest', beside a cornfield – half a mile from the A193."

He looked for a reaction among any of the audience. He saw none.

"Now we have a number of suspects with photographic interests. Derek Coates-Smythe and Mrs Hayman are both active with the camera. Mr Coates-Smythe has been taking what we might call 'life poses' for many years. Mrs Hayman prefers birds. So does Mr Paul Brown. And Ernie McCulloch bought a spanking new camera from Munns just after Christmas 1985 …"

"In the January sales," said Ernie.

"… Mrs Bridges tells me that her husband has no less than three cameras lying at home but he never uses them. However, Canon Murray has been practising the art for many years and has got several albums full of prints from his holidays down in Rye!"

Peter Bridges raised his eyebrows at the mention of the cameras and shook his head. Canon Murray affected to ignore Raynes' words.

"So," continued Raynes, "if we are looking for a budding photographer, these people are potential suspects. The important question for me was why Sophie allowed herself to be tied up. Now, of course, photography may not be the answer. It could be that this was a 'gangland killing' – or a contract killing. That would equally explain why she was tied up. In fact," said Raynes, "there is every reason to believe that the Reid brothers might well have arranged this unpleasant encounter in the woods …"

"We didn't!" said Eddie. And in case people hadn't heard, he shouted it more loudly: "We didn't!"

"I'm not apportioning blame," said Raynes. "I'm exploring a number of possibilities …"

"You're a bastard," said Eddie. "Everyone knows you're a bastard."

Canon Murray smiled grimly.

"At least give me a hearing," said Raynes.

Eddie muttered a few more obscenities about Raynes' mother.

The Inspector continued: "We might also consider in this connection Mr Zaposito who has quite a record of violence and knifing. He knew Sophie extremely well. She shopped him to the police over a killing some years ago, and Mr Zaposito vowed his revenge. He had threatened to slash Sophie's face open in the past and it turns out that he was in Grasshallows that Saturday night hoping to screw a cheque out of Sophie – possibly at knifepoint."

Raynes had been careful to avoid all mention of Linda but John looked sharply across the room at Emilio. He looked highly indignant that anyone else should be sponging on his mother for money. Linda looked fixedly at the ground.

"But," said Raynes, "if we are not talking about a gangland killing or a revenge murder (for which we might possibly suspect her son, John, and his wife, Linda), then we are left with the probability that the murder was done by one of her customers. Sophie kept an address book in which the names of many of her clients appeared. All those who had intercourse with her had a tick beside their name and their initials appeared in her diary. This information was used by her son for the purposes of blackmail."

John drank deeply from his beer.

"So it may be that the murder was done by one of her regular clients whose names appear in 'the book of life'! A known client for whom she was prepared to put on her best dress and travel without anxiety to the darkest part of the 'forest'. There to receive handsome payment for her services. Not just a 'fiver' or a 'tenner' as has been suggested. But sometimes upwards of £200. So we look to the four or five men in this room who used Sophie in her professional capacity – either as a prostitute or as a photographic model."

"The suggestion has been made that Sophie was lured to the woods for a photo session. Tied up and blindfolded. Then the real murderer took over. I have found this a very helpful theory – as you will see later."

"Once the murder was done, the murderer – or murderers – tidied up. The earth around the tree was brushed clean of foot-steps. Her clothes were removed. So was the knife. There were no fingerprints on the rope or the scarf and no means of identi-fication. A visiting card was left on the ground some fifty yards away from the tree – a card that was left either to incriminate one of the suspects or to confuse the police. Either way, it caused a lot of trouble."

Mr Coates-Smythe's face did not move an inch.

"From this we can infer that the murderer used gloves. This perhaps is not surprising – but he or she may have been in the habit of wearing gloves. It was a source of amusement to Sophie that some of her customers were so fastidious that they wore gloves. Paul Brown tells us that she even told the University students about this. I suppose with the incidence of AIDS we all have to take precautions!"

It was meant to be a joke but no one laughed.

"Once the murder was done, the villain – or villains – went straight to Sophie's flat. Mr Zaposito says that he arrived in Grasshallows at about 8.00 pm. He went directly to Riverside Road and saw a small light burning in the front room of Sophie's flat. He went up the stairs, banged on the door, shouted through the letter-box but got no answer. By the time he came downstairs, the light had been switched off ..."

"I'm not sure about the light," said Emilio.

Raynes ignored him.

"Now we know that the murderer or his associate went through Sophie's address book and diary. Five pages were torn out of her diary. Five Saturday nights between January and June 1987. Five nights when the murderer's name was mentioned. Five nights when he – or she – had been quietly lulling Sophie's suspicions. She had got quite used to meeting her killer. The killer paid well. On every Monday after the killer's visits, the amount Sophie banked was considerably up on her usual weekend takings. I have checked her building society bank books and the evidence is quite clear. Whoever her mysterious visitor was, he or she was prepared to pay well for Sophie's services, which may explain why she went so gladly to her fate."

"That is one theory," said Raynes, "but other events may have happened on those five Saturday nights. There may have been family visits. Threats, blackmail. Once again, the murderer may have had other reasons for removing those pages."

Raynes looked round the audience. Most people were staring at the floor. They did not want to appear too interested; to show any sudden reactions; to catch Raynes' suspicious eye. They were busy considering their own part in the story that was unfolding.

"However," said Raynes more cheerfully, "the flat in Riverside Road was quite busy that night. Not only was the murderer quietly leafing through her diary, tearing out any possible evidence; not only was Mr Zaposito shouting through the letterbox; but Mr Paul Brown was delivering a thank you card which he had to leave on the doormat because, after Mr Zaposito's intervention, someone blocked off the letter-box. This was very fortunate, because two other strange people were hanging about in fancy dress – or should I say, theatrical costume? – carrying a blue plastic container full of petrol. Was this designed to gut the flat in a super arson attack which would destroy all the evidence – or was it intended as a funeral pyre for Sophie herself? But if the arsonists were the murderers, why had they most inconveniently blocked the letter-box? Or did they have Sophie's key? I must confess, at this point, I became rather confused!"

Raynes smiled

"I believe that in recent times there has been an excellent performance in the Church hall of Bernard Shaw's 'St Joan', in which the Maid of Orleans was eventually burned at the stake. I am told that Mrs Hayman played the star part in this drama and that Derek Coates-Smythe, Canon Murray and even

Commander Kenworth had supporting roles. More surprisingly still, I hear that both Ernie McCulloch and Jim Reid offered a helping hand behind the scenes. So might there be some connection here?"

Raynes paused to sip some water.

"Now no murderer is going to walk in or out of Sophie's flat unnoticed. Quite a lot of people are abroad on a summer's evening on Riverside Road! How easily they might be seen! Therefore there is a strong possibility that the killer – or killers – entered the flat in disguise. Sophie's red dress, gold belt and gold shoes were found in her wardrobe as were a couple of her wigs. The suggestion is that one of the killing party was a woman – or a man dressed up as a woman – possibly in Sophie's own clothes with a wig. They changed in the flat, leaving her murder garments behind but perhaps coming out in another of Sophie's outfits. Sophie was about five foot, six inches tall so we are possibly looking for someone of that height."

There were covert glances around the room.

"Furthermore, it seems to me unlikely that someone dressed in Sophie's clothes would have entered the flat alone. The killer would have had to have a partner to make sure the coast was clear."

Several people in the room nodded. Raynes had gone far to prove his case.

"You will notice," Raynes continued, "the audacity of the killers. To murder in broad daylight. In a public park. And then to descend on the victim's flat – possibly disguised as Sophie herself. The careful planning involved. The months of preparation. The fact that they could go through the contents of Sophie's flat – looking for any tell-tale signs that they had been involved with her – possibly even looking for money or jewellery – whilst at any moment the alarm might be raised, the body be discovered and the police suddenly appear in force on the doorstep. Why not wait till it was dark? Till after midnight? Then search the flat? Why not wait and see whether the police had been alerted? Was the murderer in a hurry? Anxious to return home to London – to his wife ... or husband ... or children or" (Raynes smiled) "to his carefully prepared alibi in a certain restaurant?"

Mrs Hayman and Commander Kenworth did not smile.

"The murderer was indeed in a hurry. He or she has very little time to spare. But now he or she almost makes a mistake. For what reason I cannot imagine, he or she returns to the Meadows and places Sophie's handbag and keys in her own car. Her old Marina. At a moment when so many men are drifting round the Meadows waiting for Sophie to re-appear, this person returns to the lion's den and pops them into her car. And then bangs the door! Scoots off into the twilight. Or perhaps he doesn't scoot off at all – because he works in the Meadows?"

Ernie McCulloch shook his head.

"The murderer is so neat and tidy. Every loose end must be tidied up. That is why this case has defeated the police for over a year. The only way into this case is through motive. That is where I began and that is where I shall end."

"Did the murderer have a habit of tying people up to trees? Was he one of her secret lovers?" (He looked at Canon Murray.) "Was he determined to get his revenge for the damage she had done to his business?" (He looked at Eddie Reid.) "Someone with a long-standing grudge? Someone who hadn't been able to get as much money out of her as he had wished? Someone who liked using a knife on people?" (He looked at Emilio.) Could it have been a couple who were still hopeful that they might receive a legacy in Sophie's will – even though they knew the bulk of the estate was to go to St Benedict's?" (He looked at John and Linda.)

"People will kill each other for less than £100 if they are desperate. They may kill for nothing if they are refused. Others may kill to prevent their sordid secrets slipping out. People may murder just to eliminate an inconvenient rival." (Raynes looked pointedly at Rosalind Hayman.) "Especially if they are thinking of marriage. People may even kill just because they hate women ..." (Raynes looked at Ernie McCulloch.) "... or for religious principles ..." (He looked at Paul Brown.) "... and there was a certain element of ritual killing in the death of

209

Sophie Jack. So – once you get your motive, you get your man! Or woman!"

The room was silent as Raynes concluded his exposition.

"So those are the lines I have been following during my investigations. You will recognize the various points which I have brought up during my interviews – but none of you, I think, has seen the complete picture. Many of my questions were designed to *eliminate* suspects and I apologize for having occasionally been brutal in forcing out the truth …"

"Not half!" exclaimed Commander Kenworth with feeling.

"Shh!" said Rosalind. "He hasn't finished."

"… However, you will be glad to hear that I have brought my investigations to a successful conclusion. I know precisely who was involved in the murder of Sophie Jack and who actually killed her. This afternoon, I received a signed confession of murder from Mr James Reid …"

Eddie Reid jumped to his feet. "He didn't murder her! He didn't do it! He was in Birmingham! You've got the wrong man!"

Detective-Inspector Raynes nodded to two police officers who immediately rushed forward, grabbed Eddie and frog-marched him out of the suite, still shouting loudly.

"As I was saying," Raynes continued calmly, "Mr James Reid has been in police custody since last Thursday. It has taken a little time to get the truth out of him but at long last he has confessed. I believe the manner of his arrest has given rise to a number of complaints …"

Derek Coates-Smythe nodded gravely and looked at his fellow lawyers.

"… but when you are tracking down a particularly brutal and heartless murderer – who has a long past history of violence – then you will perhaps excuse the police for taking no chances over his arrest. I can just imagine the public outcry there would have been if one of my officers had been injured!"

There were one or two laughs at the police's expense. But it was noticeable that the atmosphere in the function suite had lightened considerably after Raynes had named the killer. Eddie Reid's outburst had somehow pricked the bubble of fear and wakened them all up. Emilio was grinning. Linda was smiling for the first time. Even Mrs Hayman and the Commander were exchanging pleasantries. Canon Murray could be heard telling Peter Bridges how much he had had to suffer from Inspector Raynes. "So unnecessary!" he kept saying. The lawyers accompanying Mr Derek Coates-Smythe turned off their cassette recorder and were exchanging contented looks now that their colleague had avoided being libelled in public.

Raynes watched them all with quiet amusement.

"Now," he said loudly over the din, "the story is not yet complete. I would like to give you a complete account of how the murder was done … which I think you will find most interesting. No one is yet free to go, but I hope you will all have a second drink and a chat and see if you can guess how the murder was done. I've given you most of the clues but I'd like you to try and put two and two together … and make five!"

Everyone laughed.

"And then, in about twenty minutes or so – when I've had a gin-and-tonic to wet my whistle … then I shall conclude my exposition in the best traditions of detective fiction. Let us see whether we have any budding Sherlock Holmes amongst us!"

Raynes went over to Coates-Smythe and talked to him briefly. The lawyer had been told that Jim Reid had made a confession but he had not yet been able to see him. He was annoyed about this.

The Chief Constable was saying nothing. He was still frightened that Raynes might humiliate him in public and he wanted to know how Raynes had succeeded where Detective-Inspector Parkinson had failed.

Canon Murray was still going on about the Inspector's rudeness. Now he was speaking to Rosalind and the Commander. "What a pity," thought Raynes, "that I can't tell them the full story!"

However Raynes had noticed that Peter Bridges was bringing him his much-needed gin-and-tonic. Bridges was smiling: "That was pretty good detective work, Inspector! I'm looking forward to hearing how you caught the beast."

"Patient stalking," said Raynes, "and a little bit of instinct." He noticed that Carlisle was hovering near at hand. "And, of course, a little help from my friends!"

His colleague smiled.

"Now, Peter," said Raynes with unaccustomed familiarity, "I promised to give you a cheque for your blasted Organ Fund!"

"So you did," said the Treasurer.

"Well, I've had my little success tonight. You must have yours."

Raynes took his cheque book out of his inside pocket. He looked in vain for a pen. Like most policemen, Carlisle had only a pencil. Finally, Peter Bridges produced his own gold biro which Raynes used with great care. He made the cheque out for £100 and signed his signature with a great flourish.

"Now who's this to be paid to?" he asked. "You or the Church?"

"To St Benedict's Church Capital Account. A bit of a mouthful, I'm afraid, but that'll make sure it gets to the right place."

Raynes wrote the inscription with incredible slowness and then handed the cheque over to the Treasurer. "A small thank-offering for all the divine inspiration I have received on this case!"

"It's a very handsome sum," said Peter Bridges. "Canon Murray will be delighted to have such support – even from a professed atheist! Shows there's hope for even the most unrepentant sinner!" He laughed and looked at the cheque before putting it in his wallet.

"Oh, Inspector," he said, "you've forgotten the date!"

"Oh, sorry," said Raynes. "How stupid of me!"

He bent down to the coffee table again, wrote in the date and handed back the cheque. By force of professional habit, the banker checked what his client had written:

"27th June 1987."

He was about to say:

"You've got the wrong date!"

But as he looked up into Raynes' face, he saw two hard dark eyes watching him like a hawk.

"It's too late, Bridges," he said. "I know it all."

33 *Inspector Raynes Explains*

No one noticed Peter Bridges being taken away. Detective-Constable Carlisle had been on hand to perform this unpleasant duty. Later, it would be his unfortunate task to break the news to Mrs Bridges. The Church Treasurer was led out of *The Green Man* and into a waiting police car to be driven to headquarters. His departure was done with complete tact and diplomacy. Carlisle returned to see Raynes getting everyone organized for the second part of his exposition.

"First of all," he said, "I would like to apologize to Mr James Reid and his brother, Eddie. I have greatly wronged both brothers by implying that they were responsible for the murder of Sophie Jack. In fact, both brothers had a genuine alibi for that night. They were together in Birmingham raiding a spare parts depot. In the course of their raid, a nightwatchman was severely injured – and has since died. You will appreciate that both brothers had every reason to keep secret their movements that night. It has taken a lot to prise the truth out of Jim Reid but eventually he has broken down and confessed. To murder. But not the murder we are discussing tonight."

There was a buzz of excitement round the room.

If it wasn't the Reid brothers, then who could it be? There were now only sixteen people in the room – fourteen men and two women. Raynes let them work it out for themselves.

"Just before I finished speaking before the interval, I said that the key to this case was – motive. Find the motive and you've found the man."

"When I first heard of the way Sophie died, my natural instinct suggested revenge. It was a revenge killing. That was what we were all supposed to think. A brutal revenge. But then I was told of the extraordinary amount of money Sophie had left behind. I automatically assumed that this would have to be the reason for her death – and so it was."

"But then Detective-Constable Carlisle told me that almost all the money had gone to a church – to St Benedict's. And my suspicions were muted. How could a donation or legacy to such a worthy cause be associated with murder?"

"I know the clergy are always fairly desperate for money but I could not believe that anyone as gentle and pastoral as Canon Murray would deliberately murder one of his parishioners in order to assist his organ appeal! Besides, the Treasurer assured me that there was plenty of money in reserve to pay for the rebuilding of the organ. In the summer of 1987, St Benedict's was worth well over £100,000 so the church would have had no problem in raising even the higher sums quoted by the organ builders. The Church Treasurer also assured me that, even after the stock market crash in October 1987, there was still sufficient cash not only to rebuild the organ but also to recast the bells."

Raynes paused and looked at Canon Murray's face. He was grey and broken. He had begun to realize what had happened. Perhaps he would at last forgive the pompous upstart?

"So," Raynes continued, "if the church did not need Sophie's money to rebuild its organ, there was no reason to be suspicious of any church official. They had received a handsome legacy and they were using it to good purpose. Like Detective-Inspector Parkinson before me, I was inclined to search for other reasons why Sophie might have been killed."

"There was indeed a strong suggestion of revenge. As I have said, Mr Zaposito and the Reid brothers had ample cause to hate Sophie – one for testifying for the prosecution in a murder trial and the other for losing their MOT licence and a lot of money. Rosalind Hayman was full of resentment and hatred for the way Sophie had carried on with her husband and broken up her marriage. Sophie's son, John, and Linda, his wife, were also prime suspects because they could not account for their movements on the night of the murder, but I could not really believe that John or Linda would choose such a diabolical way of killing his mother. Commander Kenworth and Mr Derek Coates-Smythe were both naturally suspect because of their professional association with Sophie; and Paul Brown and Ernie McCulloch were also subject to question because they were the last two people to see her alive."

"Although this has greatly upset the Chief Constable, I resolved to stir up a hornets' nest – to stimulate everyone's memories by attacking each person in turn. To assume each one was the guilty party – as perhaps they were. I was sure that this re-awakening of the case would cause great anxiety to the murderer."

"He must feel – after a year – that the danger had receded. That he was safe. He would be very upset to find that the embers were being vigorously rekindled and old skeletons taken out of their cupboards. I watched the reactions – and the inter-reactions most carefully."

"The only man who seemed completely unaffected by my investigations was the Church Treasurer, Peter Bridges. He was glad to have received the money – but not desperate. He made that quite clear to me. He also had an impeccable alibi. Each year, he goes away for the last weekend in June to attend a managers' conference in one of the south coast resorts. It seemed that he of all people was completely in the clear."

"So, inevitably, I turned back to the other suspects and began to consider the nature of the murder itself. The wounds were caused by a German hunting knife of a type once owned by Rosalind Hayman. She had used her knife to slash the tyres on Sophie's car and it had been taken away by the police. She told me that she had a mind to get another one – in Scarborough or Whitby. The possibility of getting such a knife stuck in my mind."

"And then there were the three casual slashes to Sophie's stomach. They kindled my deepest suspicions. They were so pointless. So unnecessary. She had already been strangled, so why mutilate the body? Had she had her neck slit open, it would have been a different story! Why strangle … and then mutilate? Was someone trying to make me think it was a revenge killing? And if so, why? I must tell you that I greatly dislike people making me think something. So I said to myself: 'If she is not being killed out of revenge or hatred, what is she being killed for? It must be for her money!'"

"So, as a mental exercise, I decided to consider a scenario in which the Church Treasurer might have killed her for her money. As a theory, it was a little far-fetched … but I let my imagination concoct a suitable story which would explain the murder. Suppose the Treasurer had not got the money? Suppose he had embezzled some or all of it? How many people are likely to challenge the capital account of a Church's balance sheet, especially when their treasurer is a banker? Suppose everything looked all right on paper? People would be perfectly happy. But suppose people suddenly decide to spend £60,000 or more on rebuilding the organ? What would happen then? The embezzlement would be immediately discovered. Reputations would crash. There would be a terrible scandal. So – the decision to rebuild the organ must be opposed at all costs."

"That was just a wicked thought in my mind. But then I was told by several people that the Church Treasurer had indeed done his very best to put off a decision to rebuild the organ! For two or three years, he had resisted stoutly – and then, just as suddenly, he had given way. Why? Had he indeed embezzled some of the Church's money? Was he in danger of being exposed? And had he now found a way by which his guilt might be covered?"

"I discovered that the answer to that question was: 'yes'. He had learnt at a dinner party with one of his golfing cronies, Mr Derek Coates-Smythe, that Sophie Jack was leaving St Benedict's a tidy sum in her will. How much that was, he did not know – but he made it his business to find out. I have double-checked on this. Peter Bridges pretended that Sophie was wanting to get a loan from his bank, so he phoned round the building societies to see how she stood. Banks and building societies will not normally disclose their clients' accounts to anyone – but to a reputable banker there could be no objection."

"So the figures poured out … and the Church Treasurer was amazed to find that, counting in her flat, he could gross a sum of over £100,000. All that stood between him and a clear reputation was Sophie Jack. From that day on, he abandoned all resistance to the plan to rebuild the organ. 'He collapsed like a pack of cards', said Mrs Hayman. 'We called his bluff and he just gave way'."

"We have the motive. Now let us consider the means."

"Organs take some time to rebuild; plans have to be drawn up; tenders submitted; contracts signed. A year to eighteen months is par for the course. There was no hurry to murder Mrs Jack. He could take his time, plan his methods and carefully prepare his alibi. Mr Bridges did it beautifully."

"First of all, he must make her acquaintance. Of all the suspects, he had very little to do with Sophie. Detective-Inspector Parkinson did not even consider him a suspect. That was to his advantage. She was a fellow-worshipper at St Benedict's but they did not worship at the same service. Fortunately, she was not a customer at his bank … that might have looked suspicious! He had met her once at a charity dance in the University but it is unlikely that she remembered his face or his name. Mr Bridges is happily married with a grown-up family. He has no sexual problems or frustrations so he has no need to visit people like Mrs Jack. He is a man who has a distaste for 'that sort of person'. He is fastidious. He is not likely to want any sexual involvement in his murder plan. He is not interested in Sophie's body. Only in her money."

"So how to strike up an acquaintance? He knows that his friend, Mr Coates-Smythe takes 'life poses' with his camera. So why not present himself as a budding photographer? Sophie is quite used to all sorts of cranks. As long as they pay well, she will do anything. Mr Bridges is willing to pay well. But first, he has to get a camera. He has two or three at home – but they are not the sort a professional would use. He does not go to Munn's in Grasshallows because someone might talk, but he buys an expensive piece of equipment which he hides at his office. On one occasion, he unfortunately leaves it in his car and his wife sees it. But he tells her it belongs to Mr Derek Coates-Smythe."

"Now that he has the camera, it is simply a question of phoning up Sophie and asking for a booking. He selects a Saturday evening in January. He suggests a handsome fee for Sophie's services and she naturally accepts. Whether she recognized him or not – or whether he used a false name – I do not know. It may be that since his wife was connected with amateur dramatics, he may have borrowed a wig to cover his bald head. With a pair of glasses, he would have been suitably disguised. And, of course, he was probably the man who wore gloves – so that not a fingerprint would ever be found. Mr Bridges was most thorough."

"On at least five occasions between January and May 1987, Peter Bridges met Sophie and shot a load of film. As far as I know, that film was never developed. In fact, his camera may have contained no film at all! But he 'cultivated' Sophie, allaying her anxieties, posing as a harmless eccentric who – like many others – wanted to photograph her in the nude, in suggestive positions, blindfold, hands tied, in chains, whatever ... Two or three of these sessions would have been held indoors and then, as the nights got lighter, one or two would have been done outside. Where outside? Presumably the darkest corner of the Meadows had much to commend it? For each of these sessions, Sophie was paid well over £200. As I said before, her bank book registered a substantial jump after each of these weekends. Sophie was quite happy. It was easy money. Mr X had become a trusted, regular customer."

"So, without the slightest qualm, she accepted the booking for June 27th. It would only take an hour. It would repay her handsomely. A few sordid pictures of her tied to a tree or baring her buttocks – and she will be £200 better off. What has she to lose? In the words of Paul Brown: 'It is a good one'!"

"What Sophie Jack does not know ... what Mrs Bridges does not know ... and what the police did not know was that Peter Bridges had returned from his Bank Managers' Conference to keep that assignation. This was the key to his crime The perfect alibi. Everyone knows that Peter Bridges is away at the end of June. He has been away at his Conference for the past fifteen years. So it can be safely assumed that on Saturday June 27th 1987, he is 200 miles away at some south coast resort."

"But of course he isn't!"

"In 1987, the Conference was held in Scarborough. I got this fact from a friend of mine who is also a banker. Peter Bridges was at pains to suggest Brighton or Bournemouth as possible venues but, because I didn't trust him, I again double-checked.

Thus we have Scarborough. Somewhat nearer to Grasshallows. Less time to come – and go."

"Now Mr Bridges obviously did not want to be seen or recognized whilst he was in Grasshallows. So naturally he did not bring his own car. He hired a red Escort. Once I knew where the Conference was being held, it did not take long to find out who hired a car and when. I phoned up two firms and discovered that Peter Bridges hired the Escort on the morning of June 27th. For me that was the conclusive evidence in this case. I checked the mileage with the company and it is almost precisely the distance from Scarborough to Grasshallows and back."

"Peter Bridges of course did not leave his car in the Meadows where it might have been seen. He left it on the A193 ... in the lay-by ... and crossed the fields on foot – as I suggested earlier."

"Sophie kept her appointment in her best dress and her gold shoes. She arranged herself artistically to suit her photographer. She submitted to being tied up. Blindfolded. And then, all of a sudden, a rope was cast round her neck, drawn tight and knotted. Mrs Jack struggled feebly – but in a few moments, it was all over. Mr Bridges feels her pulse. There is none. The deed is done. He comes round the tree to face his victim. Her eyes are blindfolded with a very nice scarf which he bought in Scarborough for his wife – the sort of scarf which, as Mrs Hayman said, no wife would ever think of buying for herself. So he does not have to look Sophie in the eye."

"He has thought out every detail."

"Now he takes out his hunting knife – presumably also a present from Scarborough – and slashes three times into her abdomen. Pointless – and messy. But a useful distraction for the police who love to make a great song and dance about the murder weapon."

"Mr Bridges has never done anything in his life with a knife so the job is done in a very amateurish fashion. No Jack the Ripper he! The knife is wiped on Sophie's underwear and all the messy and incriminating objects are put into a plastic bag for disposal. Her clothes and handbag are put into a different bag. All trace of the encounter is carefully brushed away. The whole operation has taken less than fifteen minutes."

"The murderer now hurries back to his car. However, even in that short time, it has been seen and noted by Mr Coates-Smythe on his way back from Picton Dale. The murderer drives down to Sophie's flat and parks his car. By this time, it must be 7.45 pm. Using Sophie's keys, he enters the flat, returns the clothes to her wardrobe and then settles down to examine her bank books, her address book and her diary. Peter Bridges is long-sighted so he puts on his spectacles and switches on a table lamp – which is seen by Emilio Zaposito."

"It must have been a nasty shock for the murderer to discover that his name appeared both in her address book and her diary. However, it would have pleased him to note that, in the address book, he figured merely as the Treasurer of St Benedict's alongside the Vicar, Canon Murray – an entirely innocent connection. He therefore did not touch the address book which contained the names of so many of her customers – who would all naturally be suspects. However, he did tear five pages out of her diary where his visits and fees were recorded."

"He must have had another nasty shock when there was a loud knocking at the door and a rough voice shouting through the letter-box. He turned off the lamp and sat for a long time waiting till the coast was clear. It must have been Peter Bridges who blocked the letter-box thereby preventing an arson attack by Commander Kenworth and Mrs Hayman which had also been carefully planned for that night."

"A little later – and very nervously, I imagine – Mr Bridges emerged from the flat, locked the door and hurried back to his hired car. Being a neat and tidy person – I can think of no other reason – he drove down to the Meadows, returned the keys and handbag to her car – and was almost seen. That was really a terribly stupid thing to do. Mr Ernie McCulloch saw someone making off in the twilight. That was the murderer."

"I must say that Mr McCulloch has been most helpful in this inquiry. It was he who spotted the visiting card of Mr Derek Coates-Smythe some fifty yards from the fatal tree. Peter Bridges had known for a long time that the lawyer was one of Sophie's customers. He knew about the photographs. He felt that the visiting card would make life rather unpleasant for Mr Coates-Smythe who had fought so hard to get the organ rebuilt against the Treasurer's unbending opposition."

"It caused a lot of trouble," said Mr Coates-Smythe. "It almost ruined my marriage and my legal practice."

"It was meant to," said Raynes. "That was the master-touch. But it also left me wondering who could have such an animus against such a distinguished lawyer. Peter Bridges was your friend; you played golf together; you and your wives had dinner together; you worshipped in the same church. But Peter had it in for you because you nearly exposed him as a crook. The more you pushed for the organ to be rebuilt, the more you pushed him into a corner. He hated you for that."

"I never realized."

"Of course not. How could you?"

"How much did he embezzle?"

"I don't know. I think it must have been over £50,000. Quite a sum. The balance sheet looked all right because it contained the historic costings of all the shares and investments. But some of them didn't exist. They'd been sold. What surprised me was that he went all the way to Croydon to get his accounts audited. 'A good London firm' he said to me. But Coulter, Veal and Blyth was just a small one-man outfit in a back office in a London suburb. That again confirmed my suspicions that the accounts were not all they might have appeared."

"Why didn't he pay it back?"

Raynes paused.

"I can only guess. But I have a feeling that he intended to pay the Church back when his endowment policies matured or when he got a golden handshake from his bank. He was looking forward very much to retirement and I fancy that at that point, he'd have put things straight. But the preceding three or four years were a dangerous time for him. Had you waited a couple more years, he'd have been home and dry and Sophie would not have been murdered."

"He's been very clever," said the Chief Constable.

"Very clever," said Raynes. "After he left the Meadows that

night, he must have driven back to Scarborough very quickly. Disposed of the knife and the blood-stained clothes. Got rid of the camera and the gloves. Had a quick wash and brush up. By 11.30 pm he was back in circulation. My friend who is a bank manager and was at the same conference tells me that he saw him at the end of the evening – but not during. Peter came in looking very pleased with himself. They thought he'd been out on the tiles for a couple of hours. 'Like a cat that's got the cream!' That's what my friend told me. But now that cream has gone a little sour!"

Raynes sat down.

The Chief Constable, who had now had time to digest the fact that one of his golfing cronies had turned out to be a scheming and ruthless murderer, stood up and said a few words of thanks and congratulation for all Detective-Inspector Raynes had achieved during his first week of service in Grasshallows. "A most promising beginning," said the Chief Constable. "A flying start. We all wish him a most happy and rewarding life in our city."

Looking at Canon Murray, Mrs Hayman and Commander Kenworth, Raynes did not think that these were sentiments likely to be deeply felt. To him, they were sheer hypocrisy. But everyone clapped and smiled.

Raynes was thinking about a tall, sad woman arranging flowers in St Benedict's. He was thinking of how carefully she constructed her display. Putting one bloom into the oasis and then standing back to see if it looked right. A number of flowers had been tried but not all had fitted. There had to be one right one at the centre and then all the others surrounded that one. It had been the same for him. Any number of suspects – but only one fitted. Once you put him in the central place, the answer sprang out at you. It was a similar case of selection and rejection. There was an art to flower-arranging and an art to detection. You either had it – or you didn't.

Raynes stood up to acknowledge the applause.

To himself he said: "Perhaps now they'll give me a decent desk?"